QUIVER

QUIVER

a novel

Julia Watts

THREE ROOMS PRESS
New York, NY

Quiver
BY Julia Watts

© 2018 by Julia Watts

This is a work of fiction. Names, characters, businesses, places, events, and incidents are either the products of the author's imaginations or used in a fictitious manner. Any resemblance to actual persons, living or dead, or actual events is purely coincidental.

ISBN 978-1-941110-66-9 (trade paperback)
ISBN 978-1-941110-67-6 (Epub)
Library of Congress Control Number: 2018940808

TRP-068

Pub Date: October 16, 2018

Young Adult Fiction: Ages 14 and up
BISAC Coding:
YAF031000 Young Adult Fiction / LGBT
YAF037000 Young Adult Fiction / Loners & Outcasts
YAF058120 Young Adult Fiction / Social Themes / Friendship
YAF058260 Young Adult Fiction / Social Themes / Values & Virtues

COVER DESIGN AND ILLUSTRATION:
Victoria Black: www.thevictoriablack.com

BOOK DESIGN:
KG Design International: www.katgeorges.com

DISTRIBUTED BY:
PGW/Ingram: www.pgw.com

Three Rooms Press
New York, NY
www.threeroomspress.com
info@threeroomspress.com

For my family,
both biological and chosen

QUIVER

LIBBY

Chapter 1

When he was young, before he got married and had us kids, Daddy used to train Tennessee Walking Horses. The horses would shy away from him at first or buck or run, but over time, he broke them so they'd canter when he said canter or jump when he said jump. Some horses were easy to break, but others fought to stay free. Daddy always says the fighters were the horses that turned out best. They had spirit, and once you corrected them so their spirit turned to obedience instead of wildness, they were the horses you could really count on.

Daddy says I'm like one of those horses.

According to Mama, I was wild when I was little. She says the firstborn is always headstrong. The children that come along after aren't in danger of thinking the world revolves around them like the firstborn is. That said, any danger I had of thinking I was the center of the universe passed a long time ago. I'm the oldest of six, and Mama's expecting number seven in the fall.

As the oldest, it's my job to help Mama with the Littles and the cooking and cleaning. But even though the older kids get the most responsibility, everybody has chores to do. Even three-year-old Charity sweeps the front porch with a broom that's taller than she is.

Since today's when Mama washes the bedclothes, my thirteen-year-old sister Patience and I are stripping the beds in the room we share, the one nicknamed the Big Girls' Room.

"Faith told me that once the baby's born, she's moving to the Big Girls' Room," Patience says, yanking the case off her pillow.

I grin. Faith is just five, hardly a Big Girl. "If Faith's gonna sleep in the Big Girls' Room, she's gonna have to stop wetting the bed." I bend over to pull the bottom sheet off the mattress. "I think Mama and Daddy are planning to keep Faith and Charity in the Little Girls' room and just add a crib in there. If the baby's a boy, he can move to the Boys' Room when he gets bigger."

Patience rolls her sheets and quilt into a big ball. "That'd make three boys in one room."

"So?" I say, rolling up my own bedding. "Boys don't care. Daddy can put in bunk beds. They can sleep stacked on top of each other like they would in the army."

Patience and I go to the Little Girls' Room to see how morning duties are going. Faith has gotten herself dressed in her blue denim jumper and has managed to strip off her sheets and quilt, but Charity is just sitting on her bed, still wearing her pink nightgown with puppies on it. Of all of us, she's the prettiest. Her hair is white-blonde and curly, and her eyes are huge and blue. She looks like a little angel even if she doesn't always act like one.

"I got dressed and stripped the bed like we're supposed to because it's Monday," Faith says. "But Charity didn't because she's the baby."

Charity's chubby cheeks turn red, and she sticks out her lower lip. "I am not the baby!"

"No, you're not," I say, trying to tamp down a tantrum. "You're getting to be a big girl."

"The baby's in Mama's tummy," Charity says.

"That's right," I say. "Now why don't you show me what a big helper you can be and take the covers off the bed?"

Charity flops on her back and rolls sideways until she's wrapped up completely in her quilt.

"Now, honestly," Patience says. "How is that being a helper?"

Her name may be Patience, but sometimes she has less of it than I do. I tickle Charity's toes, sticking out of the covers. "Now that's not getting the covers off the bed, is it? That's rolling up like a pig in a blanket."

"Pig in a blanket!" Charity giggles. "Libby's silly."

"Yes, Libby's silly," I say. My name is Liberty, but the Littles can never say it right when they start talking, so it always comes out as Libby. Over time, I've turned into Libby the same way older brothers sometimes turn into Bubba. "But we still need to clean off the bed and get you dressed. Daddy won't be silly if we're late for breakfast."

At the mention of Daddy, Charity unrolls herself from the quilt and pulls it down onto the floor. The fitted sheet and pillowcase are harder to manage, so I do those while she goes to her drawer and pulls out the pink dress she'd wear every day if we let her. Meanwhile, Patience brushes the tangles out of Faith's hair.

When Patience and I finally get down to the dining room, Daddy and the boys are already sitting at the table. Justice, who at fourteen is two years younger than me, is sitting next to Daddy and talking about his newest woodworking project. Nine-year-old Valor says "good morning" the exact same time Faith says it, and they both laugh like it's the funniest thing in the world. Most of the time we call the boys Just and Val.

"Good morning, girls. Welcome to the day!" Daddy says, holding up his coffee cup in salute. His blue eyes crinkle at the corners when he smiles. He's already dressed in his Hazlett and Sons Pest Control uniform except for the hat, which he never wears at the table because it's bad manners.

"Good morning, Daddy," Patience and I say. In our house it's a rule to start every day with "good morning" and end it with "good night."

Patience and I go into the kitchen to help with breakfast. Mama's standing at the stove over a huge pan of scrambled eggs. She's definitely the parent I look more like. She and I have the same wavy, waist-length, ash-blond hair and the high, flat cheekbones that Mama says come from the Cherokee blood in our family tree. Mama's body is wider than mine, and softer, but that's the difference between being a girl and a woman.

"Good morning, girls," Mama says. "Libby, could you take those slices of bread out of the toaster and stick in another four? Patience, go see if your daddy needs his coffee warmed. Faith, you can carry the orange juice to the table, and Charity, you can take the butter."

I set four pieces of toast on a platter that's already piled high. Mama bakes seven loaves of bread every Thursday.

We'd go broke if we had to depend on store-bought bread, we go through so much of it.

"Once those other pieces are done, you can go ahead and take out the platter," Mama says. "The eggs are about ready."

In spring and summer we have scrambled eggs for breakfast. In winter, we have oatmeal instead. The color of the food matches the season, sunshine-yellow eggs for the bright, warm months, gray oatmeal when it's cold and dark.

I bring out the toast, and Mama follows with the huge steaming bowl of eggs. We gather around the table, Mama and Daddy at either end and the kids all in between. We join hands.

"Dear Lord," Daddy says, "we thank You for this bounty that is before us, and let us use this nourishment to serve you in all that we do today. In Jesus's blessed name we pray, amen."

After the amens, there's a clatter of dishes. Mama serves Daddy first, then portions out one scoop of eggs and one piece of toast for each of us kids. Then there's the scritch-scratch of toast being buttered and the Littles slurping their milk.

"I programmed the addresses of all your appointments today into your phone," Mama says to Daddy.

He smiles. "You're a blessing to me, Becky."

"You're a blessing to me, too, James," Mama says, smiling shyly.

"Just," Daddy says, between bites of egg, "I thought I might come by and pick you up this afternoon. Let you come on a few calls with me."

"Yes, sir," Just says. He's training to become the first son to actually work at Hazlett and Sons Pest Control. So far the company has just been Daddy doing the actual pest control and Mama helping out by scheduling appointments, advertising, and bookkeeping.

"Can I go, too?" Val asks.

"In a few more years," Daddy says gently. "We need to get your schooling taken care of before we start teaching you a trade."

"School's not as fun as killing bugs," Val says, poking at his scrambled eggs with his fork.

"It's not about killing. It's about controlling. Right, Daddy?" Just says.

"That's right," Daddy says, letting Mama refill his coffee. "The Lord created bugs just like He created all the other critters folks tend to like better."

"Like kittens?" Faith offers.

Daddy grins at her. "Like kittens. Exactly. And the Lord gave us stewardship over the animals, which means we take care of them but make use of them, too. Like eating these good eggs from chickens this morning. But if there gets to be too many of a certain critter, they get to be a danger to themselves or to people. That's why it's good stewardship to control the population."

"Like when we hunt deers in deer season?" Val says.

"Just like that," Daddy says, scraping up egg with a piece of toast. "There's too many for them all to get enough to eat, so we control the population by hunting."

Mama reaches over and touches Val on the arm and says, "The plural of deer is deer, dear," and we all laugh.

"Well, that don't make sense," Val says. "Usually you add an 's.'"

"No, it doesn't make sense," Mama says. "But that's the rule."

"See," Daddy says, "that's why she gets to homeschool y'all. She's better at all that grammar stuff than I am."

Patience says, "Mama says grammar is using rules to clean up your language like you use a broom to clean up your house."

"Well, maybe that's why she's better at it than I am," Daddy says, looking at his watch. "But what I am good at is providing for my family, which I'm not gonna do if I sit here chewing the fat all day." He gets up, grabs his hat, kisses Mama like he does every morning, and says, "Have a blessed day, everybody."

After Mama's seen him to the door, she comes back to the table with the clipboard where she keeps track of everybody's chores. "Okay, kiddos," she says. "Charity, you sweep the front porch. Faith, you clear the table, then dust the living room. Just and Val, you empty all the trash cans, and Libby, you wash the dishes. Got that, everybody?"

We all say, "Yes, ma'am."

"Okay." She claps her hands once. "I'll get the first load of wash in and start supper in the crock-pot, and then I'll see everybody in the schoolroom at nine o'clock sharp."

I KNOW MY FAMILY IS DIFFERENT from other people's. Sometimes when we make a trip to Walmart, I see them: the mom with her short dyed hair and long red fingernails and makeup, talking on her cell phone while her kids, half naked in shorts and T-shirts printed with characters I don't know, run wild and tear the store apart. Mama says some of those kids probably don't even know who their daddies are. It's funny—these kids with their candy-sticky faces and handheld video games stare at us, especially at us girls with our uncut hair and long skirts. Sometimes the mothers stare, too, counting how many of us there are and shaking their heads.

Daddy and Mama moved from Johnson City to the country when I was a baby and Mama was pregnant with Just. A man at their church told Daddy he knew somebody who was trying to sell a farmhouse about an hour away. It wasn't in great shape, but the owner had been trying to unload it for a long time, so the price was right.

When Mama and Daddy drove out to see the place, God gave Daddy a vision. Daddy had been working for the Orkin pest control company in Johnson City, but his vision told him that he and Mama should buy the house, and with Mama's help, he'd run his own pest control business from home. He and Mama would have as many children as the Lord would bless them with, and Mama would stay home with us and homeschool us and, with Papa's leadership, raise us to be God's righteous warriors.

I was too little to remember it, but Mama always said the first three years in the house made her pray a lot for strength. Daddy was trying to get the business off the ground, but he was having to do odd jobs or mow people's lawns to make enough money for house payments and food. Plus, the house was in bad shape. Every day something new needed fixing. But over time, they fixed up the house, Hazlett and Sons Pest Control grew, and so did our family.

Washing dishes is my favorite chore. There's no bustling around like with sweeping or mopping. I just stand in my spot over the sink. The hot soapy water feels nice, and the white foamy bubbles are fluffy like clouds. I fall into a rhythm—wash, rinse, stack—that still leaves enough room in my brain for daydreaming. I dream about different times and places. What it would have been like to have lived in the Bible days—to wear a robe and sandals and a veil, to draw water from a well and wash clothes in the river, to hear God's voice speaking to you just as sure as you heard your own neighbor's.

It's easy to daydream about the past but hard to daydream about the future. Mama says that's because the future is in God's hands—only He knows who my husband will be—but the important thing is that I'm learning all I need to know to be a Godly wife and mother.

I don't daydream about the present either. What's the point of daydreaming about what you're doing now? Most days are busy and not much different than the day before, but there's something comforting about that. Sometimes—and this doesn't make any sense because I'm always surrounded by other people—I feel something that I think might be loneliness. Maybe I wouldn't feel this way if my closest sibling in age was a girl instead of a boy. But the girl closest to me is Patience, and there's a big difference between being thirteen and being sixteen. Talking to Mama helps, which is another reason I like morning dish duty. Mama always comes in to start supper in the crock-pot while I'm finishing the dishes, and so unless something happens with the Littles, we get a few minutes to talk, just the two of us.

She comes in as I'm scrubbing the egg pan, which I always save for last because it makes the water the dirtiest.

"One load in, six to go!" she says, going to the refrigerator and opening the door.

"You gotta start somewhere," I say. Laundry is a never-ending process at our house. Bedding gets washed on Monday, but Mama keeps a load or two of clothes washing every day but Sunday.

"Vegetable soup tonight," Mama says. "Remember when Val used to pick out the green beans and hide them in his napkin?"

I smile. "Yes, and I remember when you served him nothing but green beans for his supper the night after you caught him."

Mama is chopping onions. She's so good with a knife she doesn't even look at what she's cutting. "Everybody else was having deer burgers that night, and it broke my heart when I saw how his face fell. But sometimes you've got to make your point."

"Well, you sure made it. I think Val's eaten everything that's been put in front of him ever since."

"Can't afford to be too picky around here," Mama says, dumping onions and stew beef in a sizzling skillet. "If it's edible, you better eat it."

Because there are so many of us living on just what Daddy makes, we eat a lot of stuff worldly kids would probably turn up their noses at: rabbit stew, squirrel and dumplings, poke salad. But we turn up our noses at a lot of what those kids eat, too: I've never set foot in a McDonald's, and I don't feel any poorer for it.

The smell of the frying meat and onions makes my mouth water, but then Mama says, "Oh, dear," jerks the pan off the stove eye, and runs to the trash can. She leans over it, retching.

I step behind her and hold her hair out of the way. "Poor Mama," I say, rubbing her back while she gags.

Finally, she stands up straight, takes a deep breath, and says, "Sorry about that."

"No need to apologize for something you can't help," I say. "Why don't you sit down a minute? You want me to fix you a cup of tea?"

Mama, who hardly ever sits during the day except for meals, sinks into a kitchen chair. "That would be nice. Thank you."

"I can finish putting the soup together if the food smells are getting to you." I put the kettle on to boil.

"They are," Mama says. "I'm getting so sick this time I wonder if I'm carrying another boy. Seems like I only get sick with boys." She smiles a little, but she's still pale and sweaty. "And it's always food smells that set me off. This time it's meat cooking. With Just, it was eggs. With Val, it was peanut butter."

"I'm surprised it wasn't green beans," I say, getting a little laugh out of her.

Once the kettle whistles, I put the tea infuser in a cup and pour hot water over it. When I hand Mama the steaming cup, she says, "You're a blessing to me, Libby."

"You're a blessing to me, too, Mama."

Maybe it's because her eyes are like mine and her hair is like mine, but sometimes when I look at Mama I feel like I'm looking in a mirror that shows my life years from now. Will I be like her, pregnant again and queasy, being seen to by my teenage daughter? But when I really try to imagine my adult self, it's like the mirror fogs up, and I can't see myself at all.

CHAPTER 2

MAMA MUST BE FEELING BETTER TODAY because the smell of the ham and beans in the crock-pot is all over the house and she hasn't thrown up once. Right now we're in the school-room like we always are from nine until noon on weekdays. Mama is helping Patience with some long division problems, and I'm trying to help Val with his reading. He's smart, but he still struggles sounding out words. Faith and Charity are still too little to do much, but they still "have school" when we do. They work wooden puzzles and thread thick ropes of yarn through lacing cards and color Bible story coloring pages, trying to learn how to stay inside the lines. You can tell all this "schoolwork" makes them feel really big.

Since Just is fourteen and a boy, he sits off to himself and does his Bible study and history lessons. He's gotten too old for Mama to teach him. She can still teach me because I'm a girl, but since I'm sixteen there's not much left in the schoolbooks for me to learn. I still do a Bible lesson every day and a page or two out of my *Bookkeeping for Christian Stewardship* workbook, but other than that, I spend most of the school day helping my younger brother and sisters. Mama says helping with homeschool and working in the kitchen is the best education I could have.

"Crud, crud, crud!" Patience says. She must've messed something up on her math page because she's erased so hard she's torn the paper.

"Patience, Patience," Mama says, which is kind of a running joke in our family.

Patience sets her pencil down. "I don't even know why I have to do long division. Girls don't need to know math anyway."

"Really?" Mama says. She's smiling, but it's her challenging smile. "And how do you think I figure out how much to spend on groceries and other household expenses every month?"

"Math!" Val says.

"That's right." Mama rests her hand on Patience's arm. "And how do you think I double a recipe to feed all of y'all? Val, let Patience answer this time."

"Math," Patience says so low you can hardly hear her.

Mama picks up Patience's long blond braid and uses the end of it to tickle Patience's chin. "What's that you said?"

"Math," Patience says louder, smiling like she knows she's beat.

"Yes, ma'am!" Mama says. "So pick up your pencil and try that problem again."

After lunch (peanut butter sandwiches, like always), it's time for recess/PE. Just usually goes off to hike in the woods or do target practice with his bow. Patience has this silly exercise routine she likes to do, then she uses the rest of the time to work on whatever she's sewing. She's crazy for needlework. My job is to supervise the Littles' recess/PE. I know Mama needs her hour and a half of quiet in the afternoon so she can make phone calls and do bookkeeping for the family business, so I take the Littles outside to play and keep them out. If it's chilly, I bundle them up, and if they need to go to the bathroom, I make them "play kitty" in the woods. On rainy days we play in the barn.

Today it's nice, and as soon as I open the back door, Val and Faith and Charity run out into the yard and scramble onto the swing set. Faith and Charity get on opposite sides on the teeter-totter, and Val climbs the ladder to the slide. I always tell the Littles they can use their outside voices for recess time, which means they're extra loud. Val sings that song about climbing Jacob's ladder every time he climbs the ladder to the slide, and Charity, on the teeter-totter, yells, "We're on a rocket in space!"

"Yeah," Faith says, "and we're gonna fly past the moon and stars and all the way to heaven!"

"Say hello to the angels for me," I say. I like taking the Littles out to play because it makes me remember when I was that age and could be so deep in my imagination that it felt almost realer to me than the world I was in. Now that I'm closing in on being a grownup, I miss that feeling.

I walk over to the corner of the yard to the dog pen. Ruth and Boaz, Daddy's two hunting dogs, are curled up together in their dog house, but as soon as they see me, they run out, wagging their tails and barking their deep, hound-dog woofs. They know what's coming. I unlatch the gate of their little pan, and they run free through the backyard, nipping at each other playfully.

Daddy says Ruth and Boaz are for hunting, not petting, and that I could never be a real farm girl because I make pets out of every animal I see. But I figure the least I can do is let the dogs get out of the pen in the afternoon and run off some steam, the same as the Littles do. Daddy says it's all right with him as long as I make sure they stay away from the chickens.

The Littles have moved from the swing set to the trampoline and are playing some made-up game they call Bounce Monster. I pick up a chewed-on Frisbee and throw it for Ruth to fetch. She's a world-class fetcher and will make impossible-seeming leaps to catch it in her mouth. Boaz doesn't seem to get the whole Frisbee thing. He mostly runs behind Ruth while she fetches, barking like he's cheering her on.

While I'm watching Ruth jump for the Frisbee again, I notice something at the farmhouse next door that makes me go to the fence for a closer look. We call this house the old Dobbins place because when Mama and Daddy moved here, an old couple named Dobbins lived there. Mr. Dobbins died when I was really little, but Mrs. Dobbins stayed on by herself. She was a sweet old lady who always fussed over us kids and offered us peppermints, and sometimes Mama would pick things up for her at Walmart. Two years ago, Mrs. Dobbins's son moved her to a nursing home in Johnson City, and the old Dobbins place, a white farmhouse that doesn't look that different from ours, has sat empty ever since.

But now a big truck with MADISON MOVERS printed on its side is parked in front of the old Dobbins place, and two young men are lowering a ramp from the truck bed.

"That's a big truck," Val says from the trampoline.

"It is," I say. "It looks like we're going to have some new neighbors."

"Do they have kids?" Faith asks without stopping her jumping.

"I can't tell," I say. "The only people I see are the moving men." The two men are unloading a purple couch splashed with big red flowers. Our couch is solid tan and, like everything else in our house, very plain. What kind of people have a purple couch?

WHEN PAPA COMES HOME FROM WORK, the Littles swarm him, hugging his legs. Faith and Charity want to show him pictures they've drawn, and Val wants to tell him how he beat the high score on his Noah's Ark computer game. Mama comes out of the kitchen, wearing her apron, and says, "Now y'all give the man a little room to breathe." She places a glass of lemonade in Daddy's hand and kisses his cheek. "How was your day, honey?"

"Good." He gives her waist a little squeeze. "But so far this is the best part."

"Mine, too," Mama says. "Why don't you sit down and relax? Dinner will be ready in ten minutes. We're just waiting on the cornbread."

"Your cornbread's worth waiting for," Daddy says, sinking into his armchair. This is where my job comes in. I kneel before Daddy, unlace his work boots, and pull them off.

"Ah, now that feels good!" he says, wiggling his toes inside his socks.

"Do you want me to get you a pan of hot water with Epsom salts?" Sometimes Daddy likes to soak his feet.

"I believe I'll pass since it's almost suppertime," he says. "But I sure appreciate the good care you take of your daddy's old dogs. You know, Mary Magdalene washed Jesus's feet with her hair."

I wrinkle my nose. "That doesn't seem very sanitary for the hair or the feet."

Papa grins. "Well, we are talking about Jesus's feet here. They would've been perfect. They wouldn't have gotten stinky like your old daddy's." He grins, and I grin back.

After we've said grace at the table, we pass our bowls forward, and Mama fills each one with a ladleful of beans and ham. We pass around the wedges of cornbread.

"So," Daddy says, after everybody's been served, "how about we go around the table and everybody tells one thing about their day. Let's go youngest to oldest. Charity, you go first."

Charity smiles, showing her dimples and her tiny baby teeth. "We played Bounce Monster on the trampoline and I was the monster first and I catched Faith and Val and then they turned into monsters, too."

"But then you turned back into yourselves, right?" Daddy says. "I don't see any monsters here."

Charity and the other Littles giggle.

When it's my turn, I say, "Well, during recess today I saw a moving truck pull up in front of the old Dobbins place, so I guess we're going to have new neighbors."

"That is news," Mama says. "That place has been sitting empty a long time."

Daddy sips his milk. "I know it. I had gotten pretty used to us just being out here by ourselves. I sure hope these new folks aren't trouble, with drinking and loud parties and such. Did you get a look at them, Libby?"

"No, sir. The moving men were the only people I saw. The only thing I can tell you is they've got a purple couch."

"A purple cow?" Faith says, and everybody cracks up.

"No, silly girl," I say. "A purple couch. I wish it was a purple cow, though. I'd like to see that."

Tonight's Bible study is from Ephesians 6. We all sit together in the living room while Daddy stands in front of us and reads, "Put on the whole armor of God, that ye may be able to stand against the wiles of the devil. For we wrestle not against flesh and blood, but against principalities, against powers, against the rulers of darkness in this world, against spiritual wickedness in high places. Wherefore take unto you the whole armor of God, that ye may be able to withstand in the evil day, and having done all, to stand." Daddy always reads our Bible verses loud, clear, and not too fast. Then he reads them one more time before he starts asking questions. "What does it mean," he asks, "to 'put on the whole armor of God?'"

"Knights wore armor," Val says.

"They did," Daddy says, "and they put it on to fight for Godly causes. Now why did they wear armor in the first place?"

"To fight!" Val says at the same time Just says, "for protection."

"You're both right," Daddy says. "They put on armor to prepare for battle but also to protect themselves from being hurt by evil forces." He looks at the Littles and says, "Bad guys." Daddy looks around the room at each of us. "But we're not knights, so what does it mean when we put on the armor of God?"

"That we live the way God wants us to?" Patience says.

"Yes!" Daddy says. His eyes are shining, and his grin is wide. "We live only for the glory of God. We put on God's armor to protect ourselves from the attacks of the world. The world may try to attack us with messages about what new gadget to buy or what harlotish clothes our girls should wear, or what taxes the government says we should pay. But you know what? Because we're wearing God's armor, all the worldly evils bounce right off of us." Daddy takes a moment to make eye contact with each of us. "But does God just want us to be safe and protected and hide all quiet like a turtle in his shell?"

"No!" we all yell. Daddy doesn't mind if we yell during Bible study because it means we're excited.

"No is right!" Daddy says, pumping his fist in the air. "God doesn't want us to be like turtles. What does He want us to be instead?"

"He wants us to be his righteous warriors," Just says.

"Righteous warriors against the powers of this dark world!" Daddy says, his eyes shining with excitement. "'Onward Christian soldiers, marching as to war, with the cross of Jesus going on before!' Sing with me!"

We sing, and the Littles stomp their feet. "Onward Christian Soldiers" is an excellent song to stomp to.

Once we finish singing, Daddy says, "But wait a minute—all this talk of Christian soldiers and righteous warriors—isn't that all boy stuff? What can girls do?"

Patience raises her hand. "Girls obey God, their fathers, and then their husbands and have babies to be arrows for God's army."

"They do," Daddy says. "But they do more than just have babies. They train those babies in fear and admonition of the Lord just like your Mama does." He smiles at Mama, and she smiles back. "And because your Mama and me are raising you in the full armor of God, you'll never be afraid to stand up for what you believe in the face of evil." He looks around at each of us, then says, "Amen."

"Amen," Mama says, and then does that hand clap that means it's time to move on to the next thing. "Okay, kiddos, you've got one hour of free time before baths and showers."

Val runs straight for the Lego bin, dumps out a pile of bricks, and gets to work. Patience settles in with her knitting things, and Faith and Charity play with their baby dolls. Faith is dressing up her doll "for church," and Charity has her doll over her knee and is smacking its bottom and saying, "Bad baby! Bad baby!"

Just, who's standing next to me, says, "I feel sorry for Charity's future children. They'll get whupped so much they won't be able to sit down."

"Maybe by then she won't have a toddler's temper," I say. "So what'll it be tonight? Scrabble? Chinese checkers?"

"Scrabble."

I get the box from the game closet and sit down at the card table right when Mama comes in with a tray of lemonade and oatmeal cookies. Unless money's too tight, we always get a treat during evening free time.

It's probably boastful for me to admit this, but I'm better than Just at Scrabble. He might be a little better than me at Chinese checkers, but I'm way better at Scrabble. I know it's prideful to say so, and I know that since he's a boy I should never make him feel like he's not strong or in charge. So a lot of the time when I play, I hold back. I don't make the really good words that would score lots of points so he'll win.

But sometimes, like tonight, there's an opportunity that's just too good to pass up. I'm lucky enough to have a Q and a U and with a Y that's hanging down from where Just made *sorry*, I make *query*. It's on a double-word space, too.

"Doggone it, Libby!" he says.

I point at the word *sorry* on the board and smile back.

Littles take baths with Mama's supervision upstairs in the bathtub. Bigs take turns in the downstairs bathroom's shower stall. Each time one of us goes in to shower, Daddy sets a kitchen timer for ten minutes. My hair's so long it's hard to get it washed and rinsed in the time limit, but Daddy says it's not good to stay in the bathroom too long because it leads to temptation. I don't know what kind of temptation he means, but I guess that's because I never stay in the bathroom long enough to find out.

We get fifteen minutes of reading time before lights out. Patience is reading one of those inspirational novels for girls she likes. The girl on the cover looks like she's from the Pilgrim days. I'm reading my way through *The Chronicles of Narnia* again, which Mama says is okay because even though it's fantasy, it's Christian. I snuggle under the covers and open *Prince Caspian*.

"I still don't see why you read those little kid books when you're old enough to read books about girls our age," Patience says.

Our age? "I guess people just like what they like, and I like Narnia," I say.

"I just don't see how you can like reading something you've read a million times before."

"Not a million," I say. "A dozen at the most."

The funny thing is, reading the Narnia books always feels fresher and newer to me than the inspirational teen novels Patience loves to read. I've tried a few and if you've read one, you've read them all, even if the heroine is a cowgirl in one and a pioneer in another. All the girls have the same story: a hundred pages of praying through hardships, and then, a wedding.

Chapter 3

It's a strange feeling. I'm standing in the backyard watching the Littles climb all over the swing set and trampoline, and I hear the laughter of a child who isn't one of ours. I'm about to sneak a peek at the old Dobbins place when there's a loud crack, and a Wiffle ball sails over the fence to land at my feet. Ruth barks once at this mysterious ball that's dropped from heaven, then grabs it in her mouth and trots away.

"Ruth, that's not yours!" I shout, chasing her, and soon Faith and Charity are following me, hollering, "Not yours! Not yours!"

It's all a fun game for Ruth who's running with the ball in her mouth like it's a rabbit she's just caught. This makes me think of what Daddy says to her when they go hunting. "Drop it, Ruth," I say, and she stands still and opens her jaw enough to let the ball fall.

"Good girl." I pick up the ball, which is slimy with hound spit.

The owners of the ball are standing by the fence. A little boy around Val's age with brown shaggy hair and glasses, wearing jeans and a Lego T-shirt, and a girl who must be his older sister. She's about my height but thinner, with keen features and straight, shiny brown hair down past her shoulders. Girls in our family aren't allowed to wear jeans, but I have to say the ones she's wearing are pretty modest. They're loose and baggy, and so is her light blue T-shirt. "Hi," she says.

"Hi," I say back so softly she probably can't hear me. I walk over to the fence and hold out the ball, embarrassed that my hand is shaking. "Here. I'm afraid the dog got it kind of slobbery."

"That's okay," she says, smiling. "We used to have a Basset Hound, so we're no strangers to slobber." She takes the ball. "I'm Zo, by the way, and this is my brother, Owen."

"Zoe and Owen," I say. "Nice to meet you."

"Actually, it's Zo. Rhymes with go," she says, still smiling. "And you are?"

"Oh." It's been a long time since I needed to introduce myself to anybody. The only people I talk to outside of home are at church, and they all know me. "I'm Libby."

"Are all of those your brothers and sisters?" Owen asks, his eyes wide behind his glasses.

I've always liked the way young kids will just come right out and ask you anything. When grownups ask that question, though, it's annoying. "Yes, they are. I've got another brother and sister, too, but they're closer to my age."

Owen nods. "I like your trampoline. Would it be okay if I came over and played on it?"

Zo gives Owen a little nudge with her elbow. "Not cool, bro. You wait for an invitation. You don't invite yourself."

"Sorry," Owen says. "I'm not good at waiting."

He's so cute I speak before I think. "If your mama says it's okay, you're welcome to come play on the trampoline." As soon as it's out of my mouth, I know I should've checked with my mama first, but it's too late now. I'll just have to pray for forgiveness.

Owen is already scrambling over the fence.

"Uh, don't you need to check with your mama first?" I ask.

Zo shrugs. "It's okay. She won't mind as long as I keep an eye on him."

"You can come into the yard, too," I say, because really, what's one more?

"Thanks," she says. "But unlike Owen, I'll use the gate instead of climbing over."

Once Zo's in the yard, Ruth and Boaz tackle her with licks and wags.

"Fierce guard dogs," I say.

Zo laughs, petting a hound with each hand. She looks over to the trampoline where Owen has joined Val and Faith and Charity. "Kids are funny, aren't they?" she says. "They just jump right in. Literally, in this case."

I feel myself smile. "So are there any more of y'all? Older or younger?" I have this ridiculous thought. What if their family has the same number of kids the same ages as us? It would be like God sent us each a friend.

"Nope. It's just Owen and me, and we're eight years apart. Owen was kind of a surprise, if you know what I mean."

I'm not sure I do, but I smile anyway.

"Libby! Libby!" Faith has appeared beside me and is tugging hard at my skirt. Her face is flushed from the playing and excitement. "Did you see? Did you see the New Boy?"

"I did," I say.

Faith looks at Zo, and says, "Oh, there's a new Big Girl, too."

Zo laughs. "The New Boy is my brother, so he's not new to me. I'm Zo. What's your name?"

"I'm Faith. I'm five."

"Hi, Faith." Zo looks back at me. "I have a feeling it's going to take me a while to get everybody's names."

"Even our mama has trouble sometimes," I say. "So the boy over on the trampoline is Valor, and the baby of the family is Charity. And then somewhere around here is Patience, who's three years younger than me, and my brother Justice, who's two years younger."

"Cool names," Zo says. Her face is much thinner than anybody's in our family, and her chin and nose are pointy, but in a way that looks nice.

"Daddy believes a name should mean something," I say.

"What does Libby mean?"

"It's short for Liberty."

Zo nods. "I like it."

"Thank you," I say, feeling even shyer.

"You mind if I pull up some yard and sit?"

"Go ahead, but the dogs will be all over you."

"That's okay. I like 'em." She sits down splay-legged, like you can sit when you wear pants instead of a skirt, and both dogs are immediately in her face. She laughs, then says, "You can sit, too, you know. But I don't guess you need an invitation to sit in your own yard."

I sit with my knees together and my legs to the side, spreading my skirt around me. "It feels strange to have people next door again. Your house had been empty for more than a year."

"I hope it doesn't feel strange in a bad way," Zo says.

"No, not at all," I say. "You seem nice." Is that the kind of thing people usually say to each other?

Zo smiles. "Just wait till you get to know me better, and we'll see how nice you think I am."

"Really?"

She laughs. "No, not really. I actually am pretty nice. But I'm finding things pretty strange myself right now."

"How's that?" I hug my knees to my chest but make sure to keep my skirt arranged.

"Well, moving here. We moved from Knoxville, which isn't like New York or Atlanta or anything, but it's still a city, and this"—she gestures around her—"isn't."

"No, it's not. So why did you move? If you don't mind me asking."

"I don't mind." Zo twists a strand of hair. "There are a lot of reasons. I was unhappy at school and not doing so well, and Owen was having some school trouble, too. Mom and Dad were getting tired of life being so fast-paced, and they had this dream of a place where they could grow vegetables and homeschool Owen and me. And then Dad, who's a nurse, heard from a friend of his about a one-year replacement position at the county health department here. He got the job and found the house for rent, and things just kind of fell into place." She shrugs. "So I guess I fell into this place."

"That sounds like my parents," I say. "They moved here to homestead in the country, too. But I was just a baby, so this is the only place I can remember living."

Zo nods. "You guys homeschool, too?"

"Yes. Always have."

"This is my first time trying the homeschool thing," Zo says. "Do you like it?"

"Well, I just started this week, and I haven't done anything much yet. So yeah, I love it." She grins, and I find myself grinning back.

The back door of our house swings open. Mama hurries over to where Zo and me are sitting. Mama's smiling, but she looks nervous. "I thought I heard voices," she says. "I mean, other than the Littles' usual whooping and hollering."

I stand up. I feel like I've been caught doing something wrong. "Mama, this is Zo. Her little brother Owen's over there on the trampoline. They're our new neighbors."

Zo stands up, too, and holds out her hand just as naturally as if she meets people all the time. "Nice to meet you," she says.

"Nice to meet you, too," Mama says, but she barely takes her hand. "Are y'all getting settled in next door?"

"We're trying," Zo says. "There are lots of boxes to unpack."

"Well, Libby," Mama says, "I guess we need to get the Littles in for their nap."

"Yes, ma'am." It's twenty minutes before their usual nap time. "Owen!" Zo yells. "Time to go!"

Owen is still on the trampoline, bouncing like a kangaroo. "Five more minutes?" he asks.

"No, buddy," Zo says. "Say thank you to your new friends for letting you use their trampoline."

"Thank you," Owen says, but he sounds unhappy to be leaving.

Zo puts her arm around Owen's shoulder. "See you, Libby."

"See you."

Once the Littles have gone upstairs, Mama finds me in the kitchen mixing up some lemonade. "Want a glass?" I ask.

"Better not. Seems like every time I drink something acidic I get heartburn. One of the joys of pregnancy."

"Some water, then?"

"Surely that'll be okay since my body kind of needs it to survive." She accepts a glass of water and sits at the kitchen table. "Sit with me a minute, Libby."

I obey, pretty sure we're about to have "a talk."

"So the kids from next door," Mama says, "did they just invite themselves over?"

I swallow hard. "Kind of yes and kind of no. Owen asked if he could play on the trampoline sometime and I said sure, if his mama said it was okay. But before I knew it, he was over the fence."

Mama smiles enough that I know she's not mad. "Sounds like what a little boy would do. But Libby, you know it would've also been a good idea to ask me if them coming over was okay?"

The knowledge that I've done wrong weighs me down like a lead ball in my stomach. "Yes, ma'am. I'm sorry. I just know that you use the Littles' recess time to do your office work. I didn't want to disturb you, and everything happened so fast."

"Don't make excuses." Mama's tone is firm. "Just ask for forgiveness."

I'm trying not to cry. "Will you forgive me, Mama?"

She smiles and reaches for my hand. "I forgive you."

I take a deep breath, like I'm sucking the forgiveness into my lungs. "Thank you. I'll pray for forgiveness tonight, too."

Mama squeezes my hand. "You're a good girl. I don't know what I'd do without your help around here. So what do the new neighbors seem like?"

"They seem nice, actually. They moved here to get away from the city. They're homeschooled. I think they're kind of like us."

"Really?" Mama looks thoughtful. "Well, the girl was wearing pants, but I wouldn't say she was dressed immodestly. Did they say anything about having a church?"

"No, but I don't guess they'd have one if they just moved. And really, we didn't talk that long."

Mama rests her chin in her hands and is quiet for a minute. "Well, here's what I'm thinking. I think we'll talk to your daddy about the new neighbors tonight, and if he says it's all right, tomorrow afternoon I might take a loaf of bread over there and introduce myself to the mother. Maybe then we'll be able to see if they're the sort of folks it would be all right to socialize with a little."

The "if" makes me worry a little. "And what if they're not?"

Mama shrugs. "Well, then it's a little awkward."

"Yes, ma'am, it sure would be." Especially when one of the neighbors is an eight-year-old boy who'll shimmy over your fence because you have trampoline.

DINNER IS SPAGHETTI, WHICH MEANS IT'S definitely a bath night for the Littles. Charity already has so much sauce smeared on her face it looks like she's got a big orange clown mouth.

"We met the neighbors today," Mama says, passing the basket of rolls. "Or at least the neighbor children."

"Were they worldly little heathens?" Daddy says, like he's half joking.

"Well, Libby can tell you more about them than I can," Mama says, and suddenly I'm nervous.

I set down my fork. "They seem nice. The girl's around my age and the boy's around Val's. They moved here to get away from the city."

"What does the father do for a living?" Daddy asks, cutting his spaghetti up into tiny sticks with his fork.

"He works for the health department," I say. I hope it's not a lie to leave out that Zo's daddy is a nurse. Daddy would think being a nurse is a strange job for a man, and we're already on shaky ground just because I mentioned the health department. Daddy doesn't have much use for what he calls the secular medical establishment, and Mama has her babies here at home with just Daddy to catch them. If we get sick, it's Mama who takes care of us, not a doctor.

"Hm," he says, chewing. "And the mother?"

"She stays home," I say, "and homeschools the children." This part, I know, will please him.

"Well, that's good anyway," he says.

"I was wondering, Bill," Mama says, "since tomorrow is baking day, maybe in the afternoon I could take the new neighbors a loaf of bread. I could meet the mother and get a feel for what she's like."

"I think that's a fine idea," Daddy says, gesturing with his fork. "You're a good judge of character, and it takes a virtuous woman to recognize another one."

Daddy and Mama share the special smile they have for each other, and I go back to my spaghetti, relieved. Daddy isn't displeased with me or Mama, and he agreed to Mama's request. There was no need for scolding or correction.

I love Daddy so, so much, but my love for him is different than my love for Mama. With Mama, I can relax, but since Daddy has been anointed by God to be the patriarch of this family, my love for him is mixed with fear. I don't want to make him mad or unhappy, and I try to be worthy of his love. Sometimes when I need to ask Daddy for something or explain a wrongdoing to him, I feel a little of what it must be like to tremble before the throne of God.

ZO ANSWERS THE DOOR RIGHT AFTER Mama knocks. She's wearing jeans and a red T-shirt with a cartoon cat on it. I wonder how we must look, Mama and all of us kids, clumped together in the doorway.

"We brought you some home-baked bread as a welcoming present," Mama says.

"Thank you," Zo says. "It smells great."

"Is your mama around?" Mama asks. "I was hoping we could introduce ourselves."

"She's around back in her workshop," Zo says. "I'll take you." She comes out on the porch without putting on shoes and closes the front door behind her. We follow her to the little white outbuilding in the backyard. She knocks and yells, "Mom! Company!"

Zo's about my age, but her mama must be at least ten years older than mine. Her hair, which is straight and long like Zo's, probably used to be dark like Zo's, too, but now it's streaked with thick stripes of gray. She wears glasses and has on a loose, modest knit shirt and floral skirt. But I'm not interested in what she's wearing as much as what she's doing. She's sitting at a big wooden loom, and spilling out from it is a stretch of fabric with all the colors of a winter sunset: soft pink, dark purple, inky blue. I don't know if the cloth is a cape or a comforter or what, but it's beautiful. It makes me think of Joseph's coat of many colors.

"These are our neighbors I was telling you about," Zo says. "I guess I'll let them introduce themselves."

Zo's mom gets up and approaches Mama with her hand extended. "I'm Jen Forrester," she says. Her smile looks like Zo's.

"I'm Rebecca Hazlett, but most of the time, I'm just Becky," Mama says. "And these are my children. Are you ready for all their names? Because a quiz will follow."

I've heard Mama make this little joke dozens of times, but it always seems to put people at ease. It seems to do the trick with Mrs. Forrester, too.

"I tell you what," Mrs. Forrester says. "My eyes were starting to cross from working on that thing so long, and I know Zo made a pitcher of her famous raspberry lemonade a little while ago. Why don't I take a little break, and we can all have some lemonade in the backyard?"

"That would be very nice," Mama says. "What do you say, children?"

We all say "thank you."

As we're leaving the workshop, Zo leans over and whispers, "Don't believe everything my mom says. My raspberry lemonade's not really famous."

"Really?" I grin back at her.

"Well, at best it's famous nationally. It hasn't even begun to penetrate the international market."

She says this so seriously that for a minute I'm not sure if she's joking or not. But then she grins, and I know.

There's not enough room for all of us at the wooden picnic table in the Forresters' backyard, so Just hangs back, and the Littles run and play with Owen while Mama, Patience, Mrs. Forrester, Zo, and I sit. Zo's raspberry lemonade may not be famous, but it is good, and so are the gingersnaps she serves with it.

"I'm glad y'all came over," Mrs. Forrester says. "I've wanted to come and say hi, but Zo told me you homeschool, and I didn't want to interrupt your work."

"We keep a pretty tight schedule," Mama says, and I notice she sounds a little nervous like I was when I first met Zo. "With this many kids, you have to."

"I would think so. I don't know how you do it," Mrs. Forrester says, which is one of the things Mama hears from strangers all the time. "Just these two keep me pretty busy. You know, for the longest time, we thought Zo was going to be our only one, and then eight years later, here comes Owen!"

Mama smiles. "Well, it's not in our hands, is it? But what a blessing to have a son after waiting so long!"

"Yes," Mrs. Forrester says, but her voice sounds a little strange. "We're pretty loose in how we do our homeschooling. Too loose, some people might say. But the kids are good at working independently, and that way I also get time to work on my weaving. I sell it online and at craft shops and art fairs. This summer, if the garden does well, we're going to sell produce and crafts at the farmers' market in Knoxville."

"You do beautiful work," Mama says, and I can tell she means it. "I love to knit, but I've never tried weaving." Mama's always knitting something: booties for whatever baby's on the way, scarves and hats for winter.

"I could teach you," Mrs. Forrester says. She looks over at Patience and me. "And any of the kids who might want to learn. We could set up one afternoon a week for a weaving lesson."

"That's so nice," Mama says. "Only we should pay you for your time, and I can't offer you much."

Mrs. Forrester smiles. "I'll tell you what. If you bake us a loaf of that beautiful bread whenever you make some for yourselves, we'll call it even."

Mama grins, then looks down, a little shy. "I bake bread every Thursday."

Mrs. Forrester holds out her hand. "It's a deal, then."

Mama and Mrs. Forrester shake hands like businessmen, except they're laughing as they're doing it. "Mom, is it okay if Libby and I walk down to the creek?" Zo asks. I'm surprised to hear her include me in a special invitation.

"Sure, if her mom says it's all right."

"You may," Mama says. "But just for a few minutes. We need to round up the Littles and get them home for their nap soon."

"Yes, ma'am." I'm already getting up from the picnic table.

"May I go, too, Mama?" Patience says.

Mama nods, and for a second I feel irritated at Patience. Zo wanted me to go to the creek, not her. But I know this thought is selfish and sinful as soon as I think it. It's strange, too, that it should even occur to me. I never go anywhere without at least a sibling or two tagging along.

"The creek is the best part about where we live," Zo says, leading us across the backyard to the woods. "Well, the creek and my room, but I don't have it fixed up all the way yet. My room in our house in Knoxville was shaped just like a regular rectangular box. My room here has all these weird angles and corners."

"Our room is like that, too," I say.

"Yeah, I guess all these old farmhouses have weird-shaped rooms on the top floor," Zo says. We're in the woods now, following a path that looks like it's been well worn over the years. The afternoon sun is shining through the leaves in the trees, and I remember reading in one of my homeschool books that stained glass windows in churches had been designed so the light would shine through them like sunlight through the branches of trees.

Zo turns around to look at Patience and me, but keeps on walking, just backward. "There's this weird part of the wall that comes out at about a forty-five-degree angle over the toilet in the upstairs bathroom. Dad says a guy has to be a limbo dancer to pee in there."

I giggle, maybe a little too hard, and Patience covers her mouth with her hands and blushes.

"TMI, sorry," Zo says, smiling. "I have a tendency just to say whatever pops into my brain."

The creek isn't that deep or wide, but it is pretty. Fuzzy cattails grow beside it, and because of the spring rains, the greenish water flows steadily over the smooth creek stones.

"You wanna wade?" Zo says, kicking off her sneakers. Her toenails are painted blue. "The water's pretty chilly, but it feels good." She rolls up her jeans to just below the knee and steps in. "Anybody else coming?"

Patience's arms are crossed over her chest. "I don't want to get my feet muddy. And besides, we can't stay long."

"I might as well go in for just a minute," I say, pulling off my shoes and socks. I gather up my skirt and hold it just below my knees so it won't get wet. Why not? We're all girls here.

"You're going to get your socks all muddy when you put them back on," Patience says as I step toward the water.

"I'll walk back barefoot."

"What if you step on a bee?" Patience says.

"Then the bee will come out of it worse than I will. You're such a worrywart, Patience."

The water is cold, but the mud at the bottom feels nice and squishy between my toes. I wiggle them to make it squish more, and then I feel tiny kisses at my ankles. I look down and see little fish swimming up to me and laugh. "Minnows."

"I know," Zo says. "They like to nibble on you. It's kind of adorable. You know, in some spas in Thailand if you get a pedicure, they soak your feet in a tub of tiny fish that nibble away the dead skin."

"That's nasty!" Patience says. "And you just sit there and let them eat you?"

"Well, it's not like they're piranha or anything," I say.

"Yeah," Zo says, laughing. "It would be bad if they were, though, wouldn't it? You go in for a pedicure and come out with missing toes."

"We should be getting back," Patience says over Zo's and my laughter. "It's past time for the Littles' nap."

I don't want her to be right, but I know she is. I step out of the water and gather my shoes and socks to carry with me. Somehow my feet are colder out of the water than they were in it.

"Wading will be better in a month or so when the water gets warmer," Zo says.

I remember another experience with cold water. "Hey, Patience, do you remember how cold the water was when you got baptized? Your lips turned blue, and you couldn't catch your breath."

Patience smiles a little. "It was cold, but it was good, too. When I came out of the water I couldn't breathe, but then this clean, fresh air filled my lungs, and when I breathed it in, it was like I was a new person. Does your family go to church, Zo?"

"Not since we've moved here," Zo says as we start back down the path. "But in Knoxville we went to the United Church of Christ."

"So you're Christians?" Patience asks.

"Of course they're Christians, Patience," I say. "Why would a church be called the Church of Christ if it wasn't Christian?"

"I was just thinking about Daddy," Patience says. "He said there was churches in the cities where people didn't even believe in God."

"Like the Unitarians?" Zo says as we step out of the woods. "There are a couple of those churches in Knoxville. I think there are people who go there who believe in God, but you don't have to believe in God to go there."

I can't even imagine it. What kind of crazy church makes believing in God optional?

ZO

CHAPTER 4

"So did they invite you to come to their church and handle snakes?" Dad says.

We're sitting around the table eating homemade pizza. Spinach, mushrooms, and sun-dried tomatoes. One of the downsides of living in the country is that you can't order out for pizza, so you have to make it yourself. We've gotten pretty good at it, but we do have some dough stuck to the ceiling from where Owen tried to spin it in the air like pizza guys on TV.

"No, they were nice," Mom says. "And you'd better be, too, when you meet them."

"I'll be on my best behavior." Daddy holds his bottle of beer in the air in a salute. "And I promise not to rant about any of my favorite subjects in their presence, like how legalizing marijuana would reduce prescription drug abuse and revitalize the American agricultural economy. Or about how we are a nation of immigrants—"

"Or," I chime in to quote chapter and verse of another of Dad's favorite rants, "how the US education system is turning kids into stressed-out, test-taking drones who'll never know how to use any tool besides a number-two pencil."

"Actually," Mom says, reaching for a second slice, "I think they might agree with you on that one."

"So," Dad says to Mom, picking a piece of spinach from his beard, "what did you and Sister Praise-the-Lord talk about?'

"Her name's Becky." Mom hands Dad a napkin for beard-mopping. "And I don't know . . . we talked about the kids and weaving and knitting—"

"Ah, the stuff of the womenfolk. Grinding wheat, washing clothes in the river, that kind of thing." Dad takes a swig of his beer.

"Pretty much, yeah," Mom says. "And from the heft of that loaf of bread she brought, she actually might grind her own wheat."

Dad looks over at Owen and me. "And what about you guys? What did you think of the Godly offspring?"

"We didn't really talk," Owen says. He's already on his third slice of pizza. He only weighs eighty pounds even though he eats his weight in food every day. "We just played."

"A sensible approach," Dad says. "How about you, Zo?"

"I don't guess we talked that much either. We walked down to the creek and just kind of goofed off." But I can't look at my dad's chocolate brown eyes—so full of affection and trust and good humor—and not tell him. "There was one thing, though. Libby's sister Patience asked me if we went to church."

Dad rolls his eyes. This is clearly the kind of thing he was expecting.

"I said we hadn't gone to church here because we just moved . . ." I take a deep breath. "But that back in Knoxville we used to go to the United Church of Christ."

Mom laughs. "Yeah, on Monday nights. For yoga."

"Hey," I say, "I didn't say when or why we went there. It was just awkward, and I figured if I named a church, she'd back off, which she did."

"So much for homeschooling putting an end to peer pressure," Dad says.

I sigh. "It wasn't peer pressure exactly. It's just, well, what am I supposed to say, that my dad's an atheist and my mom dabbles in Wicca?"

Dad laughs. "Well, if you did, it would certainly put an end to the conversation."

"And to any future ones," Mom adds.

"I have to say I'm kind of surprised at you, Zo," Dad says, his tone serious all of a sudden. "It's not generally in the nature of my outspoken gender-fluid offspring to claim a more mainstream identity just to make people more comfortable."

"Yeah," Owen says. "Like remember on vacation when I begged to try a Happy Meal and you finally let me get one and then the person at the drive-through asked if it was for a boy or a girl? And then Zo started yelling into the speaker about how gender isn't—what's the word, Zo?"

"Binary," I say. "And even for cisgender kids, who's to say a girl might not prefer a Hot Wheels car to a Hello Kitty? Or vice versa?"

"Exactly," Dad says, even though he's heard me say this a million times. He and I are very indulgent of each other's rants.

I know it was weird to try to pass my family off as Christians. I'm not even sure why I said it. Some of it was to get prissy Patience off my back. But that wasn't my main reason. "I guess I didn't want so scare Libby off. She seems like a nice person."

"I understand not wanting to scare her," Mom says. "But it's hard to get to know somebody while you're hiding a big part of yourself. Especially for somebody who's not good at hiding." Mom smiles over at Dad. "You remember how Zo would play hide and seek when she was little?"

Dad laughs. "Daddy! I'm right here! Under the table!"

It's true I've never been one for hiding. I guess I'm like Dad that way. I tend to just come right out and say what I think, let people know who I really am, and if they don't like me, it's their problem. Unless they turn it into mine.

Like in third grade when I decided I wanted to be called Hugo because of a kid in a book I was obsessed with. I also wanted to marry my best friend Abby. I couldn't keep quiet about any of this, and some kids ended up telling the teacher I was calling myself Hugo and saying that Abby and I were engaged. The teacher was a total Bible Belt Betty and freaked out and called my parents in for a meeting. She expressed concerns about my "gender confusion" and suggested counseling. Mom and Dad refused. Dad refused loudly. "I spent most of third grade saying I was Batman," he said. "I suppose you'd want to cure me of that, too."

The thing that sucked worst, though, was that the teacher called Abby's mom and told her what I'd been saying. Abby's mom freaked out and wouldn't let me play with her anymore. Shortly after that, Mom pulled me out of public school and put me in a crunchy granola Montessori, which was much better. Like Dad says, you can really let your freak flag fly at Montessori.

But there's no such thing as Montessori high school—at least not in Knoxville—and I was scared to go back to the publics. Freshman year turned out to be awesome, though. I joined the orchestra and the art club and the Gay–Straight Alliance, which I was amazed even existed. The GSA was small but active. There were half a dozen gay boys, one trans girl, one lesbian, and about twenty straight girls whose hobby it was to be supportive of the gays. I don't mean to sound unkind about the straight girls. I appreciated their good intentions, but they did treat it like a hobby.

Hadley, the lesbian in the group, was supercute, with short, spiky bleached hair and a jean jacket she'd decorated in Sharpie with band names and quotations, and a chin dimple so adorable it still makes my stomach ache to think about it. One day she asked me if I wanted to go with her to Pop Culture, this hipster gourmet popsicle place across the street from school. I was too dumb to know she was asking me on a date. But soon popsicles turned into walks in the park and then into afternoons at her house or mine watching Netflix and cuddling. We were so happy. Until Hadley wasn't.

Being a lesbian was really important to Hadley, and she wanted me to say I was one, too. But if I said I was a lesbian, I'd be saying I was a 100 percent girl who only liked other 100 percent girls, and I couldn't say that.

Sometimes I feel like a boy in lipstick. Sometimes I feel like a girl with a bulge in her jeans. Sometimes I don't even feel like I have a gender—that the body that contains my personality is no more significant than the jar that holds the peanut butter. I'm fine with all of this, but Hadley wasn't. She wanted to be with a woman, not with some "amorphous thing," as she called me once when we were fighting.

Then one of the supportive straight girls in the GSA, a curvy Goth named Gwen, broke up with her boyfriend, came out as a lesbian, and came after Hadley. Gwen the Goth was a total girl, all black lace and red nail polish, and Hadley dumped me for her in a text.

After that, things went dark. I quit GSA because I couldn't stand seeing the two of them together. And after I dropped that, it was like I couldn't stop dropping things. I dropped orchestra. I stopped studying and stopped remembering to turn in assignments, and my GPA dropped from a high B to a low C. I dropped into bed as soon as I got home from school and barely moved. I also dropped about twelve pounds because even my favorite foods tasted like cotton balls, and picking up a fork seemed like too much effort. I was scary skinny, but it wasn't anorexia so much as apathy.

This is when my parents decided to send me to Ron the Therapist, a nice old gay guy with a rabbity smile like Freddie Mercury's. Ron told me he was an old-school gay and didn't know as much as he should about gender nonbinary people, but he wanted me to help educate him. He showed me pictures of his Labradoodles, and we talked about our pets, and after a few sessions I was talking not just about how Hadley broke my heart but about how easy it seemed for everybody else to be who they were and how hard it was for me to be me.

"Let me tell you a secret," Ron said, leaning forward in his cushy armchair and speaking in a stage whisper. "It's never easy. They're all faking it."

I was so wrapped up in my own darkness after the Hadley breakup that I didn't realize things had turned dark for my whole family. Mom's high school teaching job had "turned toxic," as she says, both because of government regulations and a new tyrannical principal. Dad was exhausted all the time because he was pulling twelve-hour shifts at the hospital, and Owen had started having academic trouble and had been referred for psychoeducational testing. We were all a mess.

"I don't know if Owen has ADHD or not," I remember Dad saying. "But I know we're all suffering from the effects of a culture with ADHD."

Then Dad was approached about a one-year replacement position running the health department in Grant County, a rural area mainly known for growing delicious tomatoes. A country life seemed like the solution to all our problems. Dad could have a regular eight-thirty to four-thirty job instead of working crazy hours. Because the cost of living would be cheaper, Mom could quit teaching and focus on her weaving. She could also homeschool Owen and me for the year, which would put her in charge of an educational system she could actually control. Plus, homeschooling would get me out of my high school hell and give Owen one-on-one academic help.

Dad said it would do us all good to be in the country where we could hear ourselves think and weren't always racing around to get to the next thing we had to do. Also, he said we could get bunnies, which I'm not-so-patiently waiting for.

The pace is slow here, and it's quiet. Country life makes me think of books I read when I was little, like *The Swiss Family Robinson*, where the family is shipwrecked on an island. Or the Little House books where it's just Ma, Pa, Laura, Mary, and Baby Carrie homesteading together in the middle of nowhere. That kind of living brings you close as a family, but

I've still got to wonder, did any of the Robinson kids or the Ingalls kids ever wish they could hang out with somebody they weren't related to?

I think that's why I was so quick to mislead Libby into thinking we were churchgoers. So far, she's my only social outlet.

Well, I should say my only in-person social outlet because I do have something the Robinsons and the Ingalls didn't: the Internet. And so tonight, after I help with the dinner dishes, I go up to my room.

I love my room. When we rented the house, the landlord said we should feel free to paint it and decorate it the way we liked. Mom and Dad let us pick out which rooms would be ours and told us we could make them look however we wanted. For Owen, this meant Legos everywhere. But I wanted my room to say something about me and also to be a shrine to the people who inspire me. I painted my walls electric blue because of a line from a David Bowie song, and I did a really good job except that Edgar, our black cat, ended up electric blue in a couple of spots, too.

On the electric blue walls are pictures of Bowie in several of his incarnations: Ziggy Stardust, Aladdin Sane, the Thin White Duke. I have Dad to thank for my Bowie fixation. Dad is a music freak—a vinyl freak, specifically, and as soon as I started talking about my complex feelings about gender, he pulled out a stack of Bowie albums from the seventies: *Hunky Dory*, *The Rise and Fall of Ziggy Stardust* and the *Spiders from Mars*, *Aladdin Sane*, *Diamond Dogs*. Even though it was old music, it was new to me, and as Dad said, "It has stood the test of time."

I'm not exaggerating when I say David Bowie changed my
life. In fact, you could probably divide my life into two
sections, Before Bowie (BB) and After Bowie (AB). Some of
it was the way he looked—how he'd be in a brocade dress on
one album cover, then a tailored men's suit on another, then
androgynously naked and half-human/half-dog on another.
(Not that my fluidity extends to being doglike. I love dogs,
but I don't want to eat Alpo or pee on shrubbery.)

Most of it was his music, though. So many artists have one
sound and one style, and that's it. But with Bowie, there are
so many sounds and styles, yet they're all him. No matter
what mood I'm in, there's a Bowie album that fits it.

After Hadley dumped me, I played "Life on Mars?" so
much that my mom started calling it That Damn Song. I'm
not as depressed now as I was then, so tonight it's *Scary
Monsters*, the album that always makes Dad go on and on
about what a kickass guitarist Robert Fripp is. With Bowie
blasting, I stretch out on my bed and open my laptop. Country
Internet is slower than city Internet, but after a few minutes,
I'm able to log onto Facebook to see if Claire is around.

Claire was in the GSA with me. She's a petite Thai-American
girl who, through some weird fluke of nature, was born with
boy parts. Boy parts aside, though, she's way more of a girl
than I am. She wears her straight black hair in a sleek bob and
applies her makeup artfully. Claire and I were super close
friends until the Hadley thing happened. Then, I'm ashamed
to say, I turned out to be the kind of crappy person who
ditches her friends once she has a significant other.

The fact that Hadley was extremely demanding of my
time is no excuse for my behavior, and once Hadley dumped

me, I felt like it would make me an even crappier person to go back to Claire with my tail between my legs, begging for sympathy after having neglected her forever. And so I disappeared. Fortunately, Claire found me and forgave me.

Claire's name pops up in the chat box, and I start to type.

Zo: *Howdy.*

Claire: *Is this how you talk now that you're a country mouse?*

Zo: *Yup.*

Claire: *Well, how-DEE right back atcha!*

Zo: *What R U doing?*

Claire: *Homework. Some of us don't have the luxury of hippie-dippy homeschooling.*

Zo: *Homework, huh? That's strange . . . it looks to me like you're on Facebook.*

Claire: *Doing research.*

Zo: *On FB?*

Claire: *No, hopping back and forth between research and FB. Multitasking.*

Zo: *You'd better not let your mom catch you multitasking.*

Claire: *I know, right? The woman who doesn't care if I'm trans as long as I don't let my GPA slip. So how's country life so far? Do you have bunnies yet? I <3 BUNNIES!*

Zo: *Dad got the stuff to build a hutch from the farm co-op yesterday. We're going to build it this weekend, then get the bunnies.*

Claire: *Are you afraid your cat might try to eat them?*

Zo: *Edgar? R U kidding? To catch a bunny you have to get off the couch.*

Claire: *Haha*

Zo: *Hey, did I tell you I met the girl who lives next door the other day? She's about my age.*

Claire: *Is she cute?*

Zo: *It's not like that. Her family's really religious. Uber Jesusy.*

Claire: *Yikes.*

Zo: *She's nice tho, and at least she's somebody to talk to.*

Claire: *If you're careful what you say.*

Zo: *I know.*

Claire: *She'll try to convert you, you know. That's how those people are. You can't have more than two conversations before they're trying to pressure you to come to the dark side.*

Zo: *You sound like a homophobe talking about gays.*

Claire: *The difference is the homophobes are wrong, and I'm right. Crap. Here comes my mom. Gotta go—*

Claire's name disappears from the chat box. I shut my laptop and go over to the stereo and flip *Scary Monsters* to Side B.

The big difference between Claire and me is that she's so absolute in her opinions, so sure about the way things are. Like what she was saying about Libby. Is it impossible for two people on such opposite sides of things to become friends? Maybe we could be like two sides of a vinyl record, not opposites so much as complementary.

CHAPTER 5

THIS IS WHAT AN AFTERNOON OF homeschooling looks like: me, lying in a hammock, barefoot, crunching an apple and reading *Brave New World*. Mom designed this English class for me called Special Topics in Dystopian Fiction. She got the idea because I was obsessed with all the teen dystopian novels that have come out over the past few years. She thought it would be cool for me to read what she calls "the classics of the genre," so she assigned me *1984* (which I was already inclined to like because there's a Bowie song about it), *Brave New World*, and *Fahrenheit 451*. After I read them all, I have to write a paper about them.

Since Owen's younger, Mom's pretty hands-on with his homeschooling, but with me it's mostly independent study. I read novels and write about them, read the chapters in a giganto US history book and answer questions, and use a software program for Spanish. Dad does math and biology with me after he gets home from work. Overall, it's not a bad way to be educated. It amazes me how much faster the work goes than in public school, where you waste all this time shuffling from one class to another and waiting for other people to finish.

Once I'm done with my assigned reading, I hear whooping and laughter from next door. Libby's little brother and sisters are climbing on the swing set and jumping on the trampoline while Libby watches them like a mother hen. I look after Owen sometimes, too, but watching one little kid is no big deal. Libby's got triple the responsibility.

I toss my apple core and topple out of the hammock (there is no graceful way to get out of a hammock). I walk over to the fence and wait for Libby to notice me. There's something about her that makes it seem like she'd be easy to startle, like a shy forest creature.

"Oh, hi," she says when she sees me.

"Hi back." I kind of wave with my copy of *Brave New World*.

"Are you reading that for school?" She's wearing a long-sleeved, light blue floral shirt with a long denim skirt that I guess substitutes for jeans. Her brothers, I've noticed, get to wear jeans, but they're the baggy, shapeless kind that look weird on young people. Dad jeans.

"Yes. It's a novel." She could read that right off the cover, but that's still what comes out of my mouth.

She leans on the fence. "We don't read fiction for homeschool, just textbooks and the Bible."

My dad could make a compelling argument that the Bible *is* a work of fiction, but I choose not to go there. "What do you do for English class?"

"Grammar, mostly." She wrinkles her nose like grammar's not her favorite thing. "My sister reads some Christian fiction."

I can't imagine that's very thrilling stuff. I wonder if all the plots end with a baptism.

"The only novels I read are the Narnia ones," Libby says. "I read those over and over."

"Oh, I loved those when I was a kid! Those and *The Hobbit* and the Oz books." I almost add some more modern children's fantasy novels like the Harry Potters and *The Golden Compass*, but I'm 99.9 percent sure those aren't on her approved reading list.

"I wasn't allowed to read *The Wizard of Oz* because of witchcraft."

I force myself not to roll my eyes. "Even though they kill the Wicked Witch?"

"Yes, but there's a good witch, too, and there can't be good witches. 'Thou shalt not suffer a witch to live.' Exodus twenty-two, eighteen."

"Oh, right," I say, picturing angry Christian Munchkins burning Glinda at the stake. That pink hoop skirt would flame up something crazy.

"But I've never heard of that other book you mentioned. *The Rabbit?*"

"*The Hobbit*," I say, and we both laugh. "Hobbits are little short people, kind of like dwarves but with different person-alities and furry feet. The main character in the story is Bilbo Baggins. He's this hobbit who'd rather stay home but ends up getting sucked into this big adventure. J. R. R. Tolkien wrote it. He and C. S. Lewis were best friends. I've got a copy of it in my room. I'll be right back."

When I get back to the fence, Owen's already in the Hazletts' yard and on their trampoline.

"You can come over, too," Libby says, so I shrug and climb over the fence like I'm sure Owen did. I don't guess

Libby does much fence climbing since she has to wear skirts all the time.

"Here," I say, holding out my copy of *The Hobbit.* "You can borrow it."

"Really?" She looks at it like she's afraid to touch it. "Are you sure?"

"Well, I figure it's pretty safe to loan you a book. I mean, I know where you live."

Libby laughs. "I guess you do, don't you?" She takes the book and studies the cover for a moment. "Thank you. I'll take good care of it."

"That'll be more than I've done. It's just about read to pieces."

"So are my Narnia books. I guess that means they're loved. It's like this baby doll Faith has. Its hair is one big rat's nest, and one of its eyes won't open, and its clothes are always stained with whatever Faith's been eating or drinking. But it looks so worn out because she loves it so much."

"Love wears you out," I say, thinking of Hadley and what a wreck I was by the time she was through with me.

"Of course it wouldn't be like that if the doll was a real baby," Libby says, smiling. "You can't just say my baby's a mess because I love it so much."

"No, that definitely wouldn't hold up in court," I say, and we both laugh again. Libby sits on the grass and motions for me to join her. I do.

I look over to see Owen and Libby's sisters jumping dangerously high on the trampoline. "It's amazing any kids live to see adulthood when you think about it. I don't think I'd make a very good parent."

"Of course you will," Libby says. "You learn a lot just by looking after your younger brothers and sisters."

"Yeah, well, I just have Owen, and he pretty much takes care of himself, so I don't have the experience you do. They tried to teach a little about parenting in health class freshman year, but it was a joke, like the rest of the Sex Ed unit."

"Oh," Libby says. Her cheeks flush, and she looks everywhere but at me.

"Sorry. I didn't mean to embarrass you."

"It's okay." She finally looks back at me. "Daddy says they talk about things like that in public schools. About . . . what you said and about lots of things that go against God's word." She looks at me more closely. "What's it like?"

"What? Sex Ed?"

"No." Her blush returns. "School. Just says it's like prison. When he sees a big yellow school bus, he always says, 'There goes the prison bus.' Is that what it's like?"

"Well, I can't say for sure because I've never been to prison," I say, laughing. "But I'd say school's different because you get to leave every day at three-thirty, and I'm pretty sure they don't let you do that in prison. I guess that instead of being in prison, school's more like having a job. There are some nice people but a lot of mean ones, and you do some interesting work but a lot of boring work." It's weird. I guess people who send their kids to regular schools look at families like the Hazletts and think they're all control freaks who keep their kids imprisoned in their homes. But apparently kids like the Hazletts look at the regular school kids like they're doing hard time.

"That's about what I figured," Libby says. "That it wasn't a great place but that they don't keep you chained to the wall or anything. It makes sense it would be like a job." She looks off into the distance, like she's thinking hard. "You know, I've never thought I was missing anything by not going to school, but sometimes I wonder . . . " She breaks into a shy grin, then shakes her head. "Never mind."

"It's okay. You can tell me. I won't tell anyone."

She's quiet, like she's thinking hard about whether or not to say anything. Finally, she scoots closer to me, leans forward, and whispers, "I've wondered what it might be like to have a job. When I'm an adult, I mean."

That's it? Her shocking confession? "Well," I say, "what kind of job do you think you'd like to have?"

"Oh, but that's why I didn't want to say anything. I shouldn't even be wondering about having a job because I won't have one." She speaks with such certainty, maybe more certainty than I've ever felt about anything.

"Because it's against your religion?"

Libby nods. "Married women can't work outside the home. God will choose somebody for me to marry, and then I'll have all the babies God wills, and I'll take care of them and the house and the homeschooling just like my mama does now."

"Because that's what God wants women to do?" From her voice, I can't tell whether or not she's happy about the way God has supposedly mapped out her life.

She nods again. "That's right."

"And God wants that for *all* women?"

"That's what the Bible says. And it's what Daddy and the pastor say, too."

I don't want to offend her, but I feel like I have to argue a little. "What if there was a girl who didn't want that? What if there was a girl who wanted to go to college and make lots of friends and have a career and not even get married?"

Libby looks at me hard. Her eyes are blue and intense. "I guess I'd say it shouldn't be about what she wants. It should be about what God wants."

"So if the girl didn't do what God wanted, she'd—what? Go to hell?"

"That's what the Bible says," Libby says.

"Well, that sucks."

Libby reaches out and touches my arm. "I'll pray for you, Zo. I don't want you to go to hell. I like you."

She sounds so heartfelt it's hard not to be moved even though I think hell is a bunch of horseshit. She believes in it, though, so it's real to her. "Thanks," I say. "I like you, too."

She looks down at the grass and plucks at a piece. "I don't think anybody's ever said that to me before."

I stretch my legs out and study the blue polish on my toenails, which Mom says makes them look bruised. "You know, when I think about my future, I feel kind of excited but mostly scared because it's so uncertain. Do you feel that way, too, or do you feel calm because you know God has everything planned out for you?"

"I should feel calm," Libby says, "but I don't always. Sometimes I feel scared. So I have to pray." She looks at me like she can't believe what just came out of her mouth. "I've never said that to anybody before. You're easy to talk to, Zo."

"You two sure are deep in conversation."

We must have been because I didn't even hear Mrs. Hazlett come up. She's wearing a shapeless floral jumper and a pink pair of those ugly plastic clogs nobody wears anymore. Well, nobody but her, I guess.

"Hi, Mrs. Hazlett," I say. Libby stands up, so I do, too. "My mom says you and the girls can come over tomorrow for a weaving lesson any time you want."

This gets a smile. "Tell her three o'clock works for us. Oh, and I've got a fresh loaf of bread I'll send with you when you leave." Her gaze shifts to Libby. "What's that book you've got?"

"*The Hobbit*," Libby says, handing it over. "Zo loaned it to me. Is it okay for me to read?"

Mrs. Hazlett turns the book over in her hands. "Oh, I remember this one. It has that critter in it who's kind of like a frog—what's his name?"

"Gollum?" I say.

She grins. "That's it, and he talks funny, kind of hisses. And he was a man, but he's been so eaten up with the sin of greed it's turned him into a monster."

I probably wouldn't have given Gollum such a theological interpretation, but it makes sense, so I nod.

Mrs. Hazlett hands the book back to Libby. "You can read it. Just make sure you're careful with it so you can return it to Zo in good condition."

Libby hugs the book to her chest. "Yes, ma'am."

PRINTING UP INSTRUCTIONS FROM THE INTERNET may not be the best way to learn how to build a rabbit hutch. Dad and Owen and I are in the backyard, standing in front of a bunch of wood slats and a roll of wire mesh as though staring at these items will make them spring into motion and form themselves into a viable rabbitat.

Dad flips through the instructions again, rubs his hand through his hair, and curses.

"You'd better not let the neighbors hear that," Owen says.

Fortunately, Libby and her mom and sisters are out of earshot, in Mom's workshop having a weaving lesson. Since Mom gave up on me learning to weave years ago, I opted to stay outside and help Dad and Owen build the rabbit hutch. Apparently I'm no good at that either.

To tell the truth, Dad isn't the handyman he thinks he is. He's good at making lists of supplies and driving to the Home Depot in Johnson City to get them, but once he brings them home, he doesn't necessarily know what to do with them. He abandons as many projects as he finishes, and I'm starting to worry about the rabbit hutch. Maybe we should've bought a ready-made one instead of trying to build something cool.

"Hidy!" a voice calls from the other side of the fence. I look over to see Libby's dad and her hulking oldest brother. Someday, I promise myself, I will get all of her siblings' names.

"Hey, neighbor!" Dad says, turning on the charming smile he always uses to greet strangers. "Come on over if you like. Your wife and girls are over in the shop."

Mr. Hazlett and Justice (that's his name!) come through the gate. "What're you fellers working on?" Mr. Hazlett says.

"A rabbit hutch," Dad calls back. "Though right now we're really just looking at the parts it's supposed to take to build it."

"Care if we come over and have a look?" Mr. Hazlett says. He's wearing his Hazlett and Sons Pest Control hat and uniform, so he must've just gotten off work.

"Please do," Dad calls back. "We need all the help we can get."

That's one of the cool things about Dad. He's not one of those guys whose ego won't let him admit he needs help. He refuses to buy a GPS, but he will stop to ask for directions.

Mr. Hazlett holds out his hand. "Bill Hazlett," he says.

"Todd Forrester," Dad says, taking Mr. Hazlett's big paw. Dad's not much of a hand shaker. He says it reminds him of dogs sniffing each other's butts, but if somebody sticks his hand out first, he'll still shake it to be polite.

"This is my oldest boy, Justice," Mr. Hazlett says.

Justice sticks his hand out, too. "Pleasure to meet you, sir. I like your beard. It looks like he just walked right out of the Bible, don't it, Daddy?"

Mr. Hazlett grins. "It does. Of course, there wasn't no barber shops back in those days." He looks at the wood and wire on the ground like he's sizing up the situation. "A rabbit hutch, huh?"

"Yep," Dad says.

"Rabbits for food or for pets?" Mr. Hazlett asks.

"Pets!" Owen says, with a catch in his voice. We're all vegetarians, but Owen has the softest heart of us all. One night he looked up from his salad and asked if plants feel pain. He'd probably be a vegan if it didn't mean he had to give up cheese on his pizza.

"Pets it is," Mr. Hazlett says, but he and Justice glance at each other as if Owen's desire to pet bunnies instead of eat them is somehow morally suspect. "Can I take a look at your plans?"

Dad hands Mr. Hazlett the papers. Mr. Hazlett eyeballs them for a couple of minutes. "You care if we help you'uns a little?"

"I think that would be very neighborly, thank you," Dad says.

And just like that, Mr. Hazlett takes over. He delegates jobs to Justice and Dad and gives Owen some sandpaper to smooth out rough edges in the wood "so the bunnies won't get splinters." Everybody has something to do but me.

"I'm happy to help, too," I say, like I'm asking Mr. Hazlett permission to work on my own family's project.

"I would've thought you'd be helping your mama with her weaving," Justice says in a tone I don't much appreciate.

"Mom doesn't need my help with weaving," I say. "I thought since I'm going to be taking care of the rabbits, I might as well start by helping with their housing."

"See, it's just her homemaking instinct, Justice," Mr. Hazlett says. "You shouldn't have questioned her."

I can see Dad measuring his words before he lets them out of his mouth. "I don't know if instinct has anything to do with it," Dad says. "Zo's not a bird building a nest. Zo is a person."

"That's true," Mr. Hazlett says. "We are not beasts of the field or the woods or the air. We serve a higher purpose." He reaches into Dad's toolbox and hands me a tape measure. "You can help with the measuring, okay, honey?"

I can see the conflict brewing behind Dad's eyes.

"Okay," I say to Mr. Hazlett, but it feels like I'm also agreeing with Dad that we'll keep our mouths shut in order to get this job done.

After that, no matter what Mr. Hazlett thinks our "higher purpose" is, our real purpose is this rabbit hutch. And I have to say, with Mr. Hazlett in charge, the project flows smoothly. He is very skilled at dividing a job up into steps and components for different people to do. Well, except for his tendency toward sexism. But the longer we work, the more things he lets me do.

After a while, my mom and Mrs. Hazlett and Libby and Patience and the little kids come pouring out of the workshop. Libby comes over and stands next to me. "Your mom's a good teacher," she says.

"Not good enough to make me into a weaver, but I don't think anybody is."

"She is very patient, though."

"True," I say. "The fact that I'm still alive is a testament to that fact."

Libby gives me one of those looks that says she doesn't know quite what to think of me. "Oh," she says, "my mama was telling your mama about a farm she knows where you can buy rabbits. They were talking about driving out there so you and your brother can pick a couple out."

Finally. Bunnies! "You should come with us."

Libby smiles. "Mama says she'll take everybody that wants to go who'll fit in Daddy's van."

After several minutes of trying to herd little kids who are excited about seeing bunnies, Mrs. Hazlett and Mom load Libby and Owen and the younger children into the big white windowless van with the words HAZLETT AND SONS PEST CONTROL printed on the side. Mr. Hazlett and Dad and Just stay behind with the promise that by the time we return with rabbits, we'll have a place to keep them.

It's amazing how much noise that many kids can make closed up together in a van. Faith and Charity are singing "Little Bunny Foo Foo" at the top of their lungs, and Owen and Val are babbling about Legos.

"It's so loud," I yell at Libby, who's sitting next to me.

"What?" she says. "I can't hear you. It's too loud."

I think this might actually be a joke.

Outside the farm is a messy hand-painted sign that says RABBITS BUNNIES with an arrow. It's not much of a farm, really, just a run-down trailer with a barn behind it. A toddler in a diaper is standing in the trailer's doorway. He points at our car, and in a minute, a chunky woman in a Florida–Georgia Line T-shirt steps out of the trailer and approaches the van. "Was you wanting to buy some rabbits?" she asks.

"Well, we definitely want to look, and we might want to buy a couple," Mom says.

"For kids. For pets," Mrs. Hazlett adds.

The woman nods. She's probably in her thirties but looks older. "I got some real pretty ones back there. You'uns can go on back and look, but make sure the littluns don't pick up the rabbits by themselves. They could hurt 'em."

"We will," Mrs. Hazlett says.

The inside of the barn is basically a bunny playground. The floor is covered with straw, and bunnies are hopping all over the place—brown ones, gray ones, white ones, black ones, black-and-white ones. Some of the little ones are chasing each other in what seems to be some kind of silly bunny game. One gray bunny is sitting up on its hind legs and washing its face with its little front paws. I feel like my heart is going to explode from all the cuteness.

"Now don't be loud, and don't chase the bunnies," Mrs. Hazlett tells the little kids. "They scare easily."

Mom is standing in the far corner of the barn. "Come look at this!" she calls. "But watch your step and come quietly."

We make our way over. In a wooden box full of straw is a fat caramel-colored mama nursing—I stop to count—nineteen fuzzy baby bunnies no bigger than marshmallows. It's almost a lethal overdose of cute.

Mrs. Hazlett looks down at the fuzzy nursing mother. "I know just how you feel, Mama," she says.

My mom laughs. "I bet you do. The difference between her and you, though, is that she'll pop out another litter in three months."

Mrs. Hazlett pats her rounded belly. "Nope. I can't work that fast, and neither can my husband."

"You know the old joke, don't you?" Mom says. "What did the boy rabbit say to the girl rabbit?"

"No, what's that?" Mrs. Hazlett says.

Mom grins. "This won't hurt, did it?"

Mrs. Hazlett clamps her lips together for a second, then bursts out laughing anyway.

Owen wanders around the barn inspecting each rabbit, trying to choose the right one. I decide to take a different approach. I sit in the straw on the barn floor (I'm probably sitting in rabbit poop, but I'm not going to worry about it), and I wait for a bunny who's friendly enough to come close. I want my bunny to choose me.

After a couple of minutes, a caramel-colored one makes a few tentative hops in my direction. I slowly stretch out my hand, and the bunny hops closer and gives it a sniff. Then I turn my hand over and give him a gentle pat. He doesn't move, so I stroke him. His fur is the softest thing in the world. After he's let me pet him a couple of minutes, I pick him up and set him in my lap. He settles right down and lets me keep on petting. This one's mine.

Libby sits next to me. "He's so cute. He looks just like Peter Rabbit. All he's missing is a little blue jacket."

"Maybe Mom will make him one," I say, but then I murmur to the bunny, "Just kidding, buddy. You'd hate wearing clothes, wouldn't you?"

The bunny lady (she never introduced herself) comes into the barn, and you can tell she's the one who feeds the bunnies because her presence generates a lot of interest. "Did you find any you wanted?" she says, making her way through the sea of rabbits.

"I want that one," Owen says, pointing to a white bunny with black splotches. "He looks like he has a mustache."

"I like this one, obviously," I say, nodding down at the bunny on my lap.

"Now was you wanting a breeding pair?" the lady asks.

"No!" Mom says quickly.

"Well, I'd better check 'em out, then," the lady says. "I've got so many in here it's hard to keep track of which is which." She picks up Owen's bunny and inspects his nether regions, then does the same with mine. "They're both bucks. You're good," she says.

I hold my bunny on my lap all the way home.

CHAPTER 6

"THOUGHT OF A NAME FOR YOUR bunny yet?" Mom says as she slices a banana over Owen's bowl of cereal.

"No," Owen says. "It's not fair how fast Zo thought of a name for hers."

"It was easy," I say. "He looked like a Ziggy."

"The lead singer of Ziggy Stardust and the Rabbits from Mars?" Dad says, reaching for a piece of toast.

"Exactly," I say.

"I thought about just naming him Mustache," Owen says, "but I decided that sounded stupid, so I was trying to think of names of famous people with mustaches."

"Groucho Marx," Mom says, sitting down at the table with her coffee.

"But then it would sound like he's grouchy, and he's not," Owen says. "Who else had a mustache?" He spoons up some cereal and chews thoughtfully. "Hitler had a mustache."

"And he wasn't grouchy?" Dad says.

"I don't mean to stomp on your creativity, son, but you can't name your bunny Hitler," Mom says.

"I wasn't going to," Owen says. "I was just saying he had a mustache."

"Freddie Mercury had a mustache," I say. "You could name him Freddie."

"Who's Freddie Mercury?" Owen says.

"You know, from Queen," Dad says, and starts singing 'We Will Rock You,' drumming on the table.

"Oh, I love that song!" Owen says. "Maybe I will call him Freddie."

"It beats Hitler," Dad says.

After breakfast I go to my room to dress. I shuck out of my pajamas and put on a sports bra, the only kind I can stand to wear. No itchy lace, no skinny straps that dig into my shoulders, no metal hooks that had to be designed by a hardcore misogynist. I pull on my favorite pair of boys' Levis which have been washed so many times they're as soft and thin as Kleenex. I throw on a plain white T-shirt and then, because I feel like it, pick up my eyeliner and line my eyes under the bottom lashes. I'm not going for a Goth girl look, but more of the guyliner thing—like Captain Jack Sparrow or Billie Joe from Green Day.

It's probably silly to put on eyeliner when there's nobody here but my family to see me. But it's not about how I look to other people. It's about looking how I feel.

I slip on my Vans, grab my history textbook, and head down the stairs. "Mom, I'm going to do my history down by the creek," I call. She's at the kitchen table helping Owen with his morning math. Edgar is curled up on the living room couch, sticking to his strict schedule, which includes a post-breakfast nap. I head outside and stop at the hutch for a few minutes to give the bunnies a carrot and a cuddle, then head down the path to the creek.

As soon as I'm there, I find a nice creek-side rock to sit on, slip out of my shoes, and stick my feet in the water. I open my history book to the chapter on the 1920s and start reading about Prohibition and how it caused bootlegging and bathtub gin and organized crime. No surprise there. If something is prohibited, you're going to want it a lot worse than you did before. Maybe you didn't even want it in the first place, but now that you can't have it, you've just got to.

There's a section in the chapter on the changing role of women with a picture of a flapper next to a picture of a typical Victorian woman. No question about which of these two would be more fun to hang out with. All of the Victorian woman's visible clothing is long: a heavy-looking long dress with long sleeves and an up-to-the-chin neckline. Her long hair is piled on her head in a carefully arranged up-do. She looks too rigid to bend at the waist. She's not smiling, but photography back then was too long and laborious process for anybody to look happy about it.

On the other hand, three flappers from the picture from the twenties look like someone took their picture just as they heard the punch line of a hilarious joke. The picture is black and white, of course, but I imagine their lipstick is fire-engine red. Their eyes, like mine today, are lined with kohl. Everything about them looks light, free of all the dead weight that hangs from the Victorian woman. Their hair is bobbed short—it's chin-length for two of the girls, but the third has hair as short as a boy's with an adorable little

Superman-style forehead curl. Their dresses come to just below the knee and are as baggy as sacks with plenty of room for moving around, and from the natural slump of their bodies, it's clear there are no corsets restraining them either. They look free and a little wild. Probably a lot wild for those days.

The more I look at the flappers, the more radical they seem. They were gender pioneers, tearing down the old ideas of what a woman should be and building something new. After they did, there was no going back. Hemlines rarely hit the floor again, except for evening gowns, and hair length became a matter of fashion and choice.

With my pencil I draw an arrow to the flapper with the boyish haircut and write "me." Then, before I'm even fully aware of what I'm doing, I draw an arrow to the picture of the long-haired, long-dressed Victorian and write "Libby."

"I love Bilbo," Libby says. We're sitting in her backyard while Owen plays with the Littles, as Libby calls them. "I love his funny feet and how he's always daydreaming about breakfast and doesn't feel like he's cut out to go on an adventure but he does it anyway. That's brave, isn't it? When you don't know if you're going to be able to do something but you go ahead anyway because it's the right thing to do?"

"It is," I say. It's cute how excited she is about the book. A lot of kids our age try to hide their excitement and act cool and apathetic all the time, but Libby's too innocent for that. "Those are the best stories," she says, "the ones where you don't know if the main character has what it takes to succeed. If the main character's too strong and brave and perfect, it's boring."

All of a sudden, the sky opens up like it does sometimes in spring, and the rain pelts down.

"Rain! Rain!" the Littles yell and run to us like we're human umbrellas.

"We've got to gather the animals and save them from the flood!" Faith says.

"Well, we do need to put the dogs up so they can get into their house," Libby says. "Ruth! Boaz!" The hounds run with her to the pen on the hill.

Mrs. Hazlett has appeared at the back door and is herding the children back inside.

"Mama, can Owen come in and play with Legos?" Val asks.

"Okay," Mrs. Hazlett says. "But just for thirty minutes, and then it's nap time."

I stand awkwardly in the rain, not sure what to do since Owen has been invited in and I haven't.

Libby says, "Mama, is it okay if Zo comes in, too, since she's in charge of Owen?"

Mrs. Hazlett nods, but I can't tell if she's happy with the idea or not.

The first thing I notice is how plain and uncluttered their house is compared to ours. The living room has a tan sofa with a matching armchair, a cane rocking chair, and a coffee table with the biggest Bible I've ever seen on it. The only decoration is a picture hanging over the sofa, a framed print of that old painting of a guardian angel hovering behind Hansel and Gretel-like children who are crossing a bridge.

Patience is sitting in the rocker knitting. She looks up at

me. "What happened to your eyes?"

For a second I have no idea what she's talking about, but then I remember the eyeliner. I must look like a demented raccoon. "I guess the rain smeared my eye makeup," I say.

"But why were you wearing eye makeup in the first place?" Patience asks. Something about the way she's grilling me while doing needlework makes me think of a stern grandmother.

"I just like to sometimes. I guess it's like playing dress-up."

"Aren't you a little old for playing dress-up?" Patience asks.

"Patience," Mrs. Hazlett says. "Be hospitable to our guests. Why don't you and Libby go fetch some cookies and lemonade for everybody?"

"Yes, ma'am," Patience says, and she and Libby get up and leave the room.

"Please excuse Patience," Mrs. Hazlett says. "She's just at that age, you know."

"Yes, ma'am," I say. "I remember middle school. I'm glad I never have to be that age again." Nobody, I'm convinced, can be as mean as a pack of thirteen-year-old girls.

"I remember middle school, too, and I wouldn't go back there for anything," Mrs. Hazlett says. "That's one of the reasons we homeschool. I don't want our kids to have to put up with what I did. Patience is a good girl and wants to do the right thing. Sometimes she just needs to be reminded to be humble."

Libby and Patience come in with a pitcher of lemonade, a plate of oatmeal cookies, and a tower of paper cups. Libby starts filling cups, and Patience passes out cookies.

It's all very organized. After she's finished pouring, Libby says, "Mama, would it be okay if Zo and I have our lemonade upstairs?"

"I suppose that would be all right." Mrs. Hazlett's tone sounds a little cautious. "Nap time for the Littles in twenty minutes."

"Yes, ma'am."

I follow Libby up the stairs. "Everything in your house is so orderly," I say.

"It has to be because there are so many of us." She leads me into a room that's painted the soft pink of the inside of a seashell. I close the door behind us, but Libby says, "No."

"Excuse me?"

"No closed doors is a house rule."

"Oh." I try to imagine what my life would be like if I didn't have a door I could close, but it's unthinkable. "Does that go for bathroom doors, too?"

Libby smiles. "Bathroom doors can be closed but not locked. Mama or Daddy will come knocking if one of us has been in there too long."

I'm trying to act like I think this is all normal, so I decide changing the subject is the best way to go. "So this is your room," I say, like an idiot.

"Mine and Patience's," Libby says. "We call it the Big Girls' Room." She sits down on the bed I guess is hers and gestures for me to do the same. If Mrs. Hazlett knew anything about my personal history, I'm sure she wouldn't be comfortable with me sitting on a bed with her daughter. "Faith and Charity are in the Little Girls' room, and then Val and Just are in the Boys' Room. Things might change after the baby comes, depending on whether it's a boy or a girl. But new babies usually sleep in a crib in Mama and Daddy's room for the first few months."

"There's going to be a new baby?"

"Yes. She figures probably in the middle of September."

Mrs. Hazlett always wears such baggy dresses and jumpers I guess it's hard to see her baby bump. "So this will be seven?"

Libby nods. "Daddy's hoping we get into the double digits. He says a dozen kids would suit him just fine."

I've never asked Libby directly about her family's religion, but it's turning into the elephant in the room. "So just tell me to shut up if I get too personal, but having a large family . . . it's a religious thing for you, isn't it?"

"It is. It's all over the Bible—'be fruitful and multiply' and then there's Psalm 127 that says that children are like a warrior's arrows and 'blessed is the man whose quiver is full of them.' Some families like ours call themselves Quiverfull for that reason."

"So there are lots of other families like yours?"

"Thousands." Libby props up on a pillow. "Most of them homeschool and live like it says in the Bible. They let God plan their families and train the kids to grow up to be God's righteous warriors."

I don't want to offend her, but I still feel a little of my dad's orneriness bubbling up in me. "And so the kids will all grow up and declare a holy war and kill all the people who don't believe like they do?"

Libby smiles like she's embarrassed. "No, it's not like that.

It's more like if the good people have lots of babies, then the good people will outnumber the bad people. Then the good people can run things and maybe help the bad people come to Jesus."

The way she talks, it's clear that in her mind there really are only two types of people—good with a capital G and bad with a capital B. But to me, it seems like there are very few people who fit into those neat categories. Okay, so Nelson Mandela was good with a capital G, and Hitler was bad with a capital B, but with most people, isn't it more complex than that? "So is my family on the list of bad people because we believe in different things?"

Libby winces. "It's not like that. I can still love you and your family even if you don't believe like we do. 'Love the sinner, hate the sin.'"

I've heard this phrase used too many times by homophobes who think they're not homophobic. "So we're sinners?"

"We're all sinners, Zo."

"But some of us are more sinful than others, right?"

"Well, sure, but—" She stops talking and sighs. "Zo, I've never met anybody like you before. The only people I know that I'm not related to are people who go to my church. I've always heard that families that aren't like ours are really messed up. The mothers work like men and don't love their children and dump them off to be raised by schools and daycares. The men work long hours or just pretend to so they can get drunk in bars and cheat on their wives. All anybody cares about is money and momentary pleasure. But you and your family . . . you're not like that. Your parents both seem to love you and your brother, and they seem to love each other, too. You all seem . . . nice."

"Well, my parents and my brother are nice. I can be a right pain in the you-know-where sometimes." It's funny the way I automatically censor myself around Libby. At home I would've said "ass."

Libby smiles. "No, you're nice, too. And it's confusing because you don't seem like the kind of person I'd like, but I do."

"Well, that goes both ways," I say.

Libby gives my forearm a little pat. It's a gesture that seems almost maternal. "Maybe," she says, "God brought us together for a reason."

"Maybe so," I say, though I figure that when it comes to what that reason might be, her God and my god (if I had one) would be at total cross-purposes.

IN MY ROOM AFTER DINNER, I put on *Diamond Dogs*. The cover shows a shock-haired, made-up Bowie as a naked glam rocker from the waist up and a dog from the waist down. Behind him, a hanging banner advertises "The Strangest Living Oddities." I like the idea of being a living oddity. Also, the dystopian vibe of *Diamond Dogs* matches up perfectly with my summer reading list.

Once the music's blasting, I open up my laptop. I want to see if Claire's online, but I also want to do a little non-homeschool-related research. Claire's name pops up in the chat box.

Zo: *Hey.*

Claire: *You wanna Skype? I miss your face.*

I type *Sure.*

When she appears onscreen, I realize I've missed her face, too. Her smile is radiant.

"There's my favorite person!" she says. "Hey, your hair has gotten really long."

"It doesn't look girly, does it?" I run my fingers through it. "I was going for seventies rock god, not sorority girl."

Claire laughs. "Nobody is ever going to mistake you for a sorority girl. You look good."

"You look good, too. Pretty." Claire's wearing a blue floral-print scarf with matching dangly earrings. I feel suddenly shy after calling her pretty, so I change the subject. "What's up?"

Claire rolls her eyes. "Less than nothing. I'm bored to comatoseness. Is that a word? 'Comatoseness'?"

"I don't think so. Maybe comatosity? Why are you bored? You're in a town. There's stuff to do."

Claire studies her fingernails, which are painted the same shade of blue as her earrings and scarf. "Yeah, but it's the same old stuff. And even if I did find anything here remotely interesting, I'm broke. Not even enough cash to pick out a new frock at Goodwill."

I smile at her old-fashioned language. "You're the only person I know who says 'frock.'"

"I like it. I think it sounds kind of dirty. Like . . . frock you." She gives me a close-up view of the blue nail polish on her middle finger.

I laugh. "I thought you were going to get a job this summer."

"I thought I was, too. But you'll be shocked to know that Asian trans teens are not at the top of the most wanted list for crappy summer jobs."

I bring my hands to my cheeks, *Home Alone*-style. "I am shocked."

"Apparently you can't have a trans girl serving your fro yos."

"Well, I hear that kind of thing can be transferred through yogurt," I say.

"Yeah, it turns you into a fro-yo-sexual."

I laugh even though the joke is terrible. "If this weren't a long-distance conversation, I'd have to throttle you for that one."

"Oh, would that be my PUN-ishment?"

WHILE I CHAT WITH CLAIRE, I open a new tab and Google "Quiverfull." It lists 401,000 results, so it's definitely a thing. I know every teacher I've ever had including my mom would kill me for this, but I start with Wikipedia because I've got to start somewhere. Quiverfull, the entry tells me, is a term used by certain members of the "Christian patriarchy" movement who oppose any form of birth control. It's weird to think of people embracing the word "patriarchy." Mom and Dad always say it like it's a bad thing.

"You're suspiciously quiet," Claire says. "You're multitasking, aren't you?"

"I was looking something up."

"Like what to do when your best friend tells horrible jokes?"

"No, I actually miss your horrible jokes, believe it or not. It's a word Libby used today talking about her family."

"And that word was . . . crazy?"

"No." I feel defensive of Libby for some reason. "Quiverfull."

Claire nods. "Yeah, I've heard of that before. There was a TV show about a family with all these kids. When one of the daughters got married, she hadn't even kissed the dude till they were at the altar. Wouldn't it suck if he was a terrible kisser?"

"It would. And then you'd be stuck with him."

Claire crinkles her nose into a "yuck" face. "And you'd have to have a million kids with him even if he kisses like a chameleon catching a fly."

"Eww." I hope Libby never finds herself in this situation.

"Yeah, pretty grim."

"The funny thing is, Libby and her family don't seem grim. They seem pretty happy. I mean, I don't agree with them or anything, but I'm not going to judge them if they're not hurting anybody."

Claire shakes her head, but she's smiling. "And that's the difference between you and me. If I know somebody would judge me, I have no problem judging them. Read more about what they believe. You'll end up judging them, too."

I do read more. I read blogs by Quiverfull moms about Christian homeschooling and submitting to their husbands. I read about how boys should be educated to be Christian leaders and girls should be educated only to be wives and mothers. One blogger even says the best science lab for a girl is a kitchen. I read about what Claire was talking about— about purity before marriage being God's plan and about how dating is sinful. Apparently boys are supposed to control their "urges" and girls are supposed to stay totally innocent until they get married and start popping out a baby a year for Jesus.

It's 3 a.m. when I stop reading and turn off the light. But I can't sleep. "Rapunzel" was my favorite fairy tale when I was little, and for some reason I keep picturing Libby with her long hair, a princess locked in a tower, which is supposedly to protect her from the dangers of the world. But it's really a prison.

LIBBY

CHAPTER 7

I'M A WILD SLEEPER. I WISH I could help it, but I don't think I can. I wake up in the morning with my blanket kicked off the bed and the sheet twisted around me in knots. Patience is the opposite. She slides under the covers and doesn't move all night. Our first chore in the morning is making our beds. Patience just has to smooth hers out a little, and she's done. I have to untangle my sheets and rescue the blanket from the floor and get everything all fixed.

Sometimes I feel like this is the way it is with Patience and me. Things are easier for her. She's better suited for the life God wants for us, and Daddy is always saying what a fine wife and mother she'll make.

This morning, while I'm washing the breakfast dishes and Mama is starting some stew in the crock-pot, I decide to talk to her about it. I'm always too nervous about pleasing Daddy to ask him too many questions, but I can talk to Mama about anything.

"Mama," I say, "something's been on my mind lately."

She looks up from the potato she's cutting. "What is it, hon?"

I take a deep breath. "You know how Daddy's always saying what a good wife Patience will make?"

"Yes." She dumps a cutting board full of potatoes into the pot. "He says the same thing about you."

"He doesn't say it about me as much as he says it about Patience." As soon as it's out of my mouth, I hear how whiny I sound.

She hears it, too, because she says, "Well, you know what Scripture says: 'Jealousy is as cruel as the grave.'"

"I know it sounds like I'm just jealous, but that's not really it. I guess it's more that I'm scared." I'm surprised to feel a little tickle in my throat like I'm going to cry. I swallow hard to stop it. Daddy's always saying Jesus doesn't want us to feel sorry for ourselves. He didn't feel sorry for Himself when He was suffering on the cross, so why should we feel sorry for ourselves when we're not getting some little thing that we want?

"Scared of what?" Mama says.

"Scared," I say, and the tickle in my throat has spread to my eyes, which are starting to well with tears. "Scared I won't be able to do what God needs me to do. Scared that I don't have what it takes to be a righteous woman."

"Oh, Libby." Mama stops chopping vegetables and comes over to the sink and puts her arms around me. "Don't you know that you having these doubts means you have what it takes to be righteous?"

"I don't understand," I say, letting Mama hold me. Her hair smells like flowers.

"Come sit with me at the table for a minute."

Stopping to sit in the middle of chores is unusual. I sit.

"You know," Mama says, "what God asks of us isn't easy. And sometimes it's harder than others. Like right now, carrying this baby, I'm tired all the time, and when I'm not tired, I'm throwing up. But I keep going and I don't complain because I know it's what God wants me to do."

"Yes, ma'am," I say.

"But that was just warming up to what I wanted to say to you." She clamps her lips together like she does when she's thinking real hard. "What I really wanted to say is that for some people—for some girls and women—it's a harder path than it is for others. We can't all be like Patience. For some of us, it's hard to submit, to do what our fathers or husbands tell us without question. You and me—we've got that in common."

It had never occurred to me that perfect submission was anything other than easy for Mama. She makes it all—the housework, the cooking, the mothering, the homeschooling—look so effortless, like she's a machine who was created to do it all. "You mean it's hard for you?"

Mama smiles. "It used to be. When your daddy and I first got married, I used to argue with him a lot, about the way he budgeted money, about how he did some things around the house. But we prayed together and talked to our pastor and our pastor's wife. It's right there in the Bible. Ephesians five, twenty-four. Say it with me, Libby."

We say it together: "'Therefore as the church is subject to Christ, so let the wives be to their own husbands in everything.'"

Mama pats my hand. "Talking with the pastor's wife was especially helpful. Even if I have a rebellious heart, it's my sacred duty to submit to my husband just like the church submits to God." She takes a deep breath. "Now, that being said, your daddy would admit that he's not perfect. No man walking this earth is perfect. But when I submit to your daddy, I'm also showing my submission to God because I'm doing God's will, and that means that after I leave this earth, I'll be welcomed into the arms of Jesus, the only perfect man there is. What God asks of us isn't easy, Libby, but it's worth it."

I nod. "It helps me to know it's not easy for you either."

"Most things aren't when you do them right," Mama says. "But I'm sure in two or three years, or whenever the time comes, God will lead your daddy to find a godly man for you. And when you love a godly man, you're happy to serve him." She reaches over and squeezes my hand. "And I'll tell you one thing I know about you. It's in your nature to be a wonderful mother."

I do like kids. "I don't worry about the mother part as much as the wife part."

"You'll be great. It's such a blessing I have you to help with the Littles' schooling. How's the play coming, by the way?"

"I think we'll be ready tonight." A couple of times a year we have a Family Talent Show where everybody performs a special, God-given talent. For this one, I wrote a play that the Littles are acting in. "It may turn out to be a comedy, but I didn't write it that way."

"I can't wait to see it," Mama says, rising from her chair. "Now we need to get back to work."

NOW THAT DINNER'S OVER, WE'RE SETTING up for the talent show in the backyard. Daddy and Just are hanging a sheet to use as a backdrop. Mama and Patience and I are setting up a table with a pitcher of lemonade and paper cups and cookies. I'd like to say the Littles are helping, but they're mostly just running around being excited.

Val runs up to Mama. "Mama, can I go next door and invite Owen to our talent show?"

Val and Owen are almost exactly the same age, and they really hit it off.

"I don't know, sweetie," Mama says. "Usually it's just for family. Ask your daddy what he thinks."

"Ask your daddy what?" Daddy says, coming over to the refreshment table. Mama pours him a cup of lemonade.

"I was asking if I could invite Owen over to watch the talent show."

"Hm," Daddy says, then knocks back the whole cup of lemonade. "Normally I'd say this is family-only, but seeing what kind of talent show this is, it does give us the opportunity to witness for the Lord. Go ahead. Invite him and that sister of his that runs around wearing boys' britches."

"Thank you, sir," Val says, grinning. He runs across the yard and climbs over the fence.

For some reason, the idea of Zo seeing our silly little talent show feels embarrassing.

"HEY," ZO SAYS. SHE'S GOT THE black stuff around her eyes again and is wearing a T-shirt with a big dinosaur on it that says Godzilla. I wonder if that word is blasphemy.

"Hey," I say back.

"So what's your talent?" she asks.

I can't meet her eyes. "I don't really have one. But I wrote this play for the Littles, and I'm the narrator."

"So you're a playwright."

Now I can only look at the grass. "I wouldn't say that. It's just a Bible story I turned into a little skit, is all."

"Hey, if you wrote a play, then you're a playwright," Zo says, smiling.

"I don't know about that. What if the play's not any good? If I bake a cake but it's a bad cake, then that doesn't mean I'm a baker."

"Sure it does." Zo gives me a playful little punch on the arm. "It just means you're not a very good baker."

I wonder why she wears that black stuff around her eyes. Mama says it makes her look like a raccoon. Mama doesn't think women should wear makeup, and a young girl wearing it is even worse.

"Are we ready to get this show on the road?" Daddy hollers. He can be as loud as any preacher.

We all clap and hoot until we're as loud as he is.

"Then everybody take a seat," he hollers over us, "and let's get ready for some Hazlett family entertainment!"

Everybody sits, either in lawn chairs or on the blankets that Mama and Patience and me spread on the ground. We always have to wash blankets after talent show night.

"Let us begin with a prayer," Daddy says, after everybody's settled. "Oh, most precious Lord, we thank you for this time of fun and fellowship with our family and our young neighbors who are with us this evening. We thank you for the talents you have given us, and we feel gratitude to you and not pride in ourselves for these talents. We pray for your guidance in all our work and play, that we may be pleasing in thy sight. In thy most precious name we pray. Amen."

Patience and Justice are first on stage, not that we really
have a stage. Patience is sitting at the little portable keyboard
Mama uses for piano lessons, and Just is holding his hunting
bow. The bullseye he uses for target practice is set up several
feet from where he's standing. "And now," Just says, "I'm
gonna shoot some arrows at this target while my sister plays
'The William Tell Overture.' I wanted to shoot an apple off
Val's head, but he wouldn't let me."

Over the laughter, Val yells, "No way! I know the story of
Cain and Abel."

Everybody laughs some more, and then Patience starts
playing the song, which she's been practicing all week. She
sounds good. She plays at least as well as I do, even though
she's younger than me. Mama is a good pianist, and she
wants all of us girls to be able to play so we can do music with
our children.

After Patience has played a few bars, Just raises his bow
and lets his first arrow fly. It's not a bullseye, but it's close.
During deer season, Daddy always talks about what a great
shot Just is. Just fires another arrow, then another, and the
last one hits the bullseye just as Patience plays the last note
of the song. They couldn't have timed it better.

Everybody breaks into wild applause, and Owen says,
"That was awesome!"

"Amen," Daddy says, laughing. "Amen!"

Our play is next. I motion for Val and Faith and Charity to
get up and join me, and I run up to the dog pen to get our
special guest stars. I put Ruth and Boaz on their leads and
walk them down to the stage area. Val already has on his
costume, a bathrobe, and Faith and Charity tie on the dogs'

special orange and yellow yarn collars, which match their own. We're ready to go.

I feel twice as nervous as I would without Zo in the audience, but I take a deep breath and say, "The Hazlett Family Players present 'Daniel and the Lions' Den.'"

Mama and Daddy make a big show of applauding.

"Once there was a man named Daniel who loved God very much," I recite.

"I love God very much," Val says because he's Daniel.

"He loved God so much that he prayed day and night," I say, and Val kneels and pretends to pray. "But a king named Darius didn't want Daniel to pray all the time where everybody could see him." It would be better if we had another little boy to play Darius, but since we don't, I just worked Darius's lines in with the narrator's. "Darius said"—and here I try to make my voice sound low and threatening—"If you don't stop praying in public like that, I'm going to throw you in a den of hungry lions.'" I go back to my normal voice. "But Daniel said."

Val chimes in with the rhyming line he loves: "I don't care what you say, I'm praying to the Lord anyway."

I recite, "And so King Darius said, 'I'm coming back tomorrow, and unless you change your mind, it's into the lion's den with you!' But when the king came back the next day, Daniel said . . . "

Val repeats, "I don't care what you say, I'm praying to the Lord anyway."

"And so King Darius said"—and here I make my voice low again—"'Prepare to be lion chow!'" This line gets a big laugh, which makes me feel good.

"So Daniel was thrown in the lions' den," I say.

Faith and Charity take their positions as lions along with the lion hound dogs. "Roar! Roar!" Faith and Charity say, and then Boaz barks, which also gets a big laugh.

"One of the lions was a barking lion," I say, making it up on the spot and getting another laugh. "And when Daniel entered the lions' den, he was sore afraid."

Val makes a big show of shaking and biting his fingernails.

"But then God said that since Daniel was His faithful servant, He was shutting the mouth of the lions so they would not harm him," I say.

Val walks up to Faith and Charity and pets their heads. They say, "Purr! Purr!"

"When the king opened the door of the lions' den the next day," I say, "he was shocked to see that Daniel was still alive. 'Impossible!' the king said."

"With God, all things are possible," Val says. "It was God who saved me from the lions."

"And King Darius fell to his knees," I recite, "and said, 'Daniel, will you forgive me? And will you pray with me?' And Daniel and King Darius fell to their knees and prayed, and King Darius went on to become one of the most righteous men in all the land."

Then everybody but the dogs bows or curtsies, and our audience claps really loud.

After the applause dies down, Daddy says, "Well, that play is a tough act to follow, but I believe the Littles are gonna recite the Bible verses they've been learning. And after that, I think I heard something about ice cream!"

Faith and Charity jump up and down and squeal. We don't get ice cream often.

"Okay," Daddy chuckles. "Bible verses first, then ice cream."

Charity steps forward and says, "'Be ye kind one to another.'"

"Good," Daddy says. "And what book of the Bible is that from, sweetie?"

"Um . . . Phesians?" Charity says.

"That's right," Daddy says. "Ephesians four, thirty-two. Faith, what did you learn?"

Faith steps forward. "'Children, be obedient to your parents in all things, for this is well-pleasing to the Lord.' Colossians three, twenty.'"

"Amen!" Daddy says. "What you got for us, Val?"

Val shuffles forward and mumbles, "'For God so loved the world that He gave His only begotten son that whosoever believed on Him shall not perish, but have everlasting life.' John three, sixteen.'"

"Son," Daddy says, his tone stern all of a sudden, "that's one of the first verses we teach you. What new Bible verse did you learn for today?"

"I didn't learn a new Bible verse, sir," Val says. The other Littles look nervous and back away from him.

"And why is that, son?" Daddy's voice isn't jolly like it was when he was emceeing the talent show.

"Because . . . " Val shifts around on his feet, like he does when he's nervous. "Daddy, only the Littles have to recite Bible verses, and I'm getting too big to be a Little. I'm almost ten years old. I'm closer to Patience's age than I am to Faith's, but I still get lumped in with the Littles all the time and get stuck doing little kid stuff. I'd rather do Bible drill with the Bigs. Sir."

Daddy's expression softens a little. "I hear what you're saying, son. You're growing, and you want us to recognize that. But instead of coming to me and talking calmly about how you feel, you've openly disobeyed me by refusing to learn a Bible verse. Maybe you need to go back and study the verse Faith learned. Say it again, Faith."

Faith says softly, "'Children, be obedient to your parents in all things for it is well-pleasing to the Lord.'" She always hates it when one of us gets in trouble.

"Amen," Daddy says. "Valor, I need you to step inside the house with me for a minute. Bigs, you can go ahead and get ready for your Bible drill."

Val looks grim but determined as he walks toward the back door with Daddy. Daddy is already loosening his belt.

Punishment is always sure and swift. It comes so fast you don't know what hit you, even though what hits you is always Daddy's belt. Whippings don't happen that often, though. I haven't gotten one since my age has been in the double digits. Still, I always hurt for the sibling who gets one, even though I know it's how you teach them right from wrong.

Patience and Just and me line up with our Bibles. We train in Bible drill at home and at church, and sometimes our church's team competes with other churches' teams. Daddy and Pastor always remind us, though, that it's not really about the competition. It's about learning our way around the Bible so we can use it whenever we need it.

When Daddy and Val come back, Val's lips are set in a tight line, and his face looks blotchy. I hope he didn't cry.

Daddy doesn't like for the boys to cry during a whipping, but sometimes it's hard not to. The tears spring to your eyes as soon as the belt stings your skin. Val takes his seat, and Daddy stands in front of Just, Patience, and me. "Attention!" he yells like an army drill sergeant. We stand straight, our Bibles held at our sides.

"Present Bibles!" he orders.

We all raise our Bibles to waist level, Genesis-side up.

"We'll start off easy," Daddy says. "With books instead of verses. Leviticus. Start!"

My fingers fly through the tissue-thin pages, and I'm there. I put my index finger on the first verse and step forward. The rule is that you have to say the name of the books before and after the book that's been called, and then read the first chapter and verse. "Exodus, Leviticus, Numbers," I say, loud and clear. "Leviticus, Chapter One, Verse One: 'And the Lord called unto Moses, and spoke to him out of the tabernacle of the congregation.'"

"Good job, Libby," Daddy says. If we were really playing instead of just demonstrating, I'd earn three points. "And now, Acts. Start!"

I find it right away, too. Sometimes it's like my fingers just sense where the books are, like God is guiding my hand. I have to be careful, though. I can't be first every time, or Mama will shoot me a look. It's not ladylike to be a show-off, and I should let Patience and Just have a chance to get some answers right, too. Especially Just. So I force my fingers to slow down, even though it's hard.

Daddy has moved on to verses and recites, "'When pride cometh, then cometh shame: but with the lowly is wisdom.'"

I know this is Proverbs 11:2, but I fumble a little on purpose to give one of the others a chance. Then the seconds tick away, and I still end up finding it before anybody else.

"I think it's time for ice cream," Daddy announces.

The Littles run cheering to the table, where Mama has set out a gallon each of chocolate, vanilla, and strawberry, plus a stack of cones. Owen joins the Littles, and I walk over to talk to Zo. "I hope that wasn't too boring for you," I say.

"No," Zo says. "I definitely wasn't bored." She sounds shy or nervous, I can't tell which. "Your play was the best part."

"Oh, it was nothing." Now I feel shy and nervous.

Owen comes over balancing a cone piled with a scoop of each flavor.

"Got enough ice cream there, little bro?" Zo says.

"There's never enough ice cream," Owen says, then he looks at me. "Is Val okay? Did he get a spanking?"

"Shh, Owen," Zo says, nudging him. "I told you it's none of our business."

"It's all right," I say. I look over to the swing set. Val is sitting by himself in a swing, licking his ice cream cone like he's licking his wounds. This is normal behavior for him after a whipping. He'll snap out of it in the next half hour or so. "Val's fine. He just got a whipping is all."

"Is he hurt?" Owen looks worried.

"No," I say. "Daddy's real careful. It hurts when you get it, but it don't hurt after. I bet your daddy's careful like that, too."

Owen's little brow crinkles up. "My daddy never hits me."

"Does your mama do it?" I ask. Maybe that's another one of the ways their family is different from ours.

"No," Zo says. "Our parents don't believe in corporal punishment. That's why Owen was a little freaked out by what happened tonight."

This must be an example of how worldly parents don't love their kids like Christian parents do. Mama and Daddy always say they discipline us because they love us. After he gives you a whipping, Daddy always hugs you and prays with you. "So what do your parents do when you disobey?"

Owen looks at his sister. "What do they do?"

"Well, I guess they take privileges away. Like one time when you were little, you didn't pick up your toy trains like Mom told you to and so she gathered them all up and wouldn't let you play with them for the rest of the day. And when my grades dropped last year because I stopped studying, Mom and Dad took away my phone and my laptop until I pulled my average back up to a B."

I nod like I understand even though I don't. It seems like a strange way to punish a child—to take something away when they know you're just going to give it back to them.

CHAPTER 8

SUNDAY IS THE ONLY MORNING WE all have to hurry to
get somewhere. Even though there are a lot of us to get
ready and everybody has to look extra clean and holy for
church (Daddy says "holy" is better than pretty), Mama
always cooks the biggest breakfast of the week: pancakes,
buttermilk or blueberry, with bacon when we can afford it.
Sunday breakfast is also the only time we eat in our pajamas,
so the Littles won't get their church clothes all syrup-sticky.

After we eat, Mama and Patience and I put the dishes in
soapy water to soak and get busy getting everybody ready for
church. There are faces to be washed, hair to be braided,
and shirttails to be tucked in. Somehow in the middle of all
this child-grooming, Mama also manages to get herself
ready, fixing her hair extra nice and putting on one of her
good floral-print dresses. Daddy always wears a suit and tie
to church no matter what the weather is.

The Riverside Fellowship Church is about halfway between
our house and town. The funny thing about it is that it's not
beside a river at all. It's named after the River Jordan in
the Bible.

The church building is simple, with no steeple or columns or anything. It's one of those prefab buildings made out of plain light-gray corrugated aluminum. Church members raised enough money to buy the building after years of meeting in one another's houses. Daddy says that no matter what the downtown Baptists and Methodists think, it doesn't matter what a church looks like. All that matters is what's in the members' hearts. If you let church get too fancy, he says, you might as well give up Jesus and start worshipping the Pope with the Catholics.

Our church sanctuary has light blue carpet and metal chairs with padded seats instead of pews. A huge white cross hangs on the wall behind the pulpit. On nice mornings like this one, sunlight shines through the few small windows, giving everything a holy glow. Pastor Mike says these little plain windows are better than the stained glass ones in the high churches because there's no improving on the natural light God makes. "Sonlight," he calls it.

My family takes up a whole row of seats. Nanny and Papaw sit next to Mama and Daddy. Nanny, whose long silver hair always looks pretty in a big bun, says, "Liberty, come give your nanny some sugar." I lean over for a hug and a kiss. Papaw isn't cuddly like Nanny. He sits up straight in the dark suit he always wears to church, but he gives me a little nod of greeting.

Nanny and Papaw are Daddy's parents. We eat Sunday dinner at their house every week after church. Mama's parents died in a car wreck when she was just barely grown up, and she doesn't like to talk about them.

Pastor Mike is about Daddy's age, but he's a much larger man, tall and broad-shouldered and well-padded like a

La-Z Boy recliner. Daddy says he used to play football in high school. Pastor Mike always wears a jacket and tie to preach, but he gets so worked up and sweaty he always ends up taking off the jacket and loosening the tie. When he takes the pulpit this morning, he says, "I hope everybody had a good breakfast."

Some people say "yes." One person says "cornflakes."

"I tell you, brothers and sisters," Pastor Mike says, and he starts pacing like a tiger I saw once at the zoo in Knoxville. "My wife fixed me some biscuits and gravy this morning, so I'm ready to praise the Lord till dinnertime!"

Papaw and several other people say "amen."

"I mean," Pastor Mike says, his voice getting louder, "I am full of dough and ready to go!"

Everybody laughs. Pastor Mike loves to rhyme.

"But," he says, and his voice is softer and more serious, "I didn't come here to talk to you about breakfast. I came here to talk to you about war. Because, brothers and sisters, make no mistake about it: this country is at war."

Lots of amens.

"And I'm not talking about US troops going overseas to fight the Muslims." Pastor Mike has abandoned the pulpit and is pacing across the length of the stage. "I'm talking about the war at home. I'm talking about the war that God's mighty warriors are fighting against the forces of evil right here in our own country." He takes a gulp of air. "I'm talking about the little girl in an elementary school classroom who was told by her teacher that she couldn't read her Bible during the class's free-reading time. *Free*-reading time, brothers and sisters, and yet she wasn't free to read the word of God! No doubt there were other children in that room reading about witches and vampires and all sorts of hellish creatures with the teacher's approval, but this little girl was not free to read the word of God!" He shakes his head. "This means war, brothers and sisters."

Lots more amens.

"The godless secular culture has declared war on the righteous in this country!" He's really pacing now and tugging at his tie. "It means war when children are brainwashed to worship at the altar of technology instead of the altar of the Lord! It means war when our young ladies and young gentlemen are taught that courtship is out of date and instead they should try 'sexting' and 'hookups.' I don't mean to shock you, brothers and sisters, but I'm speaking frankly because this is too important to sugarcoat. We are at war when our women are told to cast aside the sacred privilege of motherhood and to abort their babies with pills or procedures. We are at war when the highest court in our land says that a man can say 'I do' to another man, and that this sterile, Godless union can be called a marriage!"

Amens and cheers and waving hands.

Pastor Mike shucks off his jacket. "We are at war, brothers and sisters, and this is a war we have to win. And it's not going to be a short war or an easy war. It's going to be such a long, hard war that many of us may have gone to our eternal reward before we can see the end of it. That's why we have to look to our children, to teach them right, so that they and their children can win this war after we're gone. That's why"—he stops pacing and smiles—"You're gonna like this one. That's why we've got to raise them to praise

Him. Say it with me, brothers and sisters: Raise them to praise Him!"

"Raise them to praise Him!" we all say, and then we say it again and again until it turns into a chant, then a cheer. "Raise them to praise Him! Raise them to praise Him!"

I look around at my family and at all the other faces I can see, and everybody's eyes are shining, their lips moving together. Some people hold both of their hands in the air as a sign of praise. These are the times in church I love the best, when everyone is together feeling the same thing, saying the same words, so there's no fear or loneliness or doubt, just one people lifting one voice to God, whose love I feel around me like a big hug.

Pastor Mike lets us go on a long time, shouting, "Raise them to praise Him," pacing the stage and waving his arms like he's the conductor and we're the orchestra. Arms are waving everywhere, and one family is holding hands and kind of jumping up and down as they say it. Finally, Pastor Mike says, "One more time, as loud as you can, and I know some of you children can be LOUD!"

"Raise them to praise Him!" we yell.

"Amen, amen, amen," Pastor Mike says. "Now since I've got us in the fighting spirit, join me in singing 'Onward Christian Soldiers.'"

Sister Sherry, who always plays the piano at our services, bangs out the opening bar, and we start singing about Christian soldiers marching with the cross. I remember reading in one of my homeschool books that it was written by a preacher for children to march to, and singing it really does make you feel brave and strong, like you're going into battle for a just cause. Even the Littles must feel this way because when I look over and see them sing, their little feet are marching in place.

I WOULD NEVER TELL MAMA THIS because it would hurt her feelings, but Sunday dinner at Nanny's is my favorite meal of the week. I can think about it any time and make my mouth water.

I'm not saying Mama's a bad cook. Her food is always good. It's just that there are so many of us she has to fix things we can afford and that can stretch, so we end up eating a lot of the same things. Breakfast is scrambled eggs or oatmeal. Lunch is a peanut butter or pimento cheese sandwich, and supper is usually soup or stew or beans cooked in the crock-pot. All of this is good food and I'm grateful for it, but Nanny's cooking is a blessed change from the everyday. She makes food you can have your own special piece of, like fried chicken, country steak and gravy, or corn on the cob—things you need to cut with a knife or really sink your teeth into. For dessert, there's always a bright, jiggly Jell-O salad with chunks of fruit in it or a banana pudding with vanilla wafers.

Daddy says we should eat to live, not live to eat, but I don't figure it's too big a sin for me to look forward to Sunday dinner. Besides, I've noticed Daddy always puts away two or three platefuls of Nanny's cooking himself.

Nanny and Papaw still live in the same little white house where Daddy and his brother grew up. Nanny likes her house neat and clean, so as long as the weather's nice, she tells the Littles to play outside until dinner's ready. "It's not that they'd mess anything up on purpose," Nanny says. "It's just that there's so many of 'em there's no place to put 'em!"

Since today's nice, the Littles play outside, and Daddy and Just and Papaw go to set up the folding tables and chairs we always use for Sunday dinner. Mama and Patience and me go to help Nanny in the kitchen.

Nanny's kitchen is my favorite room in the world. It's bright and sunny, with yellow gingham curtains and African violets in the windowsills. The smells are always delicious.

"Let's see," Nanny says. "The sweet potatoes and the bread's warming up in the oven. Liberty, why don't you put a pot of water on for the corn?"

"Yes, ma'am," I say, happy that there's going to be corn on the cob.

"And Patience," Nanny says, "I was thinking I might get you to slice up some maters and cucumbers. You can use a knife good, can't you?"

"Yes, ma'am," Patience says.

"What can I do?" Mama asks.

"Oh, I think I've got everything under control." Nanny pats Mama's shoulder. "You look like you ought to sit down and rest a spell."

"I sat all morning at church," Mama says. "I'm happy to help."

"Well, I reckon you could mix up some lemonade for the young'uns." Nanny sounds like she doesn't really want to make Mama do anything. "I reckon I'll start slicing the ham directly. I caught Ed in here half a dozen times this morning cutting little pieces of it off with his pocket knife."

Mama laughs. "Well, I can't blame him. Your ham is awful good."

Nanny's ham is about the best thing I ever tasted. She glazes it with Coca-Cola so it's dark and sweet and sticky.

When everything's ready and spread out on the table like the Pilgrims' and Indians' first Thanksgiving, Papaw, who's sitting at one end of the table, looks over to Daddy, who's at the opposite end, and says, "Son, will you say the blessing?"

"Yessir," Daddy says, and we all bow our head and close our eyes.

"Our Father Who Art in Heaven," Daddy begins. "Thank you for bringing us together on this holy day, a day of rest from our earthly labors. Thank you, Lord, for the food here before us for the nourishment of our bodies, and we pray that we use our bodies only to thy service. In Jesus's name we pray, amen."

For a long time, there's not much talking, just food being passed and served and happily eaten. It's all so good: the sweet and salty ham, the buttery crunch of the corn, the sweet potatoes smothered in perfectly charred marshmallows. I bet more little kids would eat their vegetables if they had marshmallows on top of them.

After a while, Nanny says, "Len called the other day."

Daddy looks up from his plate. "Oh? How's he doing?"

Len is Daddy's brother. He lives in Ohio. He and Daddy don't talk to each other much.

"Well," Nanny says, "it sounded like he was doing real good. He got a promotion at the factory, and there's this girl he's seeing."

"A girl?" Daddy laughs. "He's almost forty years old, and he's going out on dates like he's a teenager? Len needs to get on with the business of what life's about."

Nanny smiles. Daddy always says he doesn't understand why she has such a soft spot for Len. "Well, he's just a late bloomer, I reckon," Nanny says.

"I reckon he would've bloomed sooner if he hadn't been so busy sowing his wild oats," Daddy says, cutting his ham into bite-sized pieces. "Did you ask him if he's going to church?"

"I did ask him." Nanny holds out the plate of corn for Val. "And he said he was going with this girl to her church. He said it's one of them churches where people can dress comfortable and sit on couches with pillows and take off their shoes if they want to. It sounded right peculiar to me, but he says it's Christian, so I reckon it's better than no church at all."

"I wouldn't be so sure about that," Daddy says. "I don't think the Lord wants us to get too comfortable. Think how many of the Seven Deadly Sins come from giving into the body's desire for comfort. Sloth, gluttony, lust—"

"I don't reckon the Lord was too comfortable when He was hanging on that cross for us," Papaw says, jabbing the air with his fork.

"Amen," Daddy says. "Did you hear that, children?" He's told us that since Papaw doesn't talk much, we should pay extra close attention when he does. His words are full of wisdom, and he makes every word count.

"Yessir," we say.

Once everybody's plates are empty and bellies are full, Nanny says, "I reckon you young'uns ought to go out and play for half an hour and make room for some banana pudding."

The Littles remember to ask to be excused but then tear out of the house like wild animals. Papaw asks Daddy and Just to come see what he's making in his workshop, and Patience and I stay to help Nanny and Mama with the dishes.

After we clear the table, Nanny turns to Patience and me. "You girls need to get some fresh air. Why don't you'uns take this bowl of scraps out to Tony?"

I love Tony. Tony is Nanny and Papaw's three-legged dog. Papaw spotted him when he was a puppy, limping along the side of a country road. Tony's solid white, and Papaw says that white dogs are good luck, so he brought him home. Now Tony lives in a lot out back and has a special doghouse with his name on it.

Outside, the Littles are playing dodgeball, and Patience and I have to do some dodging of our own to get to the dog lot. When Tony sees us coming, he barks and wags. I open the gate, and he jumps up and licks me. I scratch him behind his floppy ears.

"I'm staying out here. I don't want dog slobber all over me," Patience says. She isn't tender toward animals like I am.

I set down the bowl and Tony vacuums up the scraps, then looks up at me, wagging. I give him another good scratching before I go.

"Hey, girls!" Daddy hollers from across the yard. "Come in here and see your Papaw's handiwork!"

Patience and I walk over to Papaw's workshop, a neat little wooden outbuilding Papaw built himself. On the inside, the workshop is lit by one bare light bulb and is so small it's overcrowded with Daddy and Papaw and Just and Patience and me in there. It smells like wood shavings and oil. Men's things.

"I thought you needed to see these," Daddy says. "Ain't they beauties?"

"Yessir," Patience and I say. The crosses are stacked up on Papaw's worktable. For as long as I can remember, Papaw has made crosses like this, two nailed-together slats of wood painted white and then decorated with sayings like JESUS IS COMING. R U READY? and YOUR CHOICE: HEAVEN OR HELL? He cuts the bottoms of the crosses into points, and then once a month he puts them in the bed of his truck and drives around and "plants them" at different places on the side of the road. Tony always goes with him on these trips. He loves riding in the truck and hanging his head out of the window.

I'm still holding Tony's bowl, so I excuse myself to return it to the house. When I step into the living room, I hear Mama and Nanny in the kitchen, speaking in soft, serious voices. I know it's a sin, but I stand there silently, holding the bowl and listening.

"It seems like I just feel so bad with this one," Mama says.

"Well, it must be a boy then," Nanny says. "You got awful sick with Just and Val."

"I did, but by the time I was as far along as I am now, most of the sickness had gone away. I just hope I don't lose another one. It's so hard on everybody when you're expecting joy and you get sadness instead."

"I know it. That's why I only had the two, you know. Kept losing them, so after a while we stopped trying. I know you'd say not trying was sinful, but losing them babies was too hard on me."

"I know the Lord doesn't give us more than we can handle, but losing a baby feels like an awful test."

"I remember our old pastor told us after I'd miscarried that some babies are just too perfect for this world, that they have to fly straight up to heaven."

Angel babies. I knew about Mama's, but I never knew about Nanny's. There was one between me and Just and one before Mama got pregnant with Faith. I remember that one. Mama got real sick one night and was in the bathroom a long time, and Daddy was in there with her. I got up to check on her and knocked on the bathroom door, but Daddy told me to go back to bed. The next day he explained that the baby Mama had been carrying had gone to be with Jesus. They named the baby, which wasn't any bigger than my hand, Purity because she had been too pure for this world. We had a little service in the backyard where Daddy said a prayer and we held hands and Mama, who was pale and crying, released a pink balloon into the air. We watched it float up till it was out of sight like Baby Purity's soul in heaven.

Thinking about this has made my mind wander away from the conversation a little, but when I come back I hear Nanny saying, ". . . would disagree with me, but I don't see no harm in going to the doctor if you're feeling poorly. Both my boys was born in a hospital."

"If we're going to live like we're supposed to live— debt-free and with no help from the government—then how are we supposed to afford doctors and hospitals? Besides,

God made women to have babies. Birth isn't like having your appendix taken out. It's beautiful and natural and should be between a woman and her husband and God."

"It should be," Nanny says. "But sometimes the Lord knows people need a little extra help, and that's what He made doctors for. Now I know my son's a fine man, but I also know how stubborn he is. And I want you to promise that if anything happens to make you feel like something's bad wrong, you'll go to a doctor. You've got to think of your health, too, with all them young'uns to raise."

Mama gives a nervous-sounding laugh. "If I'd known complaining about a little nausea and lightheadedness was going to cause a disagreement between you and me, Mother Hazlett, I never would've said anything. You know I love you like you were my own mother, but maybe you should do some prayerful reflection on what you just said. I'd never go against Bill's wishes. God wants me to obey him."

"I will take it to the Lord in prayer. And I'll pray for the baby, too."

At some point I'm going to have to make a noise so they know I'm here and walk into the kitchen. But right now I'm stuck in place like my feet are glued to the floor. When I look down at the bowl in my hands, I'm holding it so tight my knuckles are white.

CHAPTER 9

"Hey." Zo is standing by the fence, and Owen is already climbing over it. It's the Littles' afternoon playtime.

"Hey," I say. She's wearing shorts today—jeans that have been cut off just above the knee. Immodest, but not as immodest as some of the shorts I've seen girls wearing in Walmart.

"We're having a cookout tomorrow night," Zo says, "and Mom and Dad wanted me to invite you."

"Oh, I don't think I'd be allowed," I say. "I'll have to help Mama with dinner."

"We're not just inviting you," Zo says, giving a shy little grin. "I should've explained it better. We're inviting your whole family."

"All of us?"

Zo laughs. "Yes. Your parents, your brothers and sisters. Your dogs if they want to come."

"There's a lot of us to feed, even without the dogs."

"My parents love to feed people."

"Well . . . " I have no idea what Daddy will say. The only socializing we do outside the family is at church. "I'll tell

Mama, and she'll talk to Daddy about it, so we'd have to let you know this evening."

DADDY HAD TO PRAY ON IT, but he ended up saying yes and quoted Scripture about loving thy neighbor. Mama made a big pan of baked beans to take, and now we're all sitting in the living room for a family meeting before we go next door.

Well, we're all sitting but Daddy, who is standing up to instruct us. "Now, their ways will not be the same as our ways," he says, looking around to make eye contact with each of us. "And some of their ways will be wrong in the eyes of the Lord. But it is our duty to serve as good examples of Christian behavior in hopes that their hearts will turn to God."

I did tell Daddy that Zo and her family had gone to church in Knoxville, but he said some churches were Christian in name only.

Daddy says, "We will be polite and well-behaved unless we are asked to do something that goes against God's laws. I don't know if their family prays before they eat, but this family does, and we will. And now let's hear a few words from your mama."

Mama stands up. "I know I don't need to tell you to say please and thank you and wait to be excused from the table until everybody's finished eating. I also don't need to tell you to say sir and ma'am or to chew with your mouths closed or keep your elbows off the table. But I'm telling you all this anyway. Because I'm your mama."

Everybody laughs, and Daddy gives Mama a squeeze and a kiss on the cheek. Then he claps his hands and says,

"All right, let's move on out" like a general commanding his troops.

Zo's family's backyard has been set up like a playground. There's a net for badminton and a plastic tub full of Frisbees and balls, and there's a tire swing hanging from a tree that the Littles make a beeline for. Zo greets me with a smile. "Wanna play badminton?"

I look over at Mama, who's talking to Zo's mother. "I should probably help get the food ready."

"Mom and Dad have that under control," Zo says. "Let's play badminton. Hey, Justice?" she calls. "You and Val wanna play badminton with us?"

Just looks surprised. "Boys against girls?"

Zo shrugs. "Sure. Why not?"

Just looks over at Val. "Let's try not to beat them too bad. It wouldn't be gentlemanly."

But it turns out there's no danger of them beating us too bad because Zo is great at badminton. I've only played maybe twice before in my life, so I'm not much help, but it's not like she needs help anyway. Some of it's the way she's dressed. In shorts, she can move faster and smoother than I can in my long skirt. But even if she had on a skirt, too, she'd be way better than me. It's like she can predict where the birdie is going to be and then hit it back with real force at an angle that makes it hard for the boys across the net.

Just and Val are scrambling to return Zo's serves. One time they're both trying to hit the birdie, and they run into each other instead. Zo laughs, but not in a mean way. The boys don't laugh at all.

After we've played a few more minutes, with Zo getting better and better and the boys getting worse and worse, Daddy comes over. "Boys," he says, "I'm going to have to take you out of the game. You need to help Mr. Forrester and me set up chairs for the picnic."

"Yessir," Just and Val say. They look relieved.

After they walk away, Zo says in almost a whisper, "So did your dad do that to rescue the boys from being beaten by a girl?"

"I don't think so," I say, though maybe she's right.

"The chairs don't need to be set up for at least half an hour," Zo says. "We weren't even keeping score."

"I know," I say. "But you are really good."

"So your family believes that guys always have to be better than girls?" Coming from somebody else this could sound mean, but Zo just sounds curious.

"No, not at all," I say, twirling the racket in my hands. "Men and women are equal in God's eyes. They just have different roles. The man is the leader and the provider, and the woman takes care of the home and children. It's like the man is God and the woman is the church."

"So physically speaking, men are the strong ones?" Zo says.

"That's right," I say.

"So how do you explain me mopping up the badminton court with your brothers?" she says, grinning.

"I don't know. Maybe because they're younger than you?" I'm smiling back, but it's to hide my confusion. "You're always asking me questions I don't know the answers to."

"Well, how about this one?" Zo gives my arm a little nudge with her racquet. "How about just you and me play badminton?"

"Okay."

After Zo has beaten me at badminton, she and Owen and me take Faith and Charity to visit the bunnies. I show them how to sit crisscross applesauce so they can each hold a bunny in their laps. Zo lifts the bunnies, who have grown a lot, out of the hutch. They both settle in the girls' laps right away. I wish we could have bunnies, too, but Ruth and Boaz would make short work of them.

"What are the bunnies' names?" Faith asks, petting her bunny's ears.

"Ziggy and Freddy," Owen says.

"Why are they named Ziggy and Freddy?" Faith asks. The girl can ask questions all day long.

"They're named after singers," Owen says.

"What kind of singers?" Faith asks.

Owen looks over at Zo like he's not sure what to say, and she says, "Rock singers."

"Do they sing about rocks?" Faith says.

"No, silly," Owen says, laughing. "Rock is a kind of music."

I barely know what rock music is except that it's loud and sinful, so I'm not surprised Faith thinks it's songs about rocks. Daddy says popular music is all about devil worship. The only songs with words we're allowed to hear or sing are hymns. We can listen to classical music, too, because if songs don't have words they can't mean anything bad. Mozart is my favorite.

Mrs. Forrester yells that we're almost ready to eat. We put the bunnies back, and Mrs. Forrester tells us she's set a bottle of liquid soap next to the garden hose if we want to wash our hands.

The food spread out on the picnic table is way different from any food I've ever seen. Mama's baked beans are there, so they're familiar, and the corn on the cob is recognizable. After that, I'm lost. There's a bowl with salad with tiny tomatoes and leaves that don't look like lettuce, and little white blobs. The strangest thing is what they're calling burgers. They're brown disks but they're smooth and squishy and don't look like any ground beef I've ever seen. I must look confused because Zo says, "It's a portobello mushroom. You put it on a bun with whatever else you'd put on a burger. It's good."

I decide I'd better take one and act like I'm enjoying it. Mama and Daddy both hate mushrooms, and the Littles aren't used to eating anything cooked by anybody but Mama or Nanny. I load up my "burger" with lettuce, tomatoes, onions, and pickles, figuring the toppings will cover up the taste of the mushroom in case it's nasty.

The Littles have been trained to be polite at all times, so they don't say anything when Mama and I are helping them fill their plates. But I can tell from the looks on their faces that they're disgusted and maybe even a little afraid. They look the same way they would if Mama and I were dipping worms and bugs onto their plates.

"Remember to eat some of everything," I whisper to Charity, and she nods with her little mouth set in a straight line, like she's trying to be brave.

Zo's family has set up a folding table with chairs next to their wooden picnic table so we can all sit together. There are pitchers on the table, and Mrs. Forrester says, "Help yourself to whatever you'd like to drink, iced tea, lemonade, or an Arnold Palmer."

"What's an Arnold Palmer?" Faith asks.

"It's half tea and half lemonade," Zo says. "It's my favorite drink."

"Why is a drink called a man's name?" Faith asks.

"Wasn't Arnold Palmer some kind of ball player or something?" Just asks.

"Golfer," Mr. Forrester says. Unlike Daddy, who wears dress shirts when he's not in his work clothes, Zo's dad always seems to be wearing a T-shirt with jeans or shorts. I think he's a nice-looking man, though. His blue eyes are twinkly and kind, and together with his long beard, make me think of Pa Ingalls in the Little House books.

"I've never had much use for golf," Daddy says. "I always thought of it as a rich man's game."

"Exactly!" Mr. Forrester says. "Rich, white country-club boys riding a little cart from hole to hole to make sure they don't accidentally get some exercise. And don't get me started on the amount of land that gets cleared just so the old boys can have their eighteen holes spaced out nice and wide!"

"I think golf looks boring," Val says.

"Me too," Daddy says. "If I'm gonna spend a day outside enjoying myself, I'd rather be out in the woods than driving a little cart over grass that looks like it's been cut by a barber."

"Exactly!" Mr. Forrester says again, laughing.

I start to relax and feel happy. If the two daddies get along, then everything is going to be fine.

Everybody has their drinks now. Zo's family is already eating, but the rest of us are looking down at our plates like we've never seen food before and have no idea what to do with it. We must be pretty obvious in our confusion because Mrs. Forrester says, "I guess I should've told you we don't eat meat."

Mama smiles. "Oh, that's fine. We don't usually eat meat except at supper. It's much cheaper that way, especially when you've got a lot of mouths to feed."

"VB Six," Mr. Forrester says.

"I beg your pardon?" Mama says.

"VB Six," Mr. Forrester repeats. "Vegetarian before six p.m. That's a thing—people who won't give up meat entirely, but they limit it to one meal a day to reduce their carbon footprint. Of course we're vegetarians twenty-four seven."

"But we're not vegans," Owen chimes in. "Because we love cheese on our pizza."

Zo's dad smiles. "We do. But it's also because I don't see anything wrong with dairy and eggs as long as they come from free-range farms instead of factory ones. Plus, Claire makes her own mozzarella."

"Really?" Mama says. "I didn't know you could make it at home."

"It's super easy," Zo's mom says. "I can show you."

"But about all the VB Sixers and the people who call themselves flexitarians, whatever that means," Mr. Forrester says. "It's good they're limiting their meat intake, I guess, but I think you should live your principles all the time, not just until you get a craving for a burger."

"Now that I can agree with," Daddy says. I glance at his plate and notice he's mainly eating Mama's bacon-topped baked beans, which none of Zo's family has on their plates. "Not the burger part because I'd eat more meat if I could afford to, but the part about living your principles. There are too many people in this world—some of them calling themselves Christians—who say one thing and then turn around and do another."

"Don't get me started on hypocrites," Mr. Forrester says. "We'll be here all night."

"No," Zo's mom says, smiling. "Don't get him started."

The mushroom burger actually tastes good if you think of it as something other than a burger. The other members of my family seem to be struggling with theirs, though. Just has covered his in ketchup but is still swallowing it with great effort. I'm pretty sure Val is biting off pieces and spitting them into his napkin, but I don't say anything even though I probably should. Mama is trying to eat but is looking a little green around the gills. At least she has the excuse of being pregnant.

"There was something we planned for the kids to do after dinner," Zo's mom says, "but we wanted to check, Bill and Becky, to see if it's all right with you."

"Ask Bill," Mama says. "He makes the decisions."

Zo's mom gets a funny look, then she gets up from the table, goes over to Daddy, and whispers in his ear. His face turns red. I guess he's not used to having a woman other than Mama that close to him. But after she says whatever she has to say, he smiles and says, "That'd be fine."

Once everybody has eaten or at least pushed the food around on their plates so it looks like they've eaten, Zo's mom says, "Owen, do you want to go get the surprise?"

He grins and jumps up from the table.

"What's a surprise?" Charity asks.

At first, it's a surprise that she doesn't know the word, but she is awful little, and our day-to-day lives are so planned out there's not much room for surprises. "It's something you didn't know was going to happen," I say. "Like that time we went to town to go to Walmart and ended up stopping at the Whippy Dip for an ice cream cone."

"Oh!" Charity says, her dimples showing as she smiles. "I like surprises!"

Owen comes around from the side of the house dragging a big plastic storage tub piled high with pink, yellow, and green balloons. I don't understand until he yells, "Water balloons!" and all the Littles go crazy and run to the tub.

"I'd better go out there and make some rules," Just says, "or they'll just throw them everywhere and it'll be over in three minutes."

I can tell he really wants to play even though he's too old for it.

"You wanna go too, Miss?" Mama asks Patience.

"No, I hate getting wet," Patience says.

"I don't mind getting wet," Zo says, "but I think I'd rather just sit here and watch them clobber each other."

"Me too," I say because I'd rather stay with Zo.

Just doesn't seem to be having much luck maintaining order. The Littles have pummeled him, and he's soaked from head to toe. Val and Owen have staked out territory in the play fort and are lobbing water balloons down on the girls, who scream and giggle.

"See, this is what I love," Zo's mom says, "seeing kids running around and playing like little lunatics instead of staring at a screen like they've been narcotized."

"Ain't that the truth," Daddy says. "We don't even have a TV. We do have a computer, but it's just for the family business."

"We have a family e-mail account, but that's all," Mama says. "The children are limited to thirty minutes of supervised computer time a week."

The Littles use their computer time to play Bible games. Patience and Just go on some of the Christian teen websites. I hardly go on the computer at all. The Internet is so huge and overwhelming that I don't know what to choose or where to go. So mostly I go nowhere.

"We keep a TV to watch movies from Netflix," Zo's dad says, "but we don't have cable."

"Of course," Zo's mom says, pouring herself more iced tea, "the at-home technology isn't the half of it these days. Kids are plugged in all the time. Once I was in a Starbucks in Knoxville and saw this young mother sitting at a table with her baby. The baby was little—no more than nine months or so. The mom was playing with her phone, and the baby got fussy. Instead of picking him up to soothe him, she handed him her phone. I guess so he could play some app game for infants. I thought, there's so much wrong with that I don't even know where to start."

Mama shakes her head. "Letting a cold piece of technology take the place of being a mother."

Zo's mom nods. "And on a more minor but still important note, letting a baby drool and bang on a phone that cost hundreds of dollars! What happened to rattles? They're cheap and indestructible."

"People worship technology," Daddy says. "But it's a false god."

"A golden calf," Zo's daddy says.

Daddy's eyebrows shoot up the way they do when he's surprised. "You know the Bible?"

Zo's dad grins. "I've read it from cover to cover. I'm sure I
don't have the working knowledge of it that you do, though."

"So," Zo's mom says, almost interrupting her husband.
"I'm going to clear the table, and then I guess we can bring
out the watermelon. I got two to make sure there's plenty."

"Well, in my opinion, you can never have too much watermelon," Daddy says.

"The girls and I will help clear." Mama gives Patience and
me a look that means to get up and help.

"Just grab what you can and we'll pile it all on the kitchen
counter," Zo's mom says. "I'll sort things out later."

Zo's family's kitchen isn't dirty but it isn't spotless either.
Mama sweeps and mops the kitchen floor every day, but it
looks like Zo's mom does it every few days. The kitchen is
also full of more stuff than ours. There's a whole bookcase
full of cookbooks, and cast iron skillets and metal pans hang
on the walls. Out of nowhere, Patience lets out a little shriek.

"What in the world?" Mama says.

"I didn't see it, then it brushed up against my leg," Patience
says, her voice shaky.

I look down and see a long-haired black cat with eyes the
color of copper pennies. I know black cats are supposed to
be bad luck and witches' pets, but I have to admit this one is
beautiful.

"That's Edgar," Zo says. "He's a big baby."

"If a black cat crossing your path was really bad luck, we'd
be a very unlucky family. Edgar gets in our way all the time,"
Mrs. Forrester says.

I reach down to pet him, but Mama says, "Don't touch an animal when you're handling food."

"Yes, ma'am," I say, straightening up.

"Mama!" It's Charity, who's standing at the kitchen door, soaking wet from the water balloon fight. "I have to go."

There's no need to ask where.

"Just a second, honey, and I'll take you to the house," Mama says.

"She can use our bathroom," Mrs. Forrester says. "She'll have to use the upstairs one, though. The downstairs toilet doesn't flush right and is on the long list of Things Todd's Meaning to Fix."

"Libby, will you take her?" Mama asks.

"Yes ma'am." I'm happy because taking her gives me the chance to see more of Zo's house. As we go up the stairs, I peek into the living room. There's the purple couch I watched the moving men unload, and there are two book-cases full of books. Framed posters hang on the wall, one of a black cat that looks like theirs, another of a dancing lady kicking her leg so you can see the fluffy petticoat under her skirt. Both posters have writing on them in a language I don't understand.

"I have to do Number Two," Charity whispers.

"Okay. I'll wait outside the bathroom. Let me know if you need help."

"I can do it all by myself," Charity says, like I've made her mad.

"You're a big girl," I say.

The second floor is laid out like the second floor of our house. I stand outside the bathroom door until I hear

Charity start singing a song about Noah and the animals. She always sings to entertain herself on the potty.

The doors to all the other rooms are open. On the right is a room with a big bed with a fluffy blue comforter. Across from me is a room with a loft bed and Legos cluttering the floor. I know the third room is Zo's.

I feel a terrible curiosity rise up inside me, like when I couldn't resist eavesdropping on Mama and Nanny on Sunday. Is this curiosity what makes females the weaker sex, prone to temptation? Is it what made Eve taste the forbidden fruit?

I feel my feet moving toward Zo's room.

I don't go in, just stand in the doorway and peek. The walls are blue, but not a normal shade like baby blue or navy. They're bright blue, brighter than I've ever known blue to be. She has a double bed all for herself, I guess, with a black comforter and pillows that are striped black and white like a zebra. There are stacked plastic milk crates full of what I recognize as record albums and an old record player balanced on top of the crates. There's a bookcase, too, but it's against the left wall so I can't see what the books are without stepping into the room, which I won't allow myself to do.

The thing I can't take my eyes off, though, is the poster hanging over the record player. It's the head and shoulders of a person. I say a person because I can't really tell if it's a man or a woman. The person is thin and pale with short spiky hair that's bright orange like a clown's. The person's eyes are closed, and one side of its face is painted like a red-and-blue lightning bolt. Its lips are painted red, and its shoulders are bony. Looking at the neck, I think I see the swell of an Adam's apple. So it is a male. Is he a clown? He doesn't look like he's trying to be funny. And why would Zo have a picture of such a person hanging in her room?

I hurry over to meet Charity when she comes out.

"All done," she says.

"Good girl."

Outside, Zo's dad is cutting the watermelon into big red wedges. Faith already has her face buried in a slice.

I sit back down at the picnic table.

"Hey," Zo says. She's attacking her watermelon slice with a fork instead of diving in face first. "You look kind of strange. Are you okay?"

When I look at Zo, I don't see the picture in her room that made me feel weird and confused. I just see my nice friend. Whatever that picture is, she can't mean anything bad by it. "I'm fine," I say, and thank her dad when he sets a slab of watermelon down in front of me.

Once we've said our goodbyes and are heading back to the house, Mama says, "That was fun." She says it cautiously, like she's nervous Daddy might correct her.

"It was," Daddy says. "They're nice folks, and they ask a lot of the right questions. They just come up with the wrong answers a lot of the time. We should all pray that their hearts will be opened to the one right answer."

ZO

CHAPTER 10

"I WISH I COULD SAY FOURTEEN is the youngest I've ever seen, but you know it isn't." Dad's been talking about a girl who came into the health department today, crying and terrified because her "monthly friend" was late. "But that's what comes of abstinence-only education."

Mom and Dad are sitting on the front porch, drinking their evening beer. Owen and I are in the yard just a few steps away from the porch, throwing a ball back and forth.

"What's ab-stin-ence only education?" Owen asks.

"It's a kind of sex education that isn't sex education at all," Mom says. Her feet are bare, and her legs are stretched across Dad's lap. "Basically it says sex is something that should be saved for marriage, so there's no need for anybody to even think about it until their wedding night."

"I bet people still think about it," Owen says, catching the ball.

"Of course they do!" Dad says. "They think about it, and they do it anyway. For adolescents and adults, sex is a drive, just like hunger. If you were really hungry and there was a big, gooey cheese pizza sitting in front of you, would you not eat it if somebody told you eating it was morally wrong?"

"If I was really hungry, I'd eat it anyway. I wouldn't be able to help myself." Owen has lost interest in our game of catch, it seems, and heads up to the porch. I follow him.

"Exactly!" Dad says, and I can tell he's climbing on his soapbox, as Mom calls it. "That's why kids need to learn how sex works and how to use protection."

"Like condoms, right?" Owen says. Most kids his age would laugh talking about condoms, but in our house talking about them is so routine they seem as boring as Band-Aids.

"Right," Dad says.

"You put those on bananas, don't you?" I say because that's how Dad demonstrates condom usage at the health department.

"Yep," Dad says. "Don't want to exchange any fluids with a banana." He looks past me for a second, then whispers, "Hey, there's a good argument for condoms right over there."

"Todd, that's awful!" Mom says.

I look where they're looking. Libby and the Littles are in the front yard blowing bubbles.

"You're right. That was below the belt," Dad says, cracking himself up. "I'm sorry. They're sweet kids, and I'm glad they exist. It's just that there are so many of them. The other night at the cookout, I ended up talking to Bill about financial stuff. I asked him how he managed to support all those kids on one income."

"Because you're nosy," Mom says.

"Yes, I am." He tickles her foot.

"He said it's a constant struggle, but he knows it's the path God has set for him. And of course, Becky can't have a job because God wants her to stay home and homeschool the kids so they won't have to go to the satanic public schools. And government assistance—even something that would just help out with milk and groceries for the kids—is out of the question because the government is godless. He runs his family like it's a small country where he's the dictator. And it's a pretty impoverished country."

Next door, Libby sees me and gives a shy little wave. She's just blown an enormous bubble, and I give her a thumbs up. Then I remember something I saw on the Internet. "Hey," I say to Mom, "I should go over and show them that trick with soap bubbles I was telling you about."

"If it's okay with their parents that you go over there," Mom says, then looks at Dad. "Lord, if they saw us drinking beer, I bet they wouldn't be coming over for a cookout ever again."

"Nope," Dad says. "They'd probably build a big brick wall between their house and ours so they wouldn't have to gaze upon our sin."

I run to my room to grab a couple of things, and then Owen and I run over to the fence. "Hi," I say.

Faith looks up at me, bubble wand in hand, and says, "Mama took us to the dollar store today, and we got sidewalk chalk and bubbles!"

"Cool," I say. "I know a trick you can do with bubbles. Wanna see it?"

"Yeah!" Faith and Charity both yell. Val is more reserved, but I can tell he's curious.

"I'll have to use one of the bottles of bubble stuff," I say.

"You can take this one." Libby grabs a bottle off the porch.
"We got a six-pack."

This makes me think of Mom and Dad drinking beer on
the porch, and I smile. "Okay, so the Internet said this
would work, but that's no guarantee." I take a glow stick
and a pair of Owen's safety scissors out of my pocket. I have
this thing about glow sticks. I get them at the Dollar Tree,
the same place the Hazletts get their bubbles and sidewalk
chalk. Sometimes at night I'll put on a Bowie album, turn
off the lights, and lie on my bed just waving the glow stick
in time with the music. It's kind of hypnotic. Purple glow
sticks are my favorite, but the one I have right now is green.

I open the bottle of bubble stuff, then use the scissors to cut
off the end of the glow stick. I pour the liquid into the bottle,
put the lid back on, and shake it. Then I remove the lid, take
out the wand, and blow a glow-in-the-dark neon-green bubble.

"Whoa," Val says, and Faith and Charity are staring at me
like I just produced a fairy from thin air.

"It worked!" Owen says.

"Yup." I blow a cluster of glowing bubbles.

Libby's eyes are almost as wide as her younger sisters'.
"They're beautiful. How do you know so much stuff, Zo?"

I shrug. "Internet." But that's not really all it is. I know
stuff she doesn't know because I live in the world. She lives
on a tiny island.

The kids take turns blowing glow-in-the-dark bubbles.
Charity has the same trouble blowing bubbles a lot of little
kids do, where she spits more than she blows, and Val steps
in to help her.

"I need to tell you something," Libby says, almost in a whisper.

"Okay."

"I did something bad the other day, and I've been feeling guilty about it ever since."

Her face is so serious it looks like she's about to confess to some terrible crime. "Does it have to do with me?"

Libby nods. "You know when we came over for the cookout and I took Charity upstairs to the bathroom?"

I can tell she's not going to say anything else until I say something, so I give her an "uh-huh."

"Well, while she was in the bathroom, I looked in your room. I didn't go inside or anything, just peeped in the doorway. I'm really sorry."

I can't help laughing. "Is that it?"

"I shouldn't have done it without your permission."

"Libby, you're my friend. You don't need to ask permission to see my room. If . . . " If what? If your parents weren't religious fanatics? I've talked myself into a corner. "If things were different, so that you and I could spend time together one-on-one, then we'd probably hang out in my room all the time."

"Really?" Libby smiles, looking amazed and confused at the same time. "I've never hung out one-on-one with anybody but my sister, and that's because we share a bedroom. Your room is . . . interesting."

"Well, when we moved here, Mom and Dad said I could fix up my room exactly like I wanted it, and that's what I did. I think I made the paint mixer guy at Home Depot mad because I kept saying I wanted electric blue and it kept turning out royal blue, and I had to keep saying, 'Brighter! Brighter!'"

"It is bright." She looks at Faith and Charity, who are chasing glowing bubbles as fast as Val can blow them. She looks back at me and whispers, "That picture over your record player . . . who is that person?"

"David Bowie." I figure it would cause problems if I called him my patron saint so I just say, "my favorite singer."

"David," Libby says. "So he's a man?"

He's both and neither and more, I want to say. So am I— all hail androgyny! Long live gender fluidity! But how could I introduce these concepts to someone who doesn't even live in the twenty-first century? It would be like trying to explain gender constructs to Laura Ingalls Wilder. So I say, "Yes, and that's a picture of him from the 1970s. He doesn't look like that anymore."

"I don't know anything about secular music. We sing church music, and we're allowed to listen to classical."

"I like classical, too," I say. "Mozart is my favorite."

"Mine, too!" Libby says, clapping her hands. "His songs are so light and airy. Like those bubbles."

"Exactly." I bet the only reason Libby's parents let her listen to classical music is that there are no lyrics and therefore nothing objectionable. But whatever the reason, I'm glad she has Mozart—one voice that doesn't preach or restrict, but just lets her feel.

I'M AT THE KITCHEN TABLE READING *Fahrenheit 451* when Mom comes in with the mail. I've read the book before—I went through a big Bradbury phase in middle school—but I'm rereading it to compare it with the other dystopian novels for my summer project.

"How's that one hitting you?" Mom nods toward the book.

"You know, it's pretty amazing how in the 1950s he was predicting how technology and entertainment would take the place of reading and thinking. And a lot of the technology in the book is like what people use today."

"Yeah," Mom says. "The only difference is that in the book, it's illegal for people to read. Now people are free to read. They just don't do it." She flips through the stack of envelopes and tosses most of them in the recycling. "All junk for the grownups," she says, "but there's a Lego magazine for Owen and three college packets for you."

She sets three big envelopes on the table in front of me, and I feel a ball of anxiety in my stomach. Since I did okay on my trial run taking the ACT, I get mail from colleges every week. Mom's take on this is always "Ooh, isn't this exciting?" but my response is closer to panic. It's like my future is calling and saying, "Decide, decide."

I know I'm being weird. Even though I love my family, I don't want to live with them the rest of my life. I do want to go to college, but what school do I choose? And what if I make the wrong choice and am unhappy when I get there? What do I major in? And what if something bad happens to me like in high school and I break down and screw up my grades? The older you get, the harder your screw-ups are to fix. Or at least it gets much less likely someone else will fix them for you.

"Aren't you going to look at them?" Mom says. She always acts like opening college packets is like opening presents.

I look at the one on top of the stack. "Not this one." I toss it into the recycling. "Texas Christian Women's University."

"Don't think they hit the demographics quite right on that one," Mom says. "And I doubt there's a Texas Atheist Gender Fluid University."

"I wish there was. But maybe not in Texas." I pick up the next envelope. "This one's from Warren Wilson."

Mom sits next to me. "Ooh, that's a nice school. Kinda crunchy, and up in the mountains near Asheville. You love Asheville."

"Asheville's cool." I tear open the envelope and flip through the look book. It's the same as all the others: photos showing off the collegiate architecture and landscaping, smiling and consistently good-looking students chatting on their way to class.

"Looks nice," Mom says.

I know she's trying to be encouraging because she's worried about how I freeze up on the subject of college, but it still rubs me the wrong way. "They hired an expensive PR firm to make sure it looks nice. And they always pick out the same kids for the pictures—blandly-attractive white kids with a token black, brown, or Asian kid to show how diverse they are. Sometimes they even throw in a kid in a wheelchair. But they're all smiling and good-looking and cisgender and thin."

"You're right," Mom says. "It's advertising. The only way to really know if you'd like a school is to visit it. Sit in on a class or two, talk to some real people."

"I know." Suddenly I feel more overwhelmed than ever. "But sometimes when I look at all these choices I supposedly have, I think, what does it matter what I decide? The polar ice caps are melting. One percent of the population has all the money and resources, and people who should be rioting in the streets are sitting like zombies in front of screens instead. What kind of future can I have anyway?"

Mom picks up my copy of *Fahrenheit 451*. "I think you've had enough dystopian fiction for today. Maybe you should go listen to some music or pet the bunnies or something."

I sigh. "Maybe I'll go sit like a zombie in front of a screen for a while."

"Good idea," Mom says. "Listen, I can remember feeling nervous at your age, too, with all of these choices spread out before me. But looking back, I feel like I almost always made the right decisions. And I think you will, too."

This should probably make me feel better than it does.

In my room, I put on *Hunky Dory*, my comfort-food Bowie album. I get on Facebook and type "feeling stressed." Immediately Claire appears on chat.

Claire: *What's eatin' ya?*

Zo: *Just life. I feel like the future is weighing so heavy on me I can't even feel the present.*

Claire: *I've told you to quit experimenting with time travel.*

Zo: *LOL*

Claire: *Step away from the TARDIS.*

Zo: *Ha I keep getting all this stuff from colleges, and it's stressing me out. I don't know where I want to go or what I want to do.*

Claire: *So when the time comes, move back to Knoxville and come to UT with me.*

Zo: *You know that's what you're doing?*

Claire: *I was told that's what I'll be doing. I can go for free since Mom works there. She told me it was an offer we couldn't afford to refuse. Especially since she and I both know Dad won't give me another penny once I turn eighteen.*

Zo: *I'm kind of jealous that you have everything so settled.*
Claire: *You can have things settled, too. Come to UT with me. We could be roommates.*
Zo: *I'll think about it. We would have fun. I gotta go, okay?*
Claire: *K*

I shut my laptop and lie back on my bed. UT would be a comfortable choice. I'd be in my hometown with my best friend. But is a comfortable choice also a cowardly choice? Part of me wants to be brave—to go to California or the Pacific Northwest, some place where the way my family thinks is the rule instead of the exception. But even if I could get into a school out there, how would my parents afford it? And what if I went there only to discover I couldn't cut it?

On my stereo, Bowie is ordering me to turn to face the strange changes. I'm trying. I really am.

CHAPTER 11

"I was thinking we ought to have y'all over for supper," Mrs. Hazlett is saying, opening a jar of maraschino cherries. "But I couldn't figure out what to feed you. It was the kids who came up with the idea of an ice cream social."

"Well, it was an inspired idea," Mom says. "You never have to force me to eat ice cream."

"Wouldn't it be funny if you did have to force somebody to eat ice cream?" Owen says. "Eat it! Eat it! It's delicious!" He mimes shoving a spoon into Val's face.

"No!" Val says, laughing. "No! Not extra sprinkles!"

"You've really put out a spread here," Dad says, and he's right. On the picnic table is a gallon each of chocolate, vanilla, and strawberry ice cream; hot fudge, caramel, and strawberry topping; and Reddi-Wip, sliced bananas, chopped nuts, rainbow sprinkles, and cherries.

"Well, Bill just finished up a big job, so we could afford to splurge a little," Mrs. Hazlett says.

"'Just a little' is right." Mr. Hazlett puts his arm around his wife. "But the Lord don't mind if we give ourselves a little treat now and then. Besides, it's Faith's birthday, and her favorite thing in the world is ice cream."

I look down at Faith, who's grinning like a jack o' lantern (even though I'm sure her family doesn't celebrate Halloween). "Happy birthday," I say.

"I'm five," Faith says. "I got to have spaghetti tonight, too."

"Wow," I say. "You're five *and* you get to have spaghetti and ice cream? Life doesn't get much better than that, does it?"

It's hard for anybody not to be in a good mood with a bowl of ice cream in front of them. Libby has made herself a sort of banana split with chocolate and vanilla ice cream, two kinds of sauce, and whipped cream. I make a similar concoction and sit with her on a blanket in the grass.

She spoons a mound of ice cream into her mouth, closes her eyes, and smiles. "It's so good," she says. "If I'm prone to one of the seven deadly sins, it's gluttony."

"It's a good one," I say, digging into my sundae. "Well, I mean, I guess it's not good because it's a sin, but you know what I mean. Eating too much is very tempting." We don't talk about sin in our house, so I feel like I'm on shaky ground.

"It is," Libby says, "especially when it's all sweet and creamy and chocolatey."

"As far as the names of the seven deadly sins go, I like sloth," I say. "It sounds like what it is, you know?" I say it as slowly and lazily as possible. "SL-OTH."

Libby laughs.

"And then there's the animal called a sloth," I say, scooping up some vanilla and hot fudge.

"I've heard of them. But I've never seen a picture of one or anything."

"Oh, you should look them up. They're really adorable—kind of smiley and sleepy-looking, and they move
super slow."

"So I guess the animal was named after the sin?"

"I guess so. It's like which came first, the sin or the sloth?
You wouldn't say sloths themselves are sinful, would you?"

Libby shakes her head. "Of course not. Animals can't sin.
They don't have souls."

She says this with such certainty. I'm not sure if anybody
has a soul. Maybe we're all just a mix of chemicals and
reflexes and instincts, whether we walk on two legs or four.
The only kind of soul I believe in is the kind James Brown
had. Or Bowie on *Young Americans* with Luther Vandross on
backup vocals.

The sugar is hitting the Littles pretty hard. They're
careening off the swing set and trampoline. Just has gone off
to do target practice with his bow and arrow, which seems
like all he ever does, and Patience is sitting on a blanket by
herself, shooting glances over at Libby and me. She always
looks at me like she's just caught me doing something wrong,
which, in her opinion, I guess I have, whether it's wearing
pants or thinking my opinion matters even though I don't
have a penis. I'm pretty sure the sock I stuff into my jeans
sometimes doesn't count.

Mom and Dad are sitting at the picnic table with Mr. and
Mrs. Hazlett. The adults take their time with their ice cream
more than the kids. The way the two couples are sitting
across from each other makes me think of teenagers in the
1950s on a double date at the malt shop. I tell this to Libby,
and she giggles like I've said something naughty.

"I'll tell you, Bill," Mom is saying, "your wife has just had three weaving lessons, and she's already doing beautiful work. The girls are coming along nicely, too."

"Well," Mr. Hazlett says, "I do have to say that my wife has always excelled in the womanly arts."

"The womanly arts?" Dad says with a smirk in his voice. "And what are those?"

Dad gets in these moods sometimes where he's not willing to keep his mouth shut and silently disagree with someone. From the sound of him, he's in one of those moods right now, which isn't good. I try to shoot Mom a warning glance, but I can't catch her eye.

"Oh, you know what I mean," Mr. Hazlett says. "Cooking, cleaning, childrearing, needlework."

"All of which can be done by men, too," Dad says.

"Well, sure, in a pinch," Mr. Hazlett says. "But these skills come more naturally to women. Like I'm guessing, Todd, that you ain't much of a weaver."

I think Mr. Hazlett was trying to be funny, but Dad doesn't smile. "I'm not, and neither is Zo. But Owen's pretty good at it. I'm a good cook, and I like to knit. I made both of my kids' baby blankets." He doesn't add that he made mine yellow and Owen's green to be gender neutral, but that might be coming.

Mr. Hazlett laughs. "I'm trying to imagine those big mitts of yours clicking a pair of knitting needles! Your beard ever get tangled up in the yarn?"

"Not yet," Dad says. Both men are grinning, but there's tension between them. It's like two dogs cautiously wagging their tails while staking out their individual territory.

"I guess what I'm saying," Mr. Hazlett says, "is that according to God's plan, men and women are supposed to be complementary, and each sex has their own tasks and abilities."

"Well, I like to think we've evolved from being a hunter-gatherer society." Evolved is an unfortunate word choice, and I can tell from the look on Dad's face that he knows it as soon as he's said it.

Mr. Hazlett's back stiffens, and Mrs. Hazlett looks over at him nervously.

"Well, 'evolve' is a word we don't really say in my house," Mr. Hazlett says. "We're concerned with the truth, not with theories." He says theories in a drawn-out, condescending way and punctuates it with finger quotes.

"I'm sorry," Dad says. "I should know that, of course. But I didn't mean it in the sense of Darwin. I just meant it in the sense of growth and change. Over the years, people have grown and changed, and so there's no need for gender roles to be so rigid anymore. Women work outside the home. Men can stay home with the kids if they want and don't have to be uptight about showing their feelings."

"You're talking about the world's way of doing things, not God's way. If you live according to Biblical principles, men are men and women are women."

"But what does that even mean?" Dad says, and I can tell from his intense eyes and his rising inflection that he's really wound up now. "I mean, gender is just a social construct, right? It varies from time to time and from culture to culture."

"It does not vary in the eyes of the Lord!" Mr. Hazlett's getting worked up, too. A vein in his forehead bulges disturbingly. "In a Christian home, the man is like God, and his wife is the holy church."

Dad laughs out loud. Maybe a little too loud. "So you get to be a deity, and she just gets to be a building?"

"Listen," Mom interrupts, putting a hand on Dad's forearm. "Maybe we should switch to a more neutral subject. The weather, maybe? Nice, isn't it? Warm but not so hot that it melts your ice cream—"

"In my house," Mr. Hazlett says, "women don't get to tell men to stop talking about what they're talking about."

"Well, we're not in your house, are we?" Daddy says, in the measured tone he uses when he's trying not to yell. "We're outside in nature that belongs to everybody, and you don't get to tell my wife to shut up."

"It's my yard," Mr. Hazlett says.

Libby and I exchange worried glances. The Littles have paused in their play to eavesdrop on the grownups' argument.

"And I did not use those words to speak to your wife," Mr. Hazlett says, his tone colder than ice cream.

"I know you didn't, Bill," Dad says, and I can tell he's trying to calm down. "Look, our kids like each other, and that's great. And I want to be a good neighbor to you, but I admit—and this is a character failing on my part—that I sometimes have difficulty respecting the views of someone I disagree with."

"Only sometimes?" Mom says, giving Dad a little chuck on the shoulder. I can tell she's trying to lighten the mood.

"Okay, most of the time," Dad says. "Agreeing to disagree isn't something that comes naturally to me."

"Me neither," Mr. Hazlett says. And I start to breathe easier now that they're working toward a truce. "But it's hard to respect somebody's beliefs when you're right and they're just flat-out wrong."

"Yes," Daddy says. "We both have strong opinions, and we both think we're right—"

"Opinion has nothing to do with it," Mr. Hazlett says. "I know I'm right because I walk with the Lord every day. Do you and your family walk with the Lord, Todd?"

Dad sighs. "No, Bill. We don't walk with the Lord."

Mr. Hazlett looks sad and shakes his head. "Then you walk with the Devil."

"No, I don't believe in him either," Dad says, "though Satanism is so silly I find it hilarious. My family and I—we walk together, along with like-minded friends. That's enough."

"It is not enough!" Mr. Hazlett says, pounding his fist on the table and making the ice cream spoons rattle in their bowls. "You're walking yourself and your wife and children right down the road to hell is what you're doing!" He looks at Dad hard, but his tone softens. "You know, at first I didn't want to have anything to do with your family. I thought you'd be a corrupting influence. But then I prayed on it, and it came to me that getting to know y'all was an opportunity. An opportunity to show you how a Christian family should act and put you on the right path. I didn't know how hard it would be, how lost you truly are." Mr. Hazlett looks like he might cry. "Will you pray with me?"

"No." Dad is getting up. It's awkward to make a smooth gesture of getting up from a picnic table because you have to swing your leg over to extricate yourself from it. "Look, Bill, what needs to happen for us to stay good neighbors is that we both need to accept each other the way we are. So here's what I am, Bill. I am a feminist vegetarian atheist socialist who votes for Democrats because that's the best you can hope for in this country. I believe in labor unions, gun control, LGBTQIA equality, contraception, and separation of church and state. I also believe, like you, in working hard, living simply, and being a good husband and father. Now if you can at least try to accept me the way I am, I'll do the same for you."

Now it's Mr. Hazlett's turn to rise awkwardly from the table. "'Judgments are prepared for the scorners,'" he says, "'and stripes for the back of fools.' Proverbs nineteen, twenty-nine." He runs a hand through his hair, agitated. "Like the First Man, I have been led into temptation by a woman. And I have been brought low by foolish children." He's pacing back and forth. "When you people moved in next door, I knew in my heart we should keep our distance. But then your wife met my wife, and she wanted to be friends." He draws out "friends" like it's a bad word.

"I'm sorry, Bill," Mrs. Hazlett says, with tears in her eyes. "I guess I was just feeling lonesome."

"Lonesome?" Mr. Hazlett says, laughing in a short little bark. "How can you be lonesome with all these children around you all day?" He looks her in the eye. "But I forgive you."

"You know, sometimes adults do need adult conversation," Mom says. "Though I can't say I care too much for the one that's going on now."

"And the children," Mr. Hazlett says, like Mom never said anything. "There's nothing to forgive there, of course. They are foolish by nature and need my leadership. And this is where I've failed. I allowed myself to be tempted into a worldly relationship, and I lost sight of my role as patriarch."

"'Tempted into a worldly relationship?'" Dad says, smirking. "Bill, did you and I have sex and I missed it somehow?"

I know Dad's gone too far, but I also know it doesn't matter because it was already too late. Mr. Hazlett's face turns as red as an overripe tomato, and he roars, "Get out! 'Blessed is the man that walketh not in the counsel of the ungodly!' Children, playtime is over. No more playing with the neighbors."

"Ever?" Faith says.

"Ever," Mr. Hazlett says.

"But Owen is my friend." Val's eyes are tearing up.

"You know better than to say 'but' to me," Mr. Hazlett says. "Your brothers and your sisters are your friends. That's enough."

It takes me longer than it should to realize what this means for Libby and me. When it hits me, I look at her, and she's trying to look like she's not crying but she is, and then I'm crying, too. Without thinking, I throw my arms around her and hug her. I guess it puts her in a terrible position because if she hugs me back, it will show disobedience to her father. She doesn't hug back, but I can feel she wants to.

"What happened?" Owen says as Dad takes his hand for us to leave.

As Mom walks past the still-crying Mrs. Hazlett, she squeezes her shoulder and says, "You know where to find me if you need me, Becky."

It's probably Dad's DNA in me, but I can't walk past Mr. Hazlett and keep my mouth shut. "You know, I like Jesus," I say. "Unlike you, he wasn't a bully."

"I'll pray for you, honey," Mr. Hazlett says. Out of somebody else's mouth, these words could sound kind, but out of his, it's just another way of saying he's right and my whole family is wrong.

"WELL, THAT WAS DEFINITELY THE WORST time I've ever had while eating ice cream," Mom says once we're in the house. She's getting a beer from the fridge.

"Hand me one of those, too, will you?" Dad says.

"I still don't understand why I can't play with Val and them anymore," Owen says.

"Well, hon," Mom opens her beer bottle, "basically it's because Val's dad and your dad had a big argument because our families believe different things."

"Why does it matter if our dads agree on stuff?" Owen says. "We just like to play."

"An excellent question," Mom says, leaning against the kitchen counter, "I guess it matters because Val's dad says it matters. And like Zo said, he's a bully. And your dad here"—she nudges Dad with her beer bottle—"isn't a bully, but he isn't always prudent about when to keep his mouth shut."

"Hey, I refuse to be bullied," Dad says. "And I refuse to be anything other than my true self even though some people might have a problem with me. In the words of the great philosopher Popeye, 'I yam what I yam.'" He tousles Owen's hair. "But I am sorry about you and Val." He looks over at me. "And about you and Libby too."

At this second I realize that while I'm absolutely furious at Mr. Hazlett, I'm a little mad at Dad, too. The feeling takes me by surprise. But really, why couldn't he just dial down his liberal outrage a notch or two? He wasn't going to change Mr. Hazlett's mind by ranting at him any more than Mr. Hazlett was going to change Dad's by preaching and praying. It was all so pointless, and the only effect of it is losing Owen and me the only friends we've made since we moved. Would it have killed Mr. Hazlett and Dad to just shut up and eat their ice cream?

"I think I need to be by myself for a while," I say.

In my room, I pull up YouTube and watch David Bowie sing "Heroes," his song about the Berlin Wall, a man-made structure that separated people who might have wanted to be friends, who might have even loved each other.

CHAPTER 12

MOM AND DAD ARE WORRIED. EVER since the thing with Libby's dad the other day, it's like I've fallen back into the habits that put me in therapy after Hadley and I broke up. I lie in my room listening to the same song over and over ("We could be heroes just for one day"), and I don't come down for meals until Mom literally begs me. It's not that I'm trying to annoy her or anything; it's just that it takes so much effort for me to move.

I know it's weird. It's not like Libby was my girlfriend or anything. But she was the only person outside my family I had here, and I think I may have been the only person she had outside her family at all. And to tear us apart like her dad did and to tear Owen apart from his little pals—the cruelty of it shatters me. The fact that Mr. Hazlett justifies his dictatorship through religion makes me think of all the families and communities and countries that have been torn apart because of people who claimed to be acting in the name of God.

"Zo, I'd like to come in." Mom's at the door.

"Okay."

She walks straight to the stereo and lifts the needle off the record. "Okay, Z, I'm doing an intervention. This album's going back to Dad's music room for a while."

"If it's bothering you, I can listen with my headphones on."

Mom slides the album into its sleeve. "Yes, but then you'd still be listening to the same damn song over and over instead of taking a shower or a walk or reading a book or talking to a friend or—dare I say it?—your mother about why you're so upset."

"I don't even know why I'm so upset," I say. "I miss Libby, but it's more than that, too."

"I know." Mom sits on the foot of the bed. "Don't forget it's not just you and Owen who lost a friend. Becky and I were getting to be pretty close, too."

"Well, you were teaching her weaving."

"Yes." Without my asking, she starts giving me a foot massage. Part of me would like to complain, but it feels too nice. "When we did the weaving lessons, I'd get all the girls settled down with their mini-looms, and then Becky and I would work on the big loom. While the girls chatted about kid things, Becky and I talked quite a bit. She's a nice person. There's more to her than her religion."

"That's how I feel about Libby, too."

"And yet you can't escape the religion with them either," Mom says. "Maybe it's because we were weaving at the time, but I kept thinking of religion for her being like a web—a big, sticky spider web. The little bug can flap his wings and struggle against it, but he's still stuck." She sighs. "Not that I'm saying Becky was struggling—she only said good things about Bill and their beliefs. It was more like she was trapped in this web and didn't even know it. She'd talk sometimes about how tired she was or how hard it was to do all she had to do, and I'd think maybe she's waking up a little bit. But then she'd get this sort of hypnotized smile on her face and say something about how a righteous life wasn't an easy life and her efforts would be rewarded in heaven."

"And meanwhile she's trapped in the web and the spider's closing in on her," I say. "I guess the spider here is Mr. Hazlett?"

"I guess so." Mom smiles. "But the analogy kind of falls apart because in the world of spiders, females are the dominant ones."

She pushes my feet from her lap and stands up. "Okay, here's what you're going to do. You're going to take a shower and put on some clean clothes. Then . . . how long has it been since you talked to Claire?"

I shrug. "Before the thing with Libby."

"Don't you usually talk to her every day?"

I nod.

"Well, then she probably thinks you're dead. Check in with her after you shower. And how are you coming with your dystopian novels?"

"I finished *Fahrenheit 451* so I guess I've read them all."

"Not quite," Mom says. "I just expanded your reading list by one book. Come down and get it once you've talked to Claire."

I turn the shower on as hot as I can stand it and let the spray beat down on my neck, shoulders, and back. As my skin reddens and the steam rises, I feel like the heat is melting something inside me that's been all tight and coiled up since the scene at the Hazletts. As I get hotter, I feel softer, and before I know it's coming, I'm crying. Hard.

Tears that feel hot, too, stream down my face, and my shoulders shake as I sob.

I scrub my body with rosemary-scented soap, then wash my face, sobbing all the time. I wet my hair and lather it up with shampoo. I think of Libby and her sisters' hair and how it's never been cut because of what some long-dead misogynist in the Bible said. I think of the Victorian women with their long, heavy, pinned-up hair and constricting undergarments. To hell with all that.

Once I'm out of the shower and dried off, I stand naked in front of the bathroom mirror and take the scissors out of the drawer by the sink. My hand is steady as I make the first cut.

I'm not a total novice at this. We've always been the kind of family that saves money by cutting hair at home, and I've trimmed Mom's hair plenty of times. This is more than a trim, though. By the time I'm done, it's about as long as my chin. It looks flapper-ish, but it could just as easily be a hipster guy's haircut, especially if I tuck it behind my ears. Depending on my mood, I can look like Clara Bow or Jack White. Once I've cleaned up my clippings, I put on boxer briefs and a sports bra, then my faded boys' Levis and a plain white T-shirt. I still feel sad, but I do feel more like me.

As soon as I get online, I see half a dozen messages from Claire, ranging from a mild *R U OK?* to *Have you been eaten by coyotes? Forced into a hillbilly shotgun wedding?*

Hey, I type. *I'm okay.*

Claire: *Where the hell u been?*

Zo: *Nowhere. Just a rough couple of days.*

Claire: *The black dog?*

Zo: *Yeah, depressed. Trying to snap out of it. Something bad happened. Libby's dad won't let us see each other anymore.*

Claire: *And this surprises you? Do you think a fanatic like him was hoping his daughter would make friends with you?*

Zo: *No, but I never talked about that stuff around them.*

Claire: *"That stuff" as in who you are?*

Zo: *Well, yeah.*

Claire: *So if she never really knew you, how was she your friend?*

Zo: *I guess I felt like deep down she could see things about me and I could see things about her. Does that sound crazy?*

Claire: *Kinda.*

Zo: *Maybe it is.*

Claire: *Can I ask you an impertinent question?*

Zo: *Since when have you felt the need to ask permission?*

Claire: *You're not in love with her, are you?*

Zo: *God! NO!*

Claire: *Okay, just asking.*

Zo: *You remember when we read* To Kill a Mockingbird *freshman year?*

Claire: *Sure. I called you Scout and you called me Dill. But that was before I came out as trans. Why do you ask?*

Zo: *I was thinking about the Radley family and how they're so religious they cut themselves off from the rest of the world. And then when Mr. Radley finds out Boo's been leaving little presents for the kids in the knothole of the tree, he seals it up so Boo can't have even that little bit of contact. That's what Mr. Hazlett's done to Libby.*

Claire: *So you're Scout, I'm Dill, and she's Boo?*

Zo: *I guess so. Libby's the only person my age I've talked to face to face since we moved here. Maybe that makes me Boo, too.*

Claire: *So you're lonely.*

Zo: *I guess I am.*

Claire: *Aren't there any clubs or anything you can join?*

Zo: *Everything's church-based. Or 4-H.*

Claire: *Gross*

Zo: *yep*

Claire: *Hey, I have an idea. My mom's going to the mountains with her boyfriend this weekend so I can use her car. What if I drove up to your quaint rural dwelling and paid you a visit?*

Zo: *Seriously?*

Claire: *Sure. As long as it's okay with your mom and dad.*

Zo: *I'll check now.*

"Yeah, I just talked to Claire. She wants to know if it would be okay if she came up for a visit this weekend."

"That would be fantastic!" Mom's smile is a mile wide. "After our troubles next door, it'll be great for you to hang out with, you know, a normal friend."

"Thanks, Mom. I'll tell her you said it was okay."

"Better than okay." Mom sets down a green bean and stands up. "Hold on a second, and I'll get you that book I was telling you about."

She disappears into the living room for a minute and comes back with a paperback—one of those smaller kinds they don't make much anymore. "Here," she says, holding it out to me. "You want to know what that tyrant next door wants the world to look like? This is it."

"Okay." I look down at the cover, which shows a female figure carrying a basket and walking alongside a high gray wall. She has on some kind of headdress that makes her look like a nun, but the long, loose gown she's wearing is bright red. "*The Handmaid's Tale?*" I say, trying to put the picture and the title together in my mind.

"Read it," Mom says. "You'll get it."

WHEN I HEAR THE CAR WHEELS on the gravel driveway, I run out onto the porch. Claire has the top down on her mom's mint green convertible and looks super chic. Her shiny black hair, which is shoulder length now, is partially covered with a leopard-print scarf. Her eyes are hidden by cat's-eye sunglasses, and her lips are candy-apple red. As soon as she parks the car, she throws off the scarf and sunglasses and screams, "Zo!" It's absurd how happy this makes me, and I run into the driveway for a hug.

She hops out of the car, and the hug lasts a good long time. Then we pull back, our hands linked, to get a look at each other.

"Wow, look at you!" I say. Last year in school, Claire started taking steps toward looking more like herself—girls' jeans and fitted tees instead of baggy boys' clothes, a pixie haircut that could work for either gender, some eye makeup and lip gloss. But now she is totally glammed up, from her little black dress to the red-polished toenails that peek out from her platform sandals.

"Cherchez la femme, right?" she says. "And look at you—the new andro haircut, the black guyliner, and black T-shirt. So brooding and handsome."

"Well, brooding anyway," I say, laughing. I hear kids playing next door. I glance over and see Libby looking at Claire and me. She turns away quickly.

"Is that them over there?" Claire half whispers.

"Never mind them," I say. "Come on in. Mom made lemonade and those no-bake chocolate-oatmeal cookies you like."

"Ooh, the crack cookies? Awesome."

We walk inside holding hands. It's like we haven't seen each other in so long we can't bring ourselves to let each other go.

We settle in my room with cookies and lemonade and Edgar, who's always loved Claire to the point of being a belly-baring slut in her presence.

"Okay," Claire says, flopping on my bed, "what Bowie album are you gonna play to celebrate my visit?"

"I'm thinking *Let's Dance*."

"Aww, but you always said that one was too mainstream."

"Yes, but it's happy and dancey."

Claire bites into a cookie. "Does that mean I make you feel happy and dancey?"

"Yes." I take the record out of its sleeve. "You're just like a Nile Rodgers guitar solo."

I put on the record and sit beside Claire on the bed. "So what's the news from the big city?"

"And what big city would that be?" Claire rolls her eyes. "Knoxville's Knoxville. But lamer now because you left and the popsicle store closed."

"That sucks. That's where Hadley and I had our first date."

"Maybe that's why it closed. The bad juju just kept

lingering."

"Is she still with Danielle?"

Claire snorts. "Are you kidding? They broke up months ago. There's been another girlfriend since then, and they broke up, too."

"Wow." I'm not sure how to feel. Part of me—a mean part—is glad things between Hadley and Danielle didn't work out, but somehow it makes me feel hurt all over again to be just one more ex-girlfriend in a chain.

"The funny thing is both Danielle and the other girl are identifying as straight now." Claire is petting Edgar, who's sitting in her lap in the roasted turkey position. "At this rate, she's got a way better track record of curing queers than any of those pray-away-the-gay ministries."

I laugh. "Well, she didn't cure me. I guess I'm a hard case."

"It must be chronic with you."

"Terminal. I'm terminally queer."

"So what do you do for fun out here in hillbilly land?" She claps her hands like she's expecting big excitement.

I shrug. "You're looking at it."

"Well, that's sad." She reaches over and takes my hand in hers again. It feels nice to be touched. "Don't you go out sometimes?"

"Sure. I go on walks, pet the bunnies."

"What's in town?"

"Well, let's just say you have to use the term town very loosely."

Claire lets me go and lifts a limp Edgar off her lap. "Let's go see it."

Riding with the top down is pretty sweet, even if Claire is

a little too happy about whizzing around the curves of the country roads.

"This is cool," she says. "It feels like a video game."

"Well, just remember we only have one life."

"I'm an excellent driver. Oh, look, cows!" She veers to the side of the road.

"Let's not run over them," I say, laughing.

When we get to what passes for downtown, Claire says, "Is this it?"

"It is." And it isn't much. There's the single red-brick building that houses the fire department and post office, the Gas 'n Go, the Rite Aid pharmacy, and the IGA grocery store. A little farther up the road is the Whippy Dip, with its old metal sign depicting a rather evilly smiling soft-serve ice cream cone.

"What the hell is a Whippy Dip?" Claire asks.

"It's an old drive-in with ice cream and burgers and stuff. It's pretty good, actually. You want to get a cone?"

"Sure, why not?" She pulls in front of the powder-blue concrete-block building. "Cookies, now ice cream. If I had to live out in the middle of nowhere like this, my ass wouldn't fit through a door."

We go up to the window and order cones from a girl wearing a startling amount of blue eyeshadow. We sit at one of the wooden picnic tables with our cones.

"I always feel kind of awkward eating an ice cream cone in public," Claire says. "You know, you're doing all these things with your tongue and lips."

"You clearly get more physically involved with your cones than I do. I just bite mine."

"Ouch!" Claire says, grinning.

Two high school-aged guys have ambled up to the Whippy Dip's window. They're big, beefy white boys with buzz cuts. Jocky types. I can feel their eyes on me and especially on Claire, and it's making me nervous.

Once they've ordered from Blue Eyeshadow Girl, the bigger of the two of them comes over to our table. I look at Claire and then over at the car, trying to formulate an escape strategy.

"Hey," Big Guy drawls, his eyes boring into Claire. "Can I ask you a question?"

"Well." Claire dabs her red lips primly with a paper napkin. "I guess that depends. Is it a polite question?"

Big Guy looks over at his buddy, then back at Claire. "I don't mean to be rude nor nothing. But are you, like, Chinese or something?"

I can tell Claire's trying not to laugh. "No, but you're on the right side of the globe."

He looks down at his feet, which are encased in boat-like sneakers. "Well, whatever you are, you're just about the prettiest girl I ever seen in this town."

"Aw, that's sweet," Claire says. "I'm from out of town. I'm just visiting my friend for the day." She pats my hand.

"Well, I hate to hear that," Big Guy says. "I was fixing to ask you if you'd like to go out with me."

"Well, thank you, that's very flattering, but I have to get back to Knoxville soon." She shoots me a let's-get-out-of-here glance.

"You live in Knoxville?" he asks.

Claire nods.

"So if I got me a football scholarship to UT, would there be other girls there that look like you?"

"Sure," Claire says, standing up and walking toward the car.

"All right," Big Guy says grinning at the good news. "Well, you'uns have a good day now."

"Well, that certainly went a different direction than I thought it would," Claire says once we're in the car.

She doesn't have to say that the direction she thought it was going would have been dangerous. But it wasn't, it's a pretty day, we're together eating ice cream cones, and we laugh about Claire's "new boyfriend" all the way back to my house.

CLAIRE COULD ONLY STAY A FEW hours, then she had to drive back home to take care of the pets. I felt good when I was with her—natural and like my best self. But now that she's gone, I feel like my worst self. Lonely. Isolated. I resist the urge to put my pajamas back on, but I do get in bed. I wonder if Libby misses me or if she just automatically accepts whatever her dad says as divine truth. The book Mom gave me is on my nightstand. In hopes of distracting myself from my real misery with a fictional depiction of misery, I pick it up.

The dystopia in *The Handmaid's Tale* is called the Republic of Gilead, and the government and laws are based on the Old Testament. Men have all the power, and women's only value comes from their fertility. The handmaids are unmarried women who have been stripped of their names and sentenced to serve as surrogate uteruses for wealthy infertile married couples. The Republic of Gilead is a theocracy where heretics—professors, progressive priests, runaway handmaids—are publicly hanged, their bodies displayed on a wall of shame for all to see.

It's pretty clear that the Republic of Gilead used to be the United States, and Mom's right that it doesn't seem that different from the America Mr. Hazlett would like to see. Poor Libby.

LIBBY

CHAPTER 13

THE NIGHT OF THE ICE CREAM social, after Daddy made Zo's family leave, he told us all to gather in the living room. Faith and Charity were crying because of Owen being sent away, but Val was holding back his tears because he's a boy. Patience and Just didn't look upset at all, and I was trying not to look as upset as I felt. It was hard to read the look on Mama's face.

Daddy stood in front of us and said, "I have failed my family. I have failed my family and myself, and I must pray for forgiveness." His voice was choked, and his eyes looked sparkly. "As Christians, it is our calling to be in the world but not of the world. We as a family have allowed ourselves to be tempted by the world in the form of our new neighbors—to pursue relationships that are not Christ-centered with people who are not Christ-centered. And the name of this pursuit is sin. In many ways, I am the guiltiest of us all because I saw what was happening, and I could have stopped it. But instead I turned a blind eye to it. There was no harm, I told myself, in letting you children play with the neighbor children or in letting my precious wife learn needlework from another wife and mother. And so I failed you as a father and a husband."

At this point, Val raised his hand. "Doesn't the Bible say we're supposed to love our neighbor?"

"It does, son," Daddy said. "And we do love our neighbors, and we will pray for them every day. We will pray that they turn from the darkness of their sinful ways to the light of the one true God."

Val raised his hand again. "If Owen and his family take Jesus as their personal Lord and savior, can we play together again?"

Daddy gave a little smile. "I don't know, son. If it's the Lord's will, you can. But that's not for us to know yet. The best thing to do is for you to play with your brother and sisters. Friends come and go, but brothers and sisters are forever."

At Daddy's orders, we spent the rest of that night in prayer and scripture reading, which we did until the Littles nodded off and had to be carried to bed.

Since then, it's been strangely quiet in our house. All of us kids have done our chores and homeschool work, and the Littles still play in the backyard in the afternoons. But there's something about the way everybody acts while working and playing that's different—like everybody's holding back a little, being polite with each other, like there's something everybody's thinking even if they're not saying it.

There's a change in Mama, too. She doesn't hum anymore while she works, and sometimes it seems like her mind is on something other than what she's doing.

Right now I'm helping her hang sheets on the clothesline. "Mama," I ask, handing her a clothespin from the basket, "Are you okay?"

She looks at me with a strange smile. "Of course. Why would you even ask me something like that?"

"Well, ma'am, it just seems like you've been a little distracted the past couple of days."

"Oh, that," Mama says, waving it off. "That's just pregnancy brain. When you get this far along, you start thinking about when the baby's gonna get here, and your mind wanders so far off you forget where you are. You'll see when you're married and having babies of your own."

"Yes, ma'am." We've hung sheets on two side-by-side clothes lines, so now we're sandwiched between two curtains of white. "Mama?" I say. "About getting married?"

"Yes?" She looks pretty standing in front of the white sheet, the breeze blowing her long hair. Almost like an angel.

"What if when I was grown up and married, my husband told me to do something I disagreed with?"

Mama smiles. "Well, it's human nature to disagree sometimes, but we also have to remember that human nature is sinful. When God sends you a husband, you vow to love, honor, and obey him at all times, not just when you feel like it."

I nod. "So you mind Daddy even when you don't feel like it?"

Mama laughs. "I do. And if I struggle with it, I get on my knees and pray about it. And the Lord and your daddy haven't steered me wrong yet." She reaches out and brushes a loose strand of hair from my face. For some reason, this makes me want to cry.

"I miss Zo," I say. "I bet you miss Mrs. Forrester, too."

"I do," Mama says, and I can hear the sadness in her voice. "But it's not easy for us to live the life the Lord wants us to live. This life is the hard part. If it wasn't hard, we wouldn't deserve our reward in heaven."

I nod and tell myself I feel better. "Okay. Thank you, Mama."

She takes both of my hands in hers. "You're welcome, honey. And it's good you're asking these questions about marriage. The time will be here before you know it. And I can't wait to hold my first grandbaby."

My stomach feels wobbly like Jell-O. "Well, you're going to have to wait a while."

"I know, but time goes by so fast. Speaking of that, it's almost lunchtime. We'd better get to the house and get out the peanut butter. Your daddy said he might stop by for lunch today, so I'll let you fix the kids' sandwiches while I make him something a little heartier. You can't expect a man to work the rest of the day on a piece of bread and some peanut butter."

Daddy comes home just as I'm opening the peanut butter jar. Patience is getting the milk cups, and Mama is staring in the refrigerator.

"Hey, girls," Daddy says as he comes into the kitchen. He gives Mama a kiss on the cheek and a pat on her pregnant belly. "I'd like y'all to stop fixing lunch and get everybody together in the living room. The Lord has put something on my heart, and I need to speak about it."

"Yessir," Patience and I say at the same time. Patience goes to get Just from the work shed, and I head off to round up the Littles.

We all sit in the living room with Daddy standing before us. "This morning I was working in a crawlspace," he says, "and my flashlight batteries give out. I was in total darkness, black as coal, black as a soul full of sin. But a few yards away from me, I could see the way out. The door was open just a tiny bit, and I could see the light shining through that little crack showing me the way. And it came to me that this is what Christians see when they die—the blackness all around them, but the light calling them toward it." Daddy's eyes are dark and intense the way they are when he's really in the spirit. "And then I felt the presence of the Lord in my heart."

"Praise Jesus," Mama murmurs.

Daddy closes his eyes and holds his palms upward. "And He said to me, 'My son, your life and your family's life have been darkened by sin. You must find your way back to the light through prayer and fasting.'" He opens his eyes. "Prayer and fasting."

Val raises his hand.

"Yes, son?" Daddy says.

"What is fasting?"

"Psalm thirty-five, thirteen: 'I humbled my soul with fasting, and my prayer returned into mine own bosom.' Fasting, son, is going a stretch of time without eating to purify yourself before the Lord."

"Oh," Val says, like he had been hoping it would be something more fun.

Faith, who is sitting next to Mama, looks up at her and asks, "But if we don't eat, won't we die?"

Mama smiles at her. "No, honey, people can go without food for a lot of days without dying."

"That's right," Daddy says. "And all we're doing is fasting twenty-four hours, from now until lunchtime tomorrow."

Just raises his hand. "Can we drink water?"

"Absolutely," Daddy says. "The body has to have water every day to survive, and besides, water cleanses and purifies."

Charity raises her hand. "Can we drink apple juice?"

Daddy smiles. "Not till lunchtime tomorrow, sweetie. So until we break our fast tomorrow at noon, let's spend the time we would usually spend eating in prayer. And I'm not just talking about bowing your head and closing your eyes. I'm talking about everybody on their knees."

I kneel on the floor and clasp my hands together and close my eyes. For a while, Daddy leads us in prayer, asking the Lord for forgiveness for our transgressions, asking Him to help us remember that our place is not in the world but above it. Then he asks us each to pray silently about what is in our hearts.

I pray for forgiveness and for help being good and doing what God and my family expects of me, especially since I think it's harder for me to be good than it is for other people. But then—and this is always my problem with long silent prayer, and I know it's a sign of my sinful nature—my mind starts to wander. I think about Zo and if she misses me the way I miss her even though I know her and her family are sinful.

But the truth is, when we were spending time with Zo's family, they never seemed sinful. They seemed to love and care for each other like my family does. And Zo's parents didn't seem selfish like sinful people are supposed to be. I remember one time Zo said her dad could make more money working in a hospital or a doctor's office in the city, but he had taken the job at the health department because he wanted to help the rural poor. And Zo's mom always has some kind of project going on, like weaving scarves for the homeless or knitting caps for kids going through cancer treatment. Are these good deeds not really good because they're not done in the name of God?

I know the Bible says good works alone aren't enough to get you into heaven, but it does seem like doing good on purpose, even if it's not in the name of God, should count for more than doing bad on purpose. I'm so deep in thought that I'm startled when Daddy says "amen."

After Daddy goes back to work, Mama fixes a big pitcher of ice water. We all have some and get back to our schoolwork. The Littles seem to be concentrating less well than usual, which is understandable. When it's time for them to go out and play, I get their sidewalk chalk and bubbles out in case they don't have a lot of energy for running around. Getting out the bubbles makes me remember the night when Zo broke a glow stick into a bottle of bubble stuff, and the bubbles lit up like magic.

When Daddy comes home, we drink some more ice water and pray some more, and then for a while we all just sit around the living room like we're not sure what to do. Finally Daddy says he reckons he'll go out to the work shed for a while, and Just and Val ask to go, too.

Once they've gone, Mama says, "Well, I'll tell you what, without supper to cook or eat or clean up after, it sure leaves a big hunk of time in your evening." She looks a little pale, and her upper lip is sweaty. "I think I'm gonna go get my crocheting things and work on the baby's blanket. Why don't y'all get out some games or paper and crayons?"

"Chinese checkers?" Patience asks, in a flat, bored tone.

"Sure," I say. "Let's just get the little girls their drawing stuff first."

When I give Faith her paper, she says, "I'm gonna draw a picture of me eating spaghetti 'cause that's what I wish I was doing."

"You're not supposed to be thinking about food," Patience says. "You're supposed to be thinking about God. Why don't you draw a picture from a Bible story instead?"

"Okay," Faith says. "I'll draw Jesus with the loaves and the fishes."

"Good idea," I say, but I can't help but laugh to myself because that story's about food, too.

When we're setting up the Chinese checkers board, Patience whispers, "I know I should have better self-control because I'm older, but I can't stop thinking about food either."

This surprises me since Patience is usually Little Miss Perfect where rules are concerned. "Me neither," I say. "For me it's that pot roast Mama makes in the crock-pot with carrots and potatoes and onions."

"Macaroni and cheese," Patience says. "I could eat a whole pan all by myself." She crinkles her forehead. "Maybe praying more would help. Let's pray." She holds her hands out to me across the table, and I take them and bow my head. But there's a loud thud in the back room, and we both startle to attention. The little girls look up from their pictures, and Charity says, "Mama?"

Mama! I jump up and run to the schoolroom with Patience right behind me. Mama is lying on the floor with her back to us, but I can tell she's conscious because she's adjusting her skirt for modesty. I kneel beside her. "Mama, are you okay?"

"Yes." She's pale and dazed-looking. "I just got a little light-headed, and the next thing I knew I was hitting the floor."

I look up at Patience. "Go get Daddy." She turns on her heels and runs.

I turn back to Mama. "You didn't hit your head, did you?"

"No. I landed on my back. I was trying to protect the baby. I think I can get up now." She starts to pull herself up.

"No," I say, even though it feels weird to tell a parent no. "Let's wait for Daddy. You don't need to get up unless you have plenty of help."

"Okay," she says, sounding tired.

Daddy comes running in, followed by Just. "What happened?" Daddy says, out of breath. "You're not losing the baby, are you?"

"No," Mama says. "I just got dizzy and I fell. Maybe you two strong men can help me up."

Daddy and Just get on either side and help lift her to a standing position. Steadying her with each step, they walk her to the armchair in the back corner of the room.

"Better?" Daddy asks.

She nods. "I think it was not eating that did it. I know it's God's will for us to fast today, but I don't think the baby understands that."

Daddy smiles and pats her belly. "Well, he's too young to understand the Lord's will. He'll need us to teach him."

"Daddy," I say, "do you think it would do any harm if I brought Mama a little glass of apple juice?"

Daddy frowns. "We have made a covenant with the Lord. Are you suggesting we break it?"

"No, sir, it's just that since Mama's expecting, it seems like she's sort of a special case."

Daddy's still frowning, but he does look thoughtful.

Mama reaches up shakily and touches his hand. "Please, Bill. I really think a little juice would help."

"All right," Daddy says, then turns to me. "Get her some juice, but don't let the Littles see you. If they see we're making an exception for your mama, they'll want exceptions made for them, too."

"Yessir," I say. "Thank you."

IT'S PROBABLY AROUND MIDNIGHT, AND PATIENCE is snoring away in the bed next to mine, but I can't sleep. Partly it's hunger. I've never felt it like this before, a big, gnawing emptiness inside me. I know this means I've been very blessed my whole life. There are people in the world who go around this empty every day.

The other thing that's keeping me awake is thinking about how I acted tonight. All my life I've been taught total obedience. But when Mama tried to get up, I told her no, and then, even crazier, I flat-out told Daddy that he should let Mama have some juice. Tonight I was disobedient, but it felt like the right thing to do.

I hear little footsteps in the hall and look up to see Faith standing in the doorway. She's in her little flowered nightgown, and her hair is all messy.

"What is it?" I whisper.

"I can't sleep 'cause my belly's so empty, and Charity keeps crying and saying her belly hurts."

"Okay," I whisper. "Go back to your room and tell Charity to be quiet, and I'll be in there in a few minutes."

I get out of bed and tiptoe out of the room, through the hall, and down the stairs. I've already disobeyed twice tonight, and I shouldn't do it again, but I can't stand to think of my little sisters—or any children—crying from hunger when there's a way to stop it.

In the kitchen, I open the refrigerator door just enough to slip out the milk. I know what I'm doing now isn't like what I did earlier. If I get caught, I'll be punished. I get three paper cups and fill them about three-quarters full of milk, then slide the jug back into the refrigerator. I walk quietly and carefully with the cups, making sure I don't spill a drop.

In their room, I give Faith and Charity each a cup. "Now drink this slowly in little sips. It'll keep you from feeling so empty." I feel a presence in the doorway, and my heart thumps in my chest. What if it's Daddy?

It's Val, barefoot in his pajamas. "What's going on?" he whispers.

I gesture for him to come inside. "Faith and Charity were too hungry to sleep, so I brought them a little milk."

"We'd better not let Just or Patience hear," Val says.

"I know," I whisper. "That's why we're being extra quiet."

Val nods. "Did you bring any milk for me?"

I hand him the third cup.

PATIENCE'S FOOD DREAM CAME TRUE. MAMA broke our fast at lunchtime today with homemade macaroni and cheese—the best I've ever had. Everybody had seconds and would've had thirds and fourths if we'd been let to. After the macaroni and cheese, Mama brought out a big bowl of chocolate pudding and everybody got to have some with a dollop of Cool Whip.

Now I'm watching the Littles play out back like their old energetic selves. My belly is full, the sun is on my face, and I feel good—too good to worry too much about sneaking down and stealing the milk last night—but I still worry a little.

I hear a soft rustling, and someone I don't recognize is standing by the fence. But then I see it's Zo, and she's cut off most of her hair.

I must look startled because she whispers, "Hey, I know I'm not supposed to talk to you, but I wanted to return this copy of *Prince Caspian* you loaned me. I'm just going to slide it under the fence." She does, and then she's gone before I can even say what I'm thinking, which is *But I never loaned you a copy of* Prince Caspian*!*

It's like Eve and the apple all over again, but once she's gone, curiosity gets the best of me. I walk over to the fence when I'm sure the Littles aren't looking, pick up the book, and tuck it into the waistband of my skirt. I go into the house and ask Patience if she can watch the Littles for a minute while I go to the bathroom.

The bathrooms are the only rooms in the house with doors that lock. I lock the door, take out the book, and try to figure out why Zo gave it to me. When I open it, there's a folded up piece of notebook paper inside. My stomach gives a little jump of fear or excitement. Maybe both.

When I unfold it, it seems like the crinkliest, noisiest paper in the world. I read:

I miss you, Libby. I can't stop being your friend just because your dad ordered me to. There's a tent set up in our backyard that Owen's been playing in during the day. If you think you can sneak out, meet me in the tent Saturday at midnight. If you can't do it or feel like it's wrong, I understand. But I'll be there at midnight waiting for you just in case.

Your friend no matter what,
Zo

Chapter 14

Once I read the note, I had no idea what to do. I could shelve the copy of Prince Caspian in my bookcase without anybody knowing, but what about the note? I had to decide fast. I was still in the bathroom with the door locked, but it was only a matter of minutes until someone would come knocking.

At first I thought about ripping the note into little pieces and throwing it into the toilet. But then I remembered our toilet clogs if you put so much as an extra sheet or two of toilet paper in it. Notebook paper would be a disaster. Daddy or Just would have to plunge it, and how would I be able to explain what regular paper was doing in the toilet?

Then another idea came to me, or maybe it was the devil whispering in my ear. I ran water in the sink like I was washing my hands and let the water soak the paper until the ink was too smeared to read. I reached into the back of the closet where Mama keeps the feminine supplies for Patience and me. It was my time anyway, so me taking a napkin wouldn't make anybody suspicious.

I unwrapped the napkin, rolled the soggy wad of paper up inside, and then wrapped the whole mess in toilet paper just like I was disposing of a feminine item. I buried it deep in the trash can, took a deep breath, and unlocked the door.

That was two days ago. Now it's Saturday, the day—or the night—Zo wants me to meet her. I've tried to go through the motions of the day without feeling too distracted, but Zo waiting for me at midnight is all I can think about. When the Littles were playing outside this afternoon, I kept sneaking glances at the tent in the yard next door.

As I stand turning the jump rope for Faith while Patience turns the other end, I think, will I or won't I? "Should I?" isn't even a question because the answer is no. Of course I shouldn't. It's disobedient and dangerous and sinful. But I miss Zo so much and we never really got to say goodbye to each other. It's like we had those play telephones kids make with tin cans and a string, and somebody came along with scissors and cut our connection.

We have deer burgers and corn on the cob for supper, but I can't eat much. Mama asks me if I'm okay, and I say yes, but my stomach and head hurt.

She gives me a knowing nod. Eve's Curse is what she calls a woman's time, but she won't say anything about it in front of the boys, so she says, "After supper I'll make you some chamomile tea."

"And then we'll have Bible study and board games," Daddy says.

I stay for the Bible study because it's required, but I ask permission to skip the board games and go to bed early. This may have been a bad idea because now I'm lying awake in bed asking myself over and over, "Will I or won't I? Will I or won't I?" like a little girl playing "he loves me, he loves me not" with a daisy.

It seems like all I've done lately is ask questions in my head, and even though I know it's sinful, some of those questions are about Daddy. I know I shouldn't question Daddy just like I know I shouldn't sneak out and see Zo tonight, but I can't help turning things over and over in my mind. I know that God acts and speaks through Daddy, but would Jesus have thrown out his neighbors just because they were different from Him? In the Bible, Jesus visits with different, unholy people all the time.

I also keep thinking how Mama got sick from fasting the other day, and it took a few minutes for Daddy to decide to bend the rules and let her have some juice. I don't think Jesus would've thought twice about it. He fed the hungry and helped the sick.

I know the Bible is the Word of God, and you can't just pick and choose and say the parts I like are true and the parts I don't like aren't. But to be honest, I have to say I like the New Testament best, especially the gospels, where Jesus talks about love and forgiveness. When Daddy does our Bible studies, he picks a lot of the Old Testament with its strict rules and punishments.

I guess what I'm saying is I love Daddy, and I know God chose him to lead our family. But I also know he's not perfect. Mama says that in marriage on earth you serve and obey an imperfect man so that in heaven you can serve and obey the one perfect man and be a true Bride of Christ.

When Patience comes in to get ready for bed she says, "I'm surprised you're still awake."

"My belly hurts, and it's making me restless."

"Didn't Mama make you some tea?" She pulls her night-gown over her head. She sleeps in her bra, which I can't stand to do.

"It helped some, but I still don't feel good."

"Well, we're not supposed to feel good when it's our time. That's what we get for Eve eating the apple."

"I guess so," I say.

"No guessing about it," Patience says, sliding under the covers. "It's right there in the Bible."

"I know it is." I hadn't meant anything by saying "guess." Sometimes Patience will really pick apart your words. "I'm going to try to get some sleep now. Good night, Patience."

"Good night, Libby."

But I don't try to sleep. I lie there thinking will I or won't I? Soon Patience's breathing is slow and even. When I look at the clock, it's ten p.m. Two hours.

What's the worst thing that could happen if I go? Well, I will have committed a sin, but if I pray for forgiveness, God will give it to me. That's in the Bible, too.

It's the earthly consequences I fear more. If I got caught, I'd be punished for the first time since I was little. And I know the punishment would be bad.

But then I think of Zo, my friend, the truest friend I've ever known, sitting in the tent waiting for me. How long will she wait if I don't show up? Fifteen minutes? Thirty? An hour? I see the hurt and disappointment on her face when she realizes I'm not coming, that I've thrown away our friendship like it was nothing.

I may be punished on earth and in hell, but I can't do that to her.

I know I can't sneak out of our bedroom window without waking Patience, so at ten till twelve I get up like I'm going to the bathroom. Probably the safest way to get out is to use the door in the basement, but it's a long walk to the basement without anybody hearing me. If somebody catches me on this floor, I'll say I was going to the bathroom. If somebody catches me going downstairs, I'll say I wanted a glass of water. Lies.

It's true what they say about sinning. Once you've made up your mind to do it, it gets easier and easier.

I tiptoe downstairs with no problem. The door to the basement is in the kitchen. It's always been creaky, but right now that creak is the loudest sound in the world. After I close the door behind me, I pull the chain to turn on the single bare bulb that lights the basement. I wish I didn't have to turn it on, but the stairs are too steep to brave in the dark.

A few household things are stored in the basement—Christmas decorations, old clothes saved for future babies—but mostly it's filled with Daddy's pest control stuff. There are stacks of boxes with pictures of skulls and crossbones and warnings: "poison" and "Keep away from children and pets." I cross through the maze of boxes to the door, unlock it, open it, tiptoe through it, and shut it softly behind me. It takes a few seconds for my eyes to adjust to the dark so that I can climb the stone steps up to ground level. I've never been outside barefoot at night before, and the grass is cool and damp under my feet.

Zo must have a flashlight in the tent because I can see it glow from across the yard. It's a blue, dome-shaped tent, and it seems too big and bright and obvious. But it's too late to turn back now, so I run barefoot through our backyard, climb the fence, and stand outside the glowing blue dome. It feels like I should knock, but how do you knock on a tent?

"Libby? Is that you?"

"Yes," I whisper.

"Well, don't just stand there. Come on in."

I bend down and step inside. Zo's sitting crisscross applesauce with her face lit up by the lantern beside her. "Have a seat," she says.

I sit down across from her. The tent's much smaller than it looks on the outside. We're so close our knees are almost touching.

She holds out a plastic bag. "Marshmallow?"

"Thank you." I take one even though I'm too nervous to eat.

"I wish we could make s'mores," Zo says, taking a marshmallow for herself. "But I figured since you're here on the down-low, it would be a bad idea to build a fire. Did you have a hard time sneaking out?"

"Yes. I was terrified. How about you?"

"Oh, I didn't have to sneak. I mean, my parents don't know you're here, but I'm free to come out here whenever I want."

She says "free" like it's something she doesn't even have to think about. "Your family and mine sure are different," I say.

"They are. And I'm sorry that turned into a problem because I really like being your friend."

I'm too shy to look at her. "I like being your friend, too."

"I feel like my dad acted pretty obnoxious at the ice cream social the other night." Zo bites off half of her marshmallow.

"Or as I've come to think of it, the ill-fated ice cream social. The thing is, he didn't mean to be rude. He's a nice person. He just has such strong beliefs and opinions that he has a hard time knowing when to be quiet."

"My daddy's the same way." I'm startled by the truth of what I say. "Except, you know, he believes different things than your dad."

"Yeah," Zo says. "They're more alike than either one of them would ever admit."

I nod. It's strange. So much of what Zo's dad believes is the exact opposite of what our family believes, and yet I have no doubt that Zo's dad is a good man. I look at Zo. "You're smart about people, aren't you?"

She shrugs. "Sometimes yes, sometimes no. Same as anybody else, I guess."

"I'm not smart about people at all," I say, finally taking a bite of my marshmallow. Holding it so long is making my fingers sticky. "I've not been around many people. Just my family and people at church. Daddy says I'm not missing much. He says the world is a sinful, hurtful place full of sinful, hurtful people."

Zo digs another marshmallow out of the bag. "Well, he's right and he's wrong. There are some nasty, hurtful people in the world, but there are some pretty great ones, too." She chews thoughtfully. "I mean, I'm not saying I'm so great or anything, but you like me, right?"

I never would've taken the risk of tonight if I hadn't. "I do."

"And I like you, too."

My face gets all hot all of a sudden.

"But I've got to tell you," Zo says, her voice sounding serious but also shaky. "If we're going to really be friends, then we've got to be honest with each other, and I have to admit that so far I've not been entirely honest with you."

The commandment echoes in my head: Thou shalt not bear false witness. "You mean you've lied to me?"

"I've never lied. I just haven't told you some things about myself because I was afraid if I did you wouldn't be my friend anymore."

I'm nervous but also curious. "You've not killed anybody, have you?"

Zo laughs. "No, nothing like that. You remember when you asked me if I was smart about people, and I said yes and no?"

I nod.

"Well, let's just say I was stupid enough about one person to fall in love and get my heart broken."

I've never heard a person my age talk about dating because in my family and church nobody believes in it. Daddy says dating is something boys and girls in worldly families do. He says dating is bad because for each person you date, you give away a little piece of your heart, so that when the time comes to marry, you won't have your whole heart to give to your husband or wife. It's sad to think that Zo might have this problem. I'm not sure what to ask, so I try, "What . . . what was his name?"

Zo smiles a little, but somehow still looks sad. "See, that's it. The person I fell in love with—the person who broke my heart—is named Hadley, and she's a girl."

Before I even know what I'm doing, I feel myself scooting away from her. I'm afraid to look at her, afraid of what I'll see. "So you're a . . . "

"Stop." Zo puts up her hand. "Don't label me, and don't back up like I'm about to attack you. I'm the exact same person you were talking to three minutes ago, but now you know one other thing about me. It's like learning my favorite color."

Except having a favorite color isn't sinful, and what she's confessed to is a big, big sin—big enough to make God destroy a whole city. "But the Bible says that"—I can't make myself say the word—"that that is an abomination."

Zo nods. "The Old Testament prohibits homosexuality, but it also prohibits lots of stuff people do now without even thinking about it, like wearing mixed fabric clothing and eating shellfish. You know what Jesus said about homosexuality? Not one word."

It's all too much. I feel like I just finished putting a giant jigsaw puzzle together and somebody came along and knocked over the table, scattering all the pieces so I don't know how to put them together again. "Somebody was visiting you the other day. I saw her—an Oriental girl. Was that her?"

Zo smiles like I've said something funny. "No, that was Claire, my best friend from Knoxville. Believe me, Hadley and I aren't on visiting terms."

"Are you sorry for what happened?"

"With Hadley? No, not really. I mean, I'd never been in love before, and I wouldn't trade that feeling for anything. What we had together was good . . . until it wasn't anymore."

She has totally misunderstood me. "I guess I meant sorry in a different way."

Zo's eyebrows go up. "Oh, like sorry as in praying for God to forgive my sin?"

I nod. Now she gets it.

"No, because I didn't do anything wrong. Other than falling in love with somebody who turned out to be kind of a jerk, but it doesn't make any difference if the jerk is a guy or a girl."

I just sit. I feel like I should go, but I can't make myself move.

"I'm sorry if I've overwhelmed you," Zo says.

"It's . . . it's a lot to take in. I've never met anybody like you before."

"And I've never met anybody like you before," Zo says, but she can't mean it the same way I do.

All of a sudden I know have to go and go now. "I need to think about what you've told me . . . and pray about it."

"Do what you've gotta do," Zo says, then she looks me right in the eyes. "I hope you'll decide you can still be my friend even if it's in a 'love the sinner, hate the sin' kind of way. I'll be here next Saturday at midnight. If you don't show up, I'll know you've decided to call it quits." Her voice sounds like she might cry, which is how I feel, too. "If you do show up, we'll talk some more."

"Okay," I say, my hand on the door flap.

"Oh, and by the way, while you're learning things about me, my favorite color's purple," Zo says.

"Powder blue," I say, and tears spring to my eyes. I crawl out of the tent and break into a run from her yard into mine.

Sneaking back in is just as scary as sneaking out, maybe even scarier now that I know what I know. I tiptoe down the dark stone steps and push open the basement door, then lock it behind me. I wend my way around the boxes of pesticide, then tiptoe to the top of the stairs and turn off the lightbulb.

I open the door to the kitchen slowly, but that just makes the creaking longer and louder. In the dim light of the appliance bulb over the kitchen stove, I see my feet are covered with damp blades of grass. If I track grass all over the floor or go to bed with grassy feet, I'll be caught for sure. I turn on the faucet so low it barely makes any noise, wet some paper towels, wipe off the grass, and hide the paper towels deep in the garbage can. I tiptoe up the stairs, past Mama and Daddy's room, and into Patience's and my room, where Patience is still asleep. If she woke up at any point and found me gone, I know she wouldn't be asleep right now. She'd be up waiting for me with Mama and Daddy.

I climb into my bed and lie down, my heart pounding so loud it feels like it's right between my ears.

"Look, Libby, look!" Patience says before I've even opened my eyes.

I can't believe I fell asleep last night, but I did. Exhaustion must have won out over all my other feelings. "What is it?" I say, sounding as groggy as I feel. I'm not sure how many hours I slept, but I doubt it was more than four.

"Look on the foot of your bed!"

I'm afraid to look, afraid I've left some kind of evidence of my crime there. But when I sit up, I see it's a rectangular package wrapped in baby-pink tissue with a white bow on top.

Patience is holding an identical package. "The card on mine says, 'To my precious Patience, from Mama.'"

I pick up mine. Presents only happen at Christmas in our house, so this is very strange. Even on birthdays we just get homemade cards from our siblings, cake and ice cream and the happy birthday song, and that's it. "My card says the same except with my name," I say.

And then it hits me. Mama must've snuck into our rooms while we slept to leave these presents. What if she had come in last night when I was gone? Suddenly my blood feels like ice water.

"Do you think it's okay to open them?" Patience asks. I can tell she's excited.

"I don't guess Mama would've left them if she didn't want us to open them."

"Okay, on three," Patience says. "One . . . two . . . three!"

I smile in spite of myself and tear into the tissue paper. It's a book, a big paperback with a beautiful old-fashioned painting on the cover showing a smiling girl in a long pink dress, holding an armload of pink flowers. The title, written in fancy gold letters, is *Modest Maidens: A Godly Girl's Guide to Virtue.*

"Isn't it pretty?" Patience says.

"It is," I say. After my adventure last night, I don't feel like a very Godly girl.

"I bet nobody else got these," Patience says, hugging the book close. "I bet we got them because we're the oldest girls."

MAMA IS IN THE KITCHEN STANDING over a huge pan of eggs. Patience runs up to her, throws her arms around her, and says, "Thank you for the book!"

"Yes, thank you," I add, but my voice sounds flat in comparison to Patience's.

Mama gives me a pretend stern look. "Don't I get a hug from you, too?"

"Of course." I hug her, and feel her baby belly against me.

"And the book's not the only surprise," Mama says. "Daddy and I have another surprise for you after church."

Patience's mouth is shaped like an O. "But I don't understand. Why is today a special day?"

"Today's a special day because you're my special girls," Mama says.

After picking at breakfast, I help clear the dishes and then put on my powder-blue church dress and braid my hair. I go help Faith and Charity get ready, too, making sure they pick church clothes instead of play clothes.

But my mind is still in the blue tent. The burden of my knowledge weighs me down like a sack of stones. To know that Zo, who I've laughed with, talked with, eaten with, is something abnormal, an abomination in the eyes of God. But the strange thing is, she's never seemed like an abomination to me. She's never been anything other than nice to my brothers and sisters and me. Daddy would probably say she was just acting nice to lure me, to trap me in her web of sin. But if she's faking, she's a really good actress.

The other sack of stones weighing me down is my guilt. I knew sneaking out was wrong even as I was doing it, and I did it anyway, which shows how depraved my soul is. The weight of my knowledge and the weight of my guilt are combined into one giant weight because they go together. If I hadn't gone and done something to feel guilty about, then I wouldn't know what I know. And now I can't un-know what I know any more than I can undo what I've done.

In the van, Patience keeps smiling, I guess because she knows she and I are going to get some kind of surprise the others won't get. In a family our size, it's rare to be singled out as special or different. It's too bad that I'm too upset to enjoy myself, but I know unhappiness is what I deserve.

Along with Nanny and Papaw, we take up our usual
whole row in the church. Pastor Mike steps up to the pulpit.
He says, "Let us pray," and I bow my head. But instead of
listening to Pastor's words, I'm saying my own prayer in my
head: Dear Lord, please forgive me for disobeying my parents and sneaking out of the house last night. I know it was
my own weak and sinful nature that led me to do this. I
know scripture tells me to honor my mother and father, but
it speaks of friendship, too, and Zo has been a good friend
to me. But after what she told me last night, I don't know
what to think of her anymore. I want to pray for her, but I
don't even know what to pray. Lord, I am lost and confused,
and I pray that you have mercy on me and lead me out of
this dark wilderness and into the light. In Jesus's name I
pray, amen.

When I raise my head and open my eyes, everybody else is
standing up and singing "Nothing but the Blood of Jesus."
They're already on the second verse, and I was so deep in
prayer I didn't even hear them.

After the service is over, Nanny squeezes my hand. "Are
you excited?" she asks.

"I guess since I don't know what the surprise is, I'm more
curious than excited."

"Well, I don't reckon it would do no harm to tell you now,"
she says, smiling. "Your mama and daddy are gonna drop
Just and the Littles at our house and then take you and
Patience to eat in town."

"To a restaurant? What for?" Sometimes in the summer
Mama takes us all to the Whippy Dip for cones. But other
than that, the last time I can remember eating in a restaurant

was a couple of years ago for Nanny and Papaw's fiftieth
wedding anniversary.

"Well, you girls must deserve a special treat," Nanny says.

Guilt burns inside me. Nobody who knew the truth would
think I deserved a treat.

Town—the closest real town, where there are stores and
places to eat—is about a thirty-five-minute drive from Nanny
and Papaw's. Daddy and Mama are in a good mood. Daddy
holds Mama's hand when he doesn't need both hands to
drive. Anybody who saw them together would know how
much they're in love.

"I hope you girls are hungry," Daddy says, "cause we're
gonna eat till we're fit to bust. Gluttony is a sin, but the Lord
wants us to celebrate special occasions. There's lots of feasts
in the Bible."

"Does the special occasion have to do with the presents we
got this morning?" Patience asks. It feels weird that it's just
her and me in the back of the van.

"It might," Mama says, smiling back at us.

"We've got us some smart girls, don't we?" Daddy says.

Mama smiles at him now. "We sure do."

We go to Shoney's, the same restaurant where we went for
Nanny and Papaw's anniversary. The girl who seats us has
dyed blond hair and purple eye makeup.

Daddy and Mama sit next to each other in the booth, and
Patience and I sit across from them. Daddy opens his menu
and says, "Now I want you girls to order anything you want,
as long as it ain't the whole menu."

The waitress who comes to take our drink order is older
than Mama and has chipped red nail polish.

"Can I get a Coke?" Patience asks.

The waitress must think Patience is asking her because she says, "Sure, honey," but really Patience is asking Daddy, who nods his permission. We hardly ever drink Cokes because they're expensive and bad for you. But Daddy orders one, too.

It feels weird to talk to the waitress because usually we just talk to each other or sometimes people at church. Talking to a stranger, even just to tell her I want a cheeseburger and onion rings, makes me feel shy, and at first I say my order so soft she has to ask me to repeat it. Patience orders a cheeseburger with French fries, and Mama and Daddy both ask for the fried shrimp with baked potato and the salad bar. I think of what Zo said about the Bible saying it's a sin to eat shellfish. It's all so confusing.

Daddy and Mama go to get their salads, and I sip my Coke and look around. The family sitting nearest to us are all wearing shorts. Over the clatter of dishes I hear secular music playing, something about taking a girl to a lake in a truck.

When Daddy and Mama sit back down, Mama has a green salad with ranch dressing and Daddy has all kinds of stuff: beets and macaroni salad and red Jell-O. He says, "So your mother and I have been talking a lot about what fine young ladies you're growing up to be."

"Thank you, sir," Patience and I say.

Daddy looks over at Mama, then at us. "And because you're getting to be such fine young ladies, it's time to start thinking about your future and how you look and behave affects your future."

Mama sets down her fork and says, "And we don't have any problem with how you look and behave. You're good, modest girls, and you're both a big help to me with the Littles and the housework, and being good at those things has already put you on the right path."

If only they knew how much I have strayed.

"That's right," Daddy says, nodding his thanks as the waitress sets down plates of shrimp in front of him and Mama, then beautiful burgers in front of Patience and me. "I think the most important thing is staying on the path you're on. Let's say the blessing."

We join hands, bow our heads, and close our eyes. Daddy says, "Lord, we thank you for this good food for the nourishment of our bodies and for this special family time together. Please guide our daughters in wisdom so that they use their bodies and souls to thy service, amen." Daddy grabs the ketchup bottle right after the amen. "The reason we wanted to take you girls out for a special meal," Daddy says, squeezing out ketchup, "is because it might not be much longer till God sends a special young man your way, and with my permission, you can commence courtship with the intent to marry."

I wonder how much longer it'll be for me. Last year a girl in our church got married on her eighteenth birthday. Last month she had her first baby. I'll be eighteen in less than two years.

"Libby, you look nervous," Mama says.

I pick up an onion ring and play with it. "It's just the way you said it, Daddy. It made me think how fast everything could happen. Courtship, marriage, babies—"

"Which are all wonderful things," Daddy says, smiling. "But don't you worry. The Lord won't put anything on you till He knows you're ready for it."

"I can't wait to be a mama," Patience says. She's almost halfway through her burger. I'm eating slower, maybe because the conversation is making me tense.

"You're gonna have to wait," Mama says, laughing. "You're only thirteen years old!"

"And waiting is part of what we want to talk about," Daddy says, gesturing at Patience and me with a shrimp. "Staying pure until marriage, never putting yourself in a situation where you could cause a young man undue temptation."

"Which is why courtship works the way it does," Mama says. "So you're always supervised or in the company of other people. When a young lady and a young man are alone together, it's a recipe for trouble."

"It sure is," Daddy says, and then he looks at Patience and then at me for what feels like a long time. "I guess what I'm trying to get at, girls, is this: I value you, and I value your purity. Whether your wedding night is three years away or ten years away, I want you to be able to give your husband your whole heart. In the meantime, I'd like to be the keeper of your hearts, to watch over you and guide you and make sure you make the right choices. And on your wedding days, I can walk you down the aisle and say"—his eyes are getting a little misty—"'here's my little girl's heart. I've kept it safe and pure so she can give it to you as your bride and helpmeet.' Can you girls make that pledge to me? That you'll stay pure until marriage and let me help you stay pure?"

"Yes, Daddy," Patience says. Her eyes are a little misty, too.

"Yessir," I say, hoping God doesn't find me a husband too soon.

"Well, that sure makes me happy and proud," Daddy says, smiling big. "Now I believe your mama wants to talk a little about the presents you found on your beds this morning."

Mama nods and pushes her plate away. She's not eaten much of her food. "That's right," she says. "So that book is a kind of workbook with questions at the end of every chapter. I want you to read a chapter every day and answer the questions. And then, on Wednesday afternoons while the Littles take their naps, the three of us will do something special, just us girls."

"What's that?" Patience says.

Mama smiles. "Every Wednesday afternoon we'll have a girls-only tea party. We'll have tea and cookies and talk about what's in the book and what God's plan for our lives is."

Patience grins, and I find myself grinning, too. It sounds cozy, and it's rare for us to get Mama's undivided attention.

When the waitress comes back around, Daddy says, "I think we'd better have three hot fudge cakes for my girls here and a piece of strawberry pie for me."

The hot fudge cake may be the best thing I've ever tasted: two layers of chocolate cake sandwiching vanilla ice cream, drenched in warm, gooey fudge sauce with whipped cream and a cherry on top. Daddy watches Patience and me eating and says, "Sweets to the sweet."

Before we leave, I excuse myself to go to the ladies' room. While I'm in the stall, I hear a voice saying, "Hey, did you hear that daddy giving his girls the purity speech in the booth behind us?"

"I heard some of it," a second voice says.

"You know my daddy gave me a speech like that," the first voice says. "Gave me a purity ring, too, but I lost it in the back seat of my boyfriend's car. The ring and my purity, too."

They both laugh.

"Hey," the first voice says, "You reckon when that daddy got his girls the hot fudge cake, he made them keep their cherries?"

More laughing.

My face burning, I wait until they're gone to leave the stall.

CHAPTER 15

I'VE READ THE WHOLE BOOK ON being a virtuous maiden, but I still feel like I've got a lot to learn. I've got the outside stuff down. I dress in a modest, feminine manner. I'm not rude or bossy, and I work to help take care of the home and my brothers and sisters. I don't watch movies or TV, and I don't read romance novels. I never think impure thoughts about any of the boys in church, and I never behave or dress in a way that might cause a brother in Christ to stumble.

It's the stuff on the inside I worry about. I try to hide it, but I know I have a rebellious heart. I ask questions in my head all the time even if I don't say them out loud. And I know it's God's plan for me to marry the man God and my daddy choose for me and to keep a Christian home and raise as many babies as the Lord sees fit to give us. But when I think of this future all I can think is, *please, not too soon* or even worse, *maybe never.* I know this is sinful and selfish.

And then there's the fact that I can't make myself stop caring for Zo even though I know she's a terrible sinner.

I may have the appearance of a virtuous maiden, but appearances are deceiving. I'm like that piece of fruit that looks good on the outside, but when you bite into it, it's rotten.

We're having our first Modest Maidens tea party, and Mama has fixed everything up real pretty. She put a rose-colored tablecloth on the kitchen table and set out a real china teapot and three china cups she's had since she was a little girl. There's a plate of butter cookies that look like little flowers and little bowls of lemon slices and sugar for the tea.

"This is so pretty," Patience says.

Once she and I sit down, Mama pours us each a cup of tea and joins us at the table. "I just feel so blessed," she says, "to have this special time with you girls." Her eyes look misty, so I know she means it. "Now I want to know what you think of the book so far."

I look down at the book, at the long-haired, long-frocked girl on the cover. "It's a pretty book," I say. "The illustrations are nice." The pages are full of other long-haired, long-frocked girls, picking flowers, sewing by a fireplace, baking bread. Leave it to me, the girl who only has the appearance of a virtuous maiden, to make a comment about the appearance of the book.

"It is lovely, isn't it?" Mama says. "And I like that in all the pictures the girls aren't just sitting around looking pretty. They're always doing something helpful."

"Yes," Patience says, "like in that fairy tale in the book with the good sister and the bad sister. I liked that part."

Mama asks Patience to read the story aloud. It's about two daughters living with their father in a little cottage. Their father is a Godly man who works the land every day but Sunday. The first daughter is pretty and knows it and doesn't help on the farm because she knows it's only a matter of time before a Godly knight asks her to marry him. The second daughter is plain and hard-working. She bakes bread, cleans the house, and milks the cow, and every day she prays to become the kind of woman God wants her to be.

One winter day a knight rides up to the little cottage. He is cold and tired and hungry and asks if he might stay in the cottage overnight and board his horse in the barn. The father sees the cross on the knight's shield and tells him he is welcome.

The first daughter can't believe her luck. All she has to do is let him see her prettiness, and she will have her knight at last. She flirts and giggles and flutters her eye-lashes. Meanwhile, her plain sister fixes the hungry knight a meal of hot stew and fresh bread and milk. After supper, the first sister sings and dances to get the knight's attention while the second sister sits in the corner reading the Bible. The next morning, the first sister shows off her newest dress while the second sister cooks a good breakfast, sweeps the cottage, and goes out to milk the cow.

Later, when the father comes in from the fields, the knight tells the father he would like to ask for the hand of one of the daughters in marriage. The first daughter overhears him and jumps for joy. She knew the knight would not be able to resist her beauty and charm. But then she can't believe her ears. The knight is asking for her sister's hand! "Long have I been on a quest," the knight says, "for a young lady who is holy, hardworking, and humble. A Godly girl who serves in gladness is a rare jewel indeed, and I have found such a jewel in your daughter, bringing my quest to a happy end."

Patience gives a satisfied smile when she finishes reading, and Mama smiles back at her. "Now that's a fairy tale I would've let you girls read when you were little," Mama says. "It's not like all those Disney princess stories where it's about getting the right dress so the prince will see you and fall in love at first sight." Mama rolls her eyes. "Those stories are about vanity and outer beauty. What's this story about?"

"Inner beauty," I say. I've never seen a Disney movie, but I know who the princesses are because I've seen their faces splashed all over everything from T-shirts to toys to towels at Walmart. Mama caught Faith and Charity looking at a nightgown with some princess on it and told them it was all foolishness and that no real girls look like that. She's right. They don't.

"Yes," Mama says, "the inner beauty that comes from the light of God. That's the kind of beauty a righteous man is interested in."

"But a girl who's courting should still be well-groomed, right?" Patience says. By worldly standards, Patience is pretty. I know she tries not to be vain, but when she looks in the mirror she has to see what fine features she has.

"Of course she should," Mama says. "She should be clean and sweet-smelling and dressed in feminine, modest clothes. Presenting a neat, clean appearance helps show a young man what kind of homemaker you'll be."

"And no boy likes a slob," Patience says, giggling. Mama laughs, too.

After the laughter dies down, Mama says, "Was there anything in the book you wanted to talk about, Libby? So far Patience and I have been doing most of the talking."

"No, ma'am," I say.

"Did you read the chapter?" Mama asks.

"I read the whole book."

Mama smiles. "Well, then, you're ahead of me. Maybe you should be asking me questions!"

The truth is I'm not sure I agree with everything in the book, but I'm afraid to say so out loud. Like the part about how wives should obey their husbands no matter what and marriage should always be until death do you part. I agree with these ideas most of the time, but what if a husband is tempted to sin and tries to get his wife to do something immoral? Obeying him then wouldn't be the same thing as obeying God, would it?

And what about the "until death do us part" thing? What if a woman's husband beats her or beats the children so bad it really hurts them? Should she still stay? The book would say that a Godly husband wouldn't do these things, but what if a woman ends up with a man who isn't as Godly as she thought he was? Should she pay for her mistake for the rest of her life? Should her children have to suffer even though they never even had a choice about who their daddy was?

It might be wrong for me to disagree with the book, but it's not like I'm disagreeing with the Bible. *Modest Maidens* was not set down by God. It was written by some lady who's just giving her interpretation of things.

My mind has wandered so far that I have to snap back to attention when Mama says we should end our ladies' tea with a prayer. She says, "Dear Lord, I thank you for blessing me with these good girls, and I pray that they will grow in their faith and become wives to Godly men and mothers to the children who will be Your faithful servants. In Jesus's name we pray, amen."

After we've cleared up from the tea party, Patience says, "That was fun. I'm excited we get to do this every week!"

I can tell that the book didn't stir up the questions in her that it did in me. She swallowed everything she was told just like it was tea and cookies. Patience is a good girl. Not like me.

EVER SINCE I WENT INTO THE blue tent, I've been different. It's like you could divide my life into two sections: Before the Blue Tent and After the Blue Tent. I guess it's like the Tree of Knowledge of Good and Evil. Once you know something, you can't un-know it.

Now that I know what I know about Zo, I should be able to write her off, to never want to see her again, but I can't. It's Saturday, and tonight she'll be waiting for me in the tent, and I'm fighting a terrible war within myself because I want to go. I want to see her even if it's for one last time. But I know what the Bible says about her and about children who lie to and disobey their parents.

Right now it's the half hour of free time before supper, and I'm sitting at the school table with Faith and Charity, coloring on coloring sheets. Mine is of Noah's ark with the rainbow over it, and I'm carefully coloring in the rainbow in the right order: red, orange, yellow, green, blue, indigo, violet.

"You're a good colorer," Faith says.

It's true. There's something about coloring that soothes me, watching the crayon transform the white of the page, being careful to stay inside the lines. It's nice, too, that your mind can wander as you color and it's not a problem like when your mind wanders in church.

As I color, I'm thinking about friendship. *Modest Maidens* says that friends are soon forgotten, but brothers and sisters are forever and are your true best friends. It's something else I'm not sure I agree with. Sitting here with Faith and Charity, I love them like I'm an extra mama to them, and I feel the same way about Val. With Just—well, I love him because he's my brother, but he's always off doing boy stuff, building things or shooting things, so we don't really spend much time together.

And then there's Patience. Because she's the sister closest to me in age, I guess it would make sense for her to be who I feel closest to. But she's not. I love her because she's my sister, but I've never felt like she's understood me. Maybe it's because I struggle and question so much, and it's all so easy for her. If we weren't sisters, I don't think we'd pick each other as friends.

Of course, you could say that Zo and me don't have much in common either, but somehow I always felt like she understood and accepted me, like she liked me as I was. And I felt the same way about her until that night in the blue tent. Now I feel like I don't understand her anymore, and how can I accept her if what she is is wrong?

I don't know if I can accept her, but I want to understand. Is that a sin?

"I'll be back in a minute," I tell Faith and Charity, setting down my crayon.

I go to my room and sit on my bed. Daddy says God speaks to him. I wish He would speak to me, too. That way,

I couldn't question it because it wouldn't be coming from a person. It would be coming from God, so I would know it was true.

I sit and wait for divine guidance, but there's nothing.

Then I see it, the Bible on my nightstand. It's like God is saying, "Where else did you expect to find guidance, you silly girl?"

I reach over and pick up my Bible. It's pure white, and its pages are lined with silver. I close my eyes and hold it in my hands. It feels warm and steadying. With my eyes still closed, I flip open the Bible at random and put my index finger on a page. I open my eyes to read the verse I'm touching, Luke 11:5: "Which of you shall have a friend, and shall go to him at midnight . . . " I gasp and put my hand on my heart.

I have to go to her, at least one last time. God has spoken.

I LIE AWAKE LISTENING TO PATIENCE breathe and watching the clock. I'm nervous but not like I was before because I know God is on my side.

Once it's ten till twelve, I slip out of bed, tiptoe down the hall, then down the stairs hoping they don't squeak. Then it's through the kitchen to the basement, light bulb on, down those stairs and out the door. When you've done something once, it's easier to do it the second time.

From the yard I see the glow from the blue tent. I run toward the light.

I'm out of breath when I open the flap. Zo looks up from a book she was reading in the lantern's dim light. "You came," she says.

"Yes." I sit down across from her. "I can't do this every Saturday night, though. It makes me a nervous wreck. It's just that last time when I left I was confused and upset about a lot of things. I didn't want to leave things like that."

"I'm glad," Zo says.

"I've been thinking a lot about what you said," I say, looking down at my lap so I don't have to make eye contact. "About how you're the same person you were before you told me you were a . . . a . . . "

"Before I told you I dated a girl?"

My face heats up. "Yes. And I guess I decided that even though I don't understand or approve of it, that one thing isn't all of who you are."

"No," Zo says. "It isn't. Just like your religion isn't all of who you are."

I think about this. Can my faith be separated from the rest of me, or does it affect every part of me, like the blood that flows through my veins?

"There's one more thing I should tell you about myself."

"Wait a second. Do you hear something?" There's a definite rustling noise outside the tent.

"I hope it's not a skunk," Zo says. "Edgar got sprayed the other day, and we had to wash him in tomato juice. There's nothing madder in the world than a cat getting a tomato juice bath!"

I laugh. But then the rustling is louder. I look up and see the shadow, not of a skunk but a person. I gasp and point, too scared to scream.

The flap opens, and the face I see is Patience's. "Sinner!" she hisses at me. "Blasphemer! Apostate!" Then she points at Zo. "Sodomite!"

"Patience," I say, wondering if it might have been better if the shadowy figure had been the murderer I feared it was. "What are you doing here?"

"What are you doing here?" she throws back at me. "Sneaking out of the house in the middle of the night—"

"You snuck out, too," I say.

"Yes, to follow you and save you from sin. Because I knew you was dishonoring God and dishonoring our mother and father." She reaches into the tent, grabs my arm, and pulls. "Come on. You have to leave this place . . . leave this person. We've got to tell Daddy what you've done."

"You don't need to do that," Zo says, her voice shaking. "I promise this will never happen again."

"Why should I believe any promises from you?" Patience says. "You're the one that dragged my sister into this pit of sin in the first place! Come on, Libby."

I take one last look at Zo who mouths, "I'm sorry." But Patience is dragging me by the arm, and I stumble out of the blue tent into darkness.

In the yard, Patience marches forward, still pulling me.

"You don't have to drag me. I'm coming with you."

She turns to look at me. "And I'm supposed to trust you after you pulled a stunt like that?"

I jerk my arm out of her grip. "Look, Patience, I'm bigger than you. If I wanted to get away from you, you couldn't stop me."

She doesn't try to grab me again. "Yeah, but I'd tell Daddy. Daddy would stop you."

It's strange to walk my secret path through the basement with Patience. I guess this is what I get for thinking something could be mine and mine alone. We go into the kitchen. I'm moving as silently as I can, but Patience is still marching, almost stomping. I want to tell her to be quiet, but I'm not really in a position to tell anybody to do anything.

Once we've made it up the stairs, I turn in the direction of our room, but Patience grabs me again and says, "No."

"What do you mean, 'no?'"

"I mean we're not going back to our room. We've got to go tell Daddy what you did."

The thought of waking Daddy to tell him about my disobedience makes my stomach hurt. "Can't it wait till first thing in the morning?"

"The truth can't wait," Patience says. "He has to know now."

There's a glint in her eyes that tells me what I already know: she's enjoying this.

The door to Mama and Daddy's room is cracked a couple of inches. Patience pushes it open the rest of the way. She stands beside Mama and Daddy's bed while I wait in the shadows. Daddy is asleep on his back, snoring. Mama has kicked off her covers and is curled up on her side, one hand resting on her growing belly.

"Daddy," Patience half whispers. When he doesn't stir, she shakes his shoulder a little.

His eyes open. "Is somebody breaking into the house? Let me get my gun." The rule is that if you or one of the other kids is sick, you wake Mama. Daddy is only to be woken for major emergencies—robberies or fires.

"No, sir," Patience says. "It's more like somebody was breaking out of the house. I caught Libby sneaking out to see that girl next door. They were sitting in a tent in her backyard talking about having an unnatural relationship."

"It wasn't like that!" I say. I accept that Patience caught me being disobedient, but why does she have to make it sound like Zo and I were on a date?

"Young lady, you do not have the right to speak unless I ask you a direct question," Daddy says. His voice is hard and cold.

"Yessir," I whisper.

"What's going on?" Mama says, her voice heavy with sleep. "Is somebody sick?"

"Sick in the soul, more like," Daddy says. "Patience caught Libby sneaking out to see that little harlot that lives next door."

"Libby?" Mama says, sitting up. "What in the world? This isn't like you."

I wonder if it is or isn't. The only way I've ever been is the way I've been told to be.

"Patience," Daddy says. "Thank you for coming to me with this. You have truly honored your mother and father. You stay here with your mama for a few minutes. Libby, you come with me to your room."

"Yessir."

Daddy stops at his closet to pull a belt from a rack. He can't take off his belt to whip me because he's wearing pajamas, I think, and for a second this strikes me as funny. I must be losing my mind.

Daddy closes the door behind us. "Now the first thing I need to know," he says, "did that girl . . . touch you?"

"No!" I say, then I remember to add "sir." "It's not like that."

"Did she make advances toward you in any way?"

"No, sir. We're friends. That's all."

Daddy's face is getting red, and a vein in his forehead bulges. "And you stayed friends with her after I forbid you from having anything to do with her?"

He has me there. "Yessir."

"And you realize that when you disobey the rules of your father you're also disobeying the rules of your Father who art in heaven?"

"But Daddy, I prayed about what to do, and I opened the Bible for guidance. And when I did, my finger landed right on a verse about going to see a friend at midnight."

Daddy's eyes have darkened with rage. "You do not use the Bible to try to justify your sinful behavior, young lady. And in this house, there is no 'But Daddy.' There is only 'yessir.' Do you understand?"

"Yessir," I say, but I wasn't trying to justify my behavior, just to explain that God told me to visit Zo. And I know that Daddy is a higher authority than me, but isn't God supposed to be a higher authority than Daddy?

He sighs. "Pull up your nightgown and bend over the bed."

I do as I'm told, but I burn with shame knowing Daddy can see my bare back, my bare legs, and the shape of my private areas under my white cotton panties. I haven't had a whipping since I was little, and back then, pulling up my clothes didn't bother me so much.

The thing about being whipped by a belt is you hear it before you feel it. There's the big whoosh of it being slung back, which probably only lasts a couple of seconds but feels much longer, and then there's the smack when it lands. And the sting. Because a belt whipping stings, stings like you've woken up a hive of angry bees. I keep my eyes shut tight. The licks that land on my bottom aren't as bad as the ones on my bare legs, especially on the back of the knees where the skin's thin and tender. One lick there cuts into me, and I bite the quilt to keep from crying out.

Daddy counts each time the belt lands on me. He stops at twelve. "Cover yourself and get up," he says, out of breath.

I do.

"This isn't the end of your punishment, you know."

"Yessir." I know there will be extra chores, no treats.

"Now get down on your knees and pray to God for forgiveness and thank Him for having parents who correct you when you stray."

Kneeling hurts because of the welts on my legs. *Dear Lord, I pray silently. Forgive me, but I have so many questions. Why did you show me a Bible verse that led me to see Zo if this was what was going to happen? Were you testing me? Did you want me to learn something? I'm not questioning You, Lord. I'm just praying for understanding. Understanding and forgiveness and help being a better girl. In Jesus's name I pray, amen.*

I lie down on my bed on my belly so the sheets won't touch my welts. There's a soft knock on the door.

"I thought you might need some medicine on your legs," Mama says.

"Will it sting?" I ask.

She smiles. "You've asked me that ever since you were little-bitty. No, this isn't the kind that stings."

"Okay."

She uses her fingertips to gently rub cool ointment where the belt hit me. When she gets to the back of my knee, she sucks in her breath. "Got you good there, didn't he?" she says. "Libby, I was trying to remember the last time you got a whipping. I was thinking it was probably when you were seven or eight." She keeps dabbing on the medicine, which does take out some of the sting.

"That sounds about right."

"So what I want to know is, why now?" She dabs medicine near the top of my legs.

"I don't know." There's so much I don't know anymore.

"Patience says that girl is a homosexual. You don't have . . . unnatural feelings for her, do you?"

"No, ma'am," I say. "I think . . . I think I just wanted a friend." The tears I held back during my whipping spring to my eyes now.

"Well, you do have a really good friend, and that's your sister. She saved you tonight." She pats my back and gets up from the bed. "Patience, come on back in here," she says.

Patience must have been standing in the hallway the whole time.

I pull down my nightgown and struggle to sit up. Patience looks as pleased as a cat full of cream.

"Now, Libby," Mama says, looking at me, then Patience, then back at me again. "I think you owe your sister a big thank you for what she did tonight."

"Thank you, Patience," I say, but I don't feel gratitude. I feel like Patience wasn't trying to save me so much as trying to get me in trouble. And she succeeded.

"That could've sounded more enthusiastic," Mama says. "How about you girls give each other a big hug?"

Patience smiles and opens her arms. I'll look like a terrible person if I don't go to her. I stand, wincing in pain, and open my arms, too. We stand there with our arms around each other, but I don't feel any warmth or affection.

"That's what I like to see," Mama says, smiling at us. "Sisters and best friends! Now we'd better get to bed. We've got to be up for church in a few hours."

Patience and I climb in our beds, and Mama flips off the lights before she leaves.

"You know you got what was coming to you, don't you?" Patience says.

"I know this family has rules, and I know the consequences of breaking them," I say, my voice cold and flat.

"And you know the consequences of breaking God's rules is way worse than getting a whipping."

"Well, Patience, I reckon that's between God and me."

As soon as I've said it, the truth hits me harder than Daddy's belt. It's not God who makes me wear long skirts and long hair and who keeps me away from everybody I'm not related to by blood or church. It's not God who makes me clean the house and take care of little kids all day and tells me that's exactly what my future will look like, too, except the house and the kids will be my husband's. My husband, who my daddy will choose for me, saying it was God who did the choosing.

None of this comes from God. It comes from people saying what they think God wants.

Does God want me to fight the curious mind, the healthy body, and the loving heart that He gave me? Because even though I know Daddy would say different, I don't think my problem is with God. It's with the men who think they speak for Him and the women who obey those men without question.

ZO

CHAPTER 16

I DIDN'T SLEEP LAST NIGHT. I was too worried about Libby. I know I have to tell Mom and Dad, and I want to like a guilty Catholic wants to confess to a priest. But Mom and Dad sleep late on Sundays, so it's a long wait till I hear them puttering in the kitchen and grinding beans for coffee.

When I drag into the kitchen, Mom says, "Pancakes or waffles?"

I shrug. "I don't care."

Mom raises an eyebrow. "Who are you, and what have you done with my child?"

She's got a point. If I don't care about pancakes or waffles, something is definitely wrong.

"I need to talk to you guys," I say, slumping into a chair at the kitchen table.

"Okay, what's up?" Dad sits down across from me.

Mom sits next to him, looking worried. "Spill," she says.

I take a deep breath. "Okay. So you know how sometimes I hang out in the tent at night?"

Mom and Dad nod.

"Well . . . last Saturday and then last night, I kind of . . . invited Libby to meet me there."

Mom and Dad shoot each other an anxious look. Mom turns to me. "And this would be without her parents' knowledge or permission?"

"That's right," I say. "You don't have to tell me it was a bad idea."

"We will anyway," Dad says, and I can tell he's getting warmed up for a speech.

"I know," I say. "And I deserve to hear it. But first I need to tell you what happened. Libby came over last night, and we kind of . . . got caught."

"Caught doing what by whom?" Mom asks.

"Caught talking, by her sister. Patience, the prissy one."

Mom winces. "What happened when she caught you?"

I feel the tears start. "She called Libby a sinner and some other Biblical-sounding slurs, and she called me a sodomite, which was kind of over the top, but she must have overheard me talking about Hadley. And then she dragged Libby away and said she had to tell their parents."

Dad is massaging the bridge of his nose, a sign he's stressed. "Zo, do you have any idea how bad this is?"

The tears start spilling out for real. "I know it's bad."

"I don't think you know how bad," Dad says. "I mean, if you disobey us, we take away your laptop for a while or give you extra chores. But by putting that girl in a situation where she was disobeying her father, you were putting her in physical danger. There was a story in the news, just the other day. This crazy fundy family whose son disobeyed them in some stupid little way. And they beat him to death." His dark eyes lock with mine. "To death."

Fear bubbles up in my stomach, and I let out a sob. "You're not helping! Telling you this was supposed to help."

Dad shakes his head. "Zo, I don't think Libby's parents have killed her, and I didn't mean to imply that they would. But you put her in a situation that isn't exactly rainbows and lollipops."

I nod. I'm crying too hard to talk.

"But just to be fair," Mom says, putting a hand on my arm. "Libby chose to break the rules of her house by coming to see you. You both made poor choices."

"I thought I was choosing friendship." My voice sounds choked, constricted.

"Well," Mom says, "I'm afraid in this situation, being a good friend to Libby means staying away from her to keep her safe."

"But I think of her over there and the lies they teach her and how she's expected to grow up to be nothing but a baby factory, and I . . . " I know it's going to sound stupid, but I say it anyway. "I want to save her."

"Of course you do," Dad says. His tone has softened. "You want to bring her over to our side. And for a while, before they decided we were hopeless heathens, Libby's family wanted to 'save us,' too. But you know what? No matter what your definition of it is, you can't save somebody who doesn't want to be saved."

Maybe Libby does want to be saved, I think, but I don't say anything. I just keep crying.

Owen pads into the kitchen in his pajamas, his face sleepy and innocent. "Hey," he says, "are we having pancakes or waffles?"

"HERE'S THE DEAL." MOM SITS ON the edge of my bed where I've been lying all afternoon. I haven't even put on music. I deserve silence and emptiness.

"Have you decided on my punishment?" My voice is flat and dead.

"Yes, we have."

"Should I hand over my laptop?"

"No. Your dad and I talked a lot. We said we thought moving to the middle of nowhere probably sounded like a great idea while you were reeling from a bad breakup. But now that you've had some time to get over Hadley, we're afraid you're too isolated. Lonely."

Lonely. Claire used that word, too. It echoes in my head, and I feel tears come to my eyes again.

Mom is holding my hand. "It's not right that Libby is the only person your age you've met since we moved. We need to fix that. We need to find ways to get you more connected, and taking away your laptop isn't going to do that. You need to talk to people even if it's just online."

I nod. "I would miss Claire."

"I know you would. Listen, I think this whole Libby thing has been a symptom of a larger problem. Owen's still fine staying home with me because he's little, but you . . . you need to be out in the world at least some of the time. And so your dad and I were discussing the possibility of buying you a used car. Something old and ugly, but safe."

I sit up in shock. "That's my punishment?"

Mom laughs. "No, we'll get to the punishment. This is a proposed solution to the problem that makes a punishment necessary. With a car, you could go visit Claire some weekends.

You could drive to Johnson City and take some dual enroll-
ment classes at the community college. You could hit the thrift
stores and the movies. If you wanted to get a part-time job to
help pay for gas, we could talk about that, too."

I can't wrap my head around how I'm supposedly being punished, yet I'm being offered a previously unheard-of level of
freedom. "But what about Dad's whole 'cars are a drain on the
environment, therefore we are a one-car family' proclamation?"

Mom smiles. "Well, that worked better when we were in
Knoxville and could take city buses. Your dad's an idealist,
but he also has a pragmatic streak. And he said he didn't
want you to turn into one of those weird homeschool kids
who can't have a conversation with anybody they're not
related to."

I let myself smile a little.

"So . . . that's the plan. For the near future." She lets go of
my hand. "In the present, however, you're being punished."

"Okay." I await my sentence.

"You know the outbuilding that's been full of trash ever
since we moved in?"

"And how Dad's been saying he's going to clean it out and
never does?"

Mom nods. "That's the one. Now you're going to clean it
out. Like Hercules cleaning the Aegean stables."

It could be worse.

"I've got some work gloves you can use," Mom says, "and
make sure you wear sturdy shoes and watch your step. There
might be broken glass or rusty nails out there."

"Well, having a nurse for a dad means I'm always up to
date on my tetanus shots."

"True." Mom pats my arm and gets up. "Why don't you go ahead and see how much you can get done before dinner? I have a feeling it's going to be a long project."

"A Herculean effort," I say, dragging myself out of bed.

"Exactly. But maybe it'll give you some time to think, which may be what you need." She looks at me like she's seeing inside me. "You've got a good heart, sweetie, and I know you miss Libby and that's why you did what you did. I miss her mom, too. But sometimes you've got to tell your heart to shut up for a minute so you can listen to your head."

I SNEEZE AGAIN. THE OLD STORAGE shed is covered with a thick layer of dust. Standing inside it, I feel like I am, too. My eyes burn, my mouth tickles, my nose and throat are itchy. Dusty boxes and broken furniture and appliances are piled from the dirt floor to the ceiling. Just being here feels like a punishment.

I'm supposed to drag out all the items and sort them into three piles: a garbage pile, a recycling pile, and a "save" pile. Whoever owned this shed never met a box he didn't like. I drag out a Fanta box, a MoonPie box, and a Little Debbie box. I stomp them flat with my steel-toed work boots and start the recycling pile. I don't know if I'm going to find anything worth saving.

Worth saving.

I think about what Dad said about Libby's family wanting to save us and us wanting to save them. But what we wanted to save each other from was very different. I guess Libby's family wanted to save us from sin and hell, but what did I want to save Libby from? Her father. Belief in a God that closes you off instead of opening you up. A future identical to her mother's present.

But no matter what Dad thinks, I never felt like Libby's number one motivation was to save me. I felt like she just liked me even if she didn't understand why. But it doesn't matter. Our friendship can't be saved. It has to be thrown away like an old electric fan, something that's too broken to be fixed.

If a punishment is supposed to cause both thoughtfulness and unhappiness, then this is a great one. After an hour of work, I'm sneezy, dusty, sweaty, and miserable. I've also learned that for whoever lived here before us, this shed operated as a sort of mausoleum for used appliances. In addition to the fan, I've added a toaster, a hand mixer, and a can opener to the garbage pile. I wonder why the owner kept them. Did he mean to get around to fixing them one day, or could he not bear to part with the cherished memories of all the bread toasted and cans opened?

I find a cardboard box of bills and receipts from before I was born and add them to the recycling pile. I'm at least starting to clear a path. I lean over to examine another box and jump backward with a gasp.

It's full of magazines of a very specific type. The woman on the cover has big goopy eye makeup and big red hair and big bare boobs. Like the bills and receipts, the magazine is dated before my birth. The topless redhead is probably a grandmother now. Porn before you were born, I think.

The question is what to do with it. I stare at the redhead as if she'll answer my question, and a spider from the depths of the box crawls across her face. The physical condition of the magazines is so gross I'm not even tempted to examine them more closely. Since they're paper, I guess I should recycle them, but I don't want to put them out in the pile where Owen might see them.

I hear Dad starting up the lawnmower and go out to him. He turns off the mower when he sees me. "What's up?"

"Uh . . . I found something questionable in the shed."

He raises an eyebrow. "Questionable like a dead body?"

"Not that questionable."

Dad follows me out to the shed. When I show him the box, he laughs. "So the old dude living out here had a porn stash. Bless his heart."

"I wasn't sure what to do with them," I say. "I didn't want to put them out where Owen could see."

Dad picks up the box. "I'll take them down to the basement until it's time to haul off the recycling." He grins. "I didn't know I was asking you to clean out a porn and appliance warehouse."

"Me neither," I say.

Dad's face turns serious. "I hope you don't think we're being too hard on you by making you do this. But your mom and I felt like this was a bad enough error in judgment that there needed to be consequences."

I nod. "I had it coming."

Dad smiles. "Okay, it's officially become awkward to stand here being parental while holding a box of pornography."

I smile back. "Yeah."

"Why don't you work another hour, then knock off for the day and shower? You look like you've been rolled in sweat and dipped in dust."

"I kind of have."

Dad carries off the box. I figure one night after a few beers he and Mom will end up looking at it and laughing at the dated hairstyles and settings. I wonder what Mr. Hazlett would do if one of his kids discovered a stash of porn in an outbuilding. Do a ritual to cast out demons or just burn the building down because it's been so corrupted by evil?

I drag out an old landline phone and the remains of a vacuum cleaner. Laughing with Dad made me feel better. I know we're still friends, that he loves me even though I do stupid stuff. I wonder if Libby feels that way about her dad or if she just feels afraid.

LIBBY

CHAPTER 17

I WAS PRETTY SURE WHAT DADDY meant when he said my punishment wouldn't be over after the whipping. I was right. I've been tomato-staked.

Tomato-staking, the way Daddy explains it, is like this. If you let a tomato plant grow the way it wants to grow, the vines will crawl everywhere, and the fruit will fall to the ground and rot. If you want the plant to grow up right, reaching toward heaven instead of falling into the dirt, you've got to stake it. You drive a wooden stake into the ground and tie the plant to it so it's not growing the way it wants to grow. It's growing the way you make it grow.

Daddy says the child is the plant and the parent is the stake. Being tomato-staked means there's never a moment, except in the bathroom, when I'm out of Mama's sight. I can't even take the Littles out in the yard by myself anymore. Patience has temporarily moved out of our room and in with the Little Girls so at night Daddy can lock me in the bedroom from the outside. I can't leave until Daddy unlocks the door in the morning. The hardest part is when I need the bathroom. Daddy put a bucket in the corner.

Mama reminds me at least once a day that the tomato-staking is temporary, that it'll last until the Lord tells Daddy he can trust me again. Then the lock will come off my door, my sister can come back, and I can go outside without supervision.

I pray for that day to come soon. And I pray for forgiveness and understanding. But I'm pretty sure I'm going to get it from the Lord before I get it from Daddy.

The one good thing about being tied to Mama is that I can help her a lot. She never complains. Complaining is not something that's supposed to happen in our family because it's not Christlike. But even though she doesn't complain, I can tell Mama doesn't feel good. She looks tired, and her hands and ankles are swollen, which she says always happens when she's pregnant in the summer.

Right now Mama's at the ironing board, ironing Just's Sunday suit while I help the Littles with their Bible workbook. She looks like the iron's too heavy for her. "Mama," I say, "why don't you let me finish the ironing and you can sit down and help the Littles?"

She smiles. "It would feel good to sit." She sets down the iron. "Make sure you do a good job on Just's suit. He wants to look like a big man at the leadership conference."

"I know. He can't stop talking about it." Daddy's going to a Christian Leadership Weekend in the mountains of North Carolina this weekend, and he's decided Just is old enough to go with him and learn with the other men.

Mama sits down with a sigh and slips off her shoes, which is strange for her. "It's hard to believe Just is old enough to go with your daddy. Before we know it, Val will be big enough to go, too." She pats her belly. "It's good there's another little one on the way. Y'all are growing up too fast."

"I'm a big girl," Faith says.

"You sure are, honey," Mama says. "Show me how a big girl colors her Bible story picture."

There's a lot to do before Daddy gets home. He and Just are leaving this evening and will drive late into the night. Since it's a campout, they'll stay together in a tent, and we're packing all the food they'll need.

After I finish the ironing, I start filling the cooler. Mama's made a dozen hard-boiled eggs and a gallon jug of sweet tea, and there's a pack of assorted lunchmeats, a squeeze bottle of mustard, and a loaf of bread.

"Just said there's a mother-daughter weekend next year, but it's at a hotel instead of in the woods," Patience says. "Maybe me and you and Mama can go."

"Maybe," I say, but I don't see it happening. Mama will still be nursing a baby, and Daddy likes her at home. "The mother-daughter one isn't called a Leadership Weekend, is it?"

Patience rolls her eyes. "Of course not. We're girls. We're not leaders. You're really weird sometimes, you know, Libby?"

I know.

IT FEELS STRANGE FOR DADDY NOT to be here in the evening. He got home right after Mama and Patience and I finished our Modest Maidens tea, and he and Just were out of the house within thirty minutes. They both seemed really excited and in a good mood, but Daddy did take a minute to give me a stern look and say, "Now you mind your mama while

I'm gone, and don't leave her side. You're still staked even if I'm not here."

I said, "Yessir."

After he stopped looking at me, he was in a good mood again.

Now, with the menfolk gone, Mama's looking around like she's not quite sure what to do. "Well, I guess it's a Girls' Night In," she says.

"I'm not a girl," Val says.

Mama smiles at him. "No, you're not, honey. I'm sorry."

"Daddy said I'm the man of the house while him and Just are gone." Val puffs out his chest like a rooster.

"And you'll do a good job," Mama says. "I guess I need to figure out supper."

"Why don't you let us cook for you?" I suggest. She looks so tired and a little lost.

"Is it Mother's Day again already?" Mama asks, smiling.

"No, but you look like you need a rest. Put your feet up and let us cook."

"Well, these feet would sure appreciate it. If they keep swelling like they are, I'm gonna have to buy new shoes. I went up two sizes when I was pregnant with you, Val."

Patience and I do most of the cooking, but we give the Littles things to do so they'll feel like they're helping. We boil two boxes of spaghetti noodles, heat up a jar of sauce, and toss it all together in a big bowl. We make buttered toast sprinkled with garlic powder, and I stir up some brownie mix and put it in the oven for dessert later.

Supper feels like a party. The spaghetti and garlic toast are delicious, and without Daddy here, there's more talking and more laughter than there is normally when everybody, even Mama, is trying hard to be on their best behavior. I love Daddy, but with him gone, it's more relaxed. It's like a vacation. It's not that you don't love your home or your regular life, but it's nice to have a little break.

After we've done the dishes, Mama reads us a Bible story. She picks one the Littles love—about Jesus and the loaves and the fishes. She doesn't comment on it, or preach about it like Daddy does; she just reads the story. After that, we have brownies and board games, and Charity isn't very charitable when she beats me and Patience at Candyland. She laughs and jumps up and down yelling, "I win! You lose!" until Mama has to lecture her about being a good sport and a lady.

Once the Littles are in bed, Mama and Patience and I sit in the living room with mugs of chamomile tea.

"I am thankful for this restful evening," Mama says, holding her mug in both hands. "I've been praying for strength a lot lately. You'll see how it is when you're wives and mothers. Sometimes, especially when you're pregnant, you get so tired . . . so tired you feel like you can't do this anymore, any of it. And that's when you have to confess your weakness to the Lord and ask him to send you strength." She wipes under her eyes, where there are little tears.

I can't remember the last time I saw Mama cry.

"Sorry," she says. "Hormones."

"It's okay." I reach out and take her hand. It's so swollen I can't even feel the bones. "You're just tired."

"I am," Mama says. "I don't usually admit it, but I am. It'll be okay. I've just got to keep on going."

"Like the Hebrews on their way to the Promised Land," Patience says. "They were tired, but they kept on going because they knew God was leading them in the right direction."

"That's right," Mama says. She hasn't let go of my hand. "I think I might turn in early tonight. It's gonna feel strange to stretch out in that big bed all by myself."

I bet it will. Sleeping locked up alone has felt strange, too. In our family, nobody is used to being alone. "I guess if you're going to bed, I should get ready, too, so you can lock me in," I say.

Mama looks at me a little strangely, then says, "Maybe we won't lock you in your room while your daddy's gone. I agreed that you needed to be punished, but the locking you up part"—she stops, looks like she's not sure if she should go on—"I probably shouldn't tell you this, but I told your father I wasn't sure I agreed with it."

"Mama!" Patience gasps. "God acts through Daddy!"

"I know He does," Mama says. "And this is probably just me being weak and sinful, but I kept thinking, what if you got sick in the night, Libby, and we couldn't hear you and you couldn't get out? Or what if there was a fire?"

I had never thought of this, and when I do, I shudder. "Oh," I say.

"Yes, so no locking you in your room till your daddy gets back. Maybe by then he'll decide your punishment has gone on long enough."

"Mama, I don't think it's good that you're going against Daddy's wishes," Patience says. "The church is supposed to do what God says. When he gets home, I might have to tell him you disobeyed him."

Mama sighs and rubs her temples. "Patience, if you feel the Lord is leading you to tell your daddy on me, then by all means, do it. But first you need to think about whether you want to tell your daddy because the Lord wants you to or if you just want to because you're a tattletale." She pulls herself up out of her chair and says, "Good night, girls" while me and Patience sit there with our mouths hanging open.

I HEAR THE THUNK AND KNOW something's wrong. I jump out of bed and check the Little Girls' room. Faith and Charity are asleep, but Patience is sitting up. "Did you hear something?" she asks.

I nod and head toward the boys' room. Patience follows me. "I hope nobody's trying to break into the house," she whispers. "If just one person found out Daddy's gone and we're all by ourselves—"

"Shh," I say, because I think I hear something again. It's not coming from the boys' room, but from Mama's.

I knock softly on her door, but there's no answer. When I push the door open, I see her on the floor. The first thing I notice is that her nightgown has ridden up so her underwear is showing. The second thing is that she's shaking, hard.

"Mama!" I cry. "Mama!"

She doesn't respond. I sit on the floor and cradle her head so she won't bump against the nightstand or bed frame. Her eyes are open, but she doesn't seem to see me.

Patience is crying. "What are we gonna do? We've got to call Daddy."

"Daddy's in the mountains of North Carolina by now. He probably can't get a phone signal, and even if he could, he's too far away to help us." Mama's eyes look unseeing and hor-rified at the same time. She looks like she's staring into the pits of hell. "We've got to call an ambulance."

"But Daddy says no doctors and no hospitals—"

"I'm sure God will understand that this is an emergency, and Daddy might, too, if he was here. Mama's phone is in the kitchen. Call nine-one-one."

Patience runs. I'm holding Mama like she's a baby and saying, "It's okay, it's okay," even though I know it's not. Her shaking has slowed down, but she's still staring glassy-eyed at something beyond me. I pull down her nightgown for modesty.

Patience comes back, out of breath. "They say they're on a call right now, but they can be here in forty minutes."

The nearest hospital is half an hour away, which means it could be well over an hour before Mama's seen by a doctor. "That's too long." And then, maybe because God puts it in my head, I know what I have to do. "Come here, Patience. You hold Mama like I'm doing now, and I'm going to get help."

Patience narrows her eyes. "Where?"

"Next door."

"From those people? I don't think it's a good idea, Libby. I think we should pray—"

There's no time to argue. I slip a pillow under Mama's head and get up. "Okay, you stay with Mama and pray, and I'm going next door for help."

"Those people are sinners!" Patience yells, but I'm already halfway down the stairs. Sinner or not, Zo's dad is a nurse.

When you bang on somebody's door at one-thirty in the morning, they don't answer right away. After what feels like hours, Zo's face peeks out the window beside the door and looks surprised.

She opens the door. She's wearing light-blue pajamas. "Libby?"

"We need help. We need your daddy. Something's wrong with Mama."

"I'll get him," Zo disappears and after what feels like an eternity, even though I know it's seconds, she comes back with Mr. Forrester. He's wearing plaid pajama pants and a T-shirt that says Guinness Beer. His hair is all crazy.

"Let me grab my bag from my car, and you can take me to her," he says. "Is your father home? He's not gonna shoot me, is he?"

"He's on a trip," I say.

"Well, that's a relief," Mr. Forrest says as we follow him to his car. I lead them into the house and up the stairs and into Mama's bedroom. Mama's still lying on the floor, and Patience is on her knees, praying and crying beside her.

"All right, I need you to scoot out of the way," Mr. Forrest says to Patience. He squats next to Mama. "Mrs. Hazlett?" He's almost yelling. "Mrs. Hazlett?"

No response.

"Okay," he says, "let me get this blood pressure cuff on her." He wraps a band around her arm and squeezes a rubber bulb attached to it. Then he says, "Her blood pressure is through the roof. When was the last time she saw her doctor or midwife?"

"We don't use those," I say. "Daddy catches the babies."

"Well, he's not catching this one," he says. "Zo, my car keys are in the dresser in my bedroom. Grab them, tell your mom what's going on, then drive the car right up to the Hazletts' front porch."

Zo runs.

"I don't know," Patience says. "I don't know if this is a good idea." Her voice is shaking, and her face is wet with tears.

"You got any better ones?" I say. "Listen, Patience, you stay here with the Littles and see if you can get Daddy on the phone. I'm gonna go with Mama to the hospital."

"I think that's a solid plan," Mr. Forrester says.

"Hospital," a small, weak voice says. It takes me a minute to realize it's coming from Mama.

"Yes, Mama," I say. "We're taking you to the hospital."

"Baby?" she says.

I'm not sure how to answer, so I look at Mr. Forrester.

"The hospital's the best place for you and the baby," he says. "They'll take good care of both of you."

The car horn honks, and we all just about jump out of our skins.

"Okay, Mrs. Hazlett," Mr. Forrester says. "I don't think you should to try to walk, so I'm going to carry you to the car. Put your arms around my neck, okay?"

"Uh—" Mama is frozen.

"It's okay," he says. "It's a medical emergency."

She links her arms around his neck, and he lifts her up, one arm supporting her back and the other the back of her knees. It's weird to see Mama being carried like a bride over a threshold by a man who isn't her husband. "My purse," she says, and I grab it.

I didn't even know Zo could drive, but there she is, behind the wheel of the car.

"Libby, you get in the front seat," Mr. Forrester says. "I'll ride with your mom in the back. Now, Mrs. Hazlett, I'm going to lay you down on the backseat. Let's get you on your left side because that can help with your blood pressure."

In the backseat is something I never thought I'd see: my mother, in just her nightgown and underwear, lying with her head on a strange man's lap. I tell myself what Mr. Forrester told her earlier: it's a medical emergency.

"What will they do at the hospital?" I ask him.

"The first thing they'll do is give her some medicine to try to get that blood pressure down," he says.

Medicine. That's not too bad. I hadn't realized how scared I was until I sat still. I look over at Zo, who's as calm as if she drives to the hospital at 2 a.m. all the time. Her pajamas have cartoon robots on them like something a little boy would pick out.

The ride to the county hospital is long, but once we get there, things move so fast I can barely keep up. Mr. Forrester has Zo pull up right in front of the door labeled Emergency. He jumps out of the car and says he'll be back with help. In less than a minute, he's here with a big, burly guy pushing an empty wheelchair.

They help Mama into the chair, and Mr. Forrester says, "Libby, you come with me. Zo, go park and then meet us in the waiting room."

The ER waiting room has more people than you'd think at two-thirty in the morning. A thin, pale old man sits with a woman who's probably his daughter and struggles to breathe even though he's hooked to an oxygen tank. A mother holds a red-stained towel to her little boy's nose. Mr. Forrester takes my arm and leads me to the front desk where a lady with short, spiky hair sits.

"I'm a nurse," Mr. Forrester tells the lady, "and I'm pretty sure the pregnant lady who just got wheeled in is having eclamptic seizures. This is her daughter. She's probably in better shape to fill out the forms than her mom is."

The lady nods and reaches for a clipboard, which she shoves at me. "Fill it out, front and back." I can tell she says this a million times a day. "And I'll need to make a copy of your mom's insurance card."

"We don't have insurance," I say. "Daddy doesn't believe in it."

The lady gives Mr. Forrester a look.

"I'm not her dad," he says. "I'm just their neighbor. Trust me—her dad believes a lot of things I don't."

I sit down and start filling out the form, but pretty quickly I realize there's stuff about Mama I don't know. She's still sitting in the wheelchair, glassy-eyed but conscious.

"Mama, what's your middle initial?" I ask.

"J," she says, her voice weak and shaky. "For Jeanette, my grandmother."

"That's pretty." I write down J. This is the first time I've ever heard Mama mention her grandmother. I ask her the questions on the form. Does she have any allergies? Has she ever had surgery?

"I had my tonsils out when I was a kid."

It's strange to think of Mama as a little girl, of what she was like before she met Daddy and became his helpmeet and our mother. Somehow it's easier to picture Daddy as a little boy than Mama as a little girl, maybe because Daddy talks about his childhood and Mama never mentions hers.

A lady in scrubs calls Mama back almost immediately after I turn in the form. Mr. Forrester pushes Mama in her wheelchair, and Zo, who just got back from parking the car, and I follow them. The lady in scrubs has a nametag that reads Donna. She leads us to a room with a narrow bed and a lot of machines. It smells like antiseptic.

"Now, Mrs. Hazlett," Donna says, "we're gonna get you in that bed, and then we'll see if we can figure out what's going on with you." She looks at Mr. Forrester. "Do you think you can help your wife into the bed?"

"I can help, but she's not my wife," he says.

"I'm not here to judge, sir," Donna says. "I'm here to help."

Mr. Forrester and I get on either side of Mama and help her into bed. Donna puts a blood pressure cuff around Mama's arm. She squeezes the bulb a few times, her eyes widening. "Two-thirty over one-twenty," she says. "That's dangerously high. I'm gonna get the doctor."

When Donna comes back, I'm surprised to see the doctor with her is a woman. She has black hair and brown skin that really stand out against the whiteness of her coat. "Mrs. Hazlett, I am Dr. Nasour." Her accent is from somewhere far away. "When was the last time you saw your obstetrician?"

"I don't have one," Mama says.

"Midwife?" Dr. Nasour asks.

"No."

"It's a religious thing," Mr. Forrester says. "I'm her neighbor. Her daughter came to get me when her mother collapsed."

"Well, it's a good thing you did," Dr. Nasour says to me, then she turns to Mama. "Mrs. Hazlett, I assure you I mean no disrespect for whatever your religious beliefs may be, but on the basis of your blood pressure, I am admitting you to the hospital."

"No," Mama says. "We can't pay."

"We'll figure that part out," Dr. Nasour says. "If I turned

you away in your condition, I would be violating the Hippocratic Oath."

Mr. Forrester, Zo, and I follow Mama as she's wheeled out of the ER and into a room with a bed, an armchair, a chest of drawers, and a TV. All of a sudden, I feel dizzy. It's like I've been spinning and spinning, but now that I'm slowing down, I can feel the effects.

Zo touches my shoulder. "Are you okay?"

I nod. "Just tired. And scared."

"Me, too," Zo says.

I look down and notice Zo's feet. "You're not wearing shoes," I say.

She smiles a little. "I guess at the time shoes didn't seem like a priority."

Mr. Forrester drapes his arm around Zo's shoulder. "Now that we've got Mrs. Hazlett where she needs to be, we should probably get back home to bed."

"Here," Zo says, handing me her phone. "Why don't you borrow this so you can call your sister and your dad?"

Tears spring to my eyes. I don't want them to go, but I know I can't ask them to stay. "Thank y'all so much for helping us," I say, and without even deciding to do it, I give Zo a big hug and her daddy one, too. I've never hugged any man but my daddy, but it feels like a regular hug, warm and comfortable.

A pair of nurses, a big one and a little one, comes in. One puts in a catheter so Mama doesn't have get up to go to the bathroom, and the other puts in an IV for the medicine that's supposed to help her blood pressure. I hold Mama's hand while they stick things into her.

"Now the bag connected to the IV is magnesium sulfate," the big nurse says. "It might make her talk kinda crazy, but maybe she's so tired she'll just go to sleep. You can sleep in that chair if you want to, honey. The doctor will come in the morning."

I'm tireder than I can ever remember being, but I can't imagine relaxing enough to fall asleep. When the nurses have gone, I call Patience on Zo's phone.

"I don't want to talk to you. I want to talk to my sister" is how she answers the phone.

"This is your sister. I borrowed Zo's phone."

"Oh. How's Mama?"

"They're keeping her here overnight to try to get her blood pressure down."

"They're keeping her? Who's gonna make breakfast for the Littles in the morning?"

"You, I guess. Did you talk to Daddy?"

"No. I called and called, but I can't get an answer."

"Probably he's so far out in the woods he can't get a signal," I say.

"Probably." Patience's voice is choked. "I just . . . feel afraid. I don't know where Daddy is, and Mama's in the hospital, and we don't know if the baby's all right. Do you think God is testing us?"

"I don't know. Just keep on trying to get Daddy, and pray for Mama. And take care of the Littles, okay?"

I hang up and sit in the armchair and watch Mama. Her eyes are closed, but I can't tell if she's asleep or not. Her face and hands are so swollen. I don't know why I never wondered if this meant something was wrong. I guess we just trusted

God that everything would be okay.

I must doze off a little, then I hear Mama say, "Libby?"

"Yes, Mama?"

Her eyes are about half open. "Am I dying?"

"No, but you're sick, and you're on some kind of medicine that's making you feel weird."

"I think I'm dying," she says. "I think this is what dying feels like." She closes her eyes and murmurs, "I always thought he'd save me."

"Jesus?" I ask.

She laughs a little like I made a joke. "Jesus," she says. "Jesus and your daddy. Your daddy and Jesus."

I don't know what to say, and she doesn't say anything else. I curl back up in the chair and try to sleep.

THE DOCTOR THIS MORNING IS DARK and foreign, too, but this time it's a man, Dr. Kumar. "Mrs. Hazlett," he says, looking at her chart, "I don't think your blood pressure has reduced adequately from the magnesium sulfate. I'm afraid the only cure for your condition is delivery of the baby."

Mama looks scared. "The baby's not ready. I'm right at seven months."

"The baby will be premature," the doctor says, "but it will have an excellent chance of survival. If the baby stays inside you, Mrs. Hazlett, your and the baby's chances for survival drop to zero."

Tears fill Mama's eyes. "But this isn't how it's supposed to happen. I'm not supposed to be making these decisions. My husband should be here to decide."

Dr. Kumar looks at Mama, and I can see real kindness in his eyes. "Madam, the only choice to make here is between life and death. I am sure your husband would want for you to choose life."

Mama is full-out crying now, and I pass her a tissue from the box on the chest of drawers. "He would," she says.

Dr. Kumar gives her a pat on the arm. "Very good, then. We'll get the nurse to prepare you for an emergency C-section. I'm afraid your blood pressure is so high, we will have to put you under general anesthesia. But don't worry. We'll take good care of you."

As soon as the doctor leaves, Mama sobs harder, like she's been holding it in so he won't see her. "They're going to cut the baby out of me, Libby."

"It'll be okay, Mama."

"It's not natural. Nothing here is natural."

I know what she means. Everything is plastic and cold and has that antiseptic smell. I don't know what to say, so I just repeat, "It'll be okay."

Soon the big nurse and the little nurse are back. "We've just got to get her prepped for her procedure," the big one tells me. "You can't go in with her, so why don't you go down to the cafeteria and get yourself something to eat?"

I try to remember the last time I ate or drank. Yesterday evening, I guess. "I don't have any money," I say.

The big nurse reaches in her pocket and pulls out an orange slip of paper. "Why don't you take this? It's a ticket for a free meal in the cafeteria. It's not the best food in the world, but it eats."

"Thank you," I say. It's strange. Daddy always talks about how bad people in the world are, but here everybody's been so nice.

I follow the signs to the cafeteria. It looks like what I imagine a school cafeteria would look like, with a long table of hot food: eggs and bacon and sausage. But what catches my eye are the little boxes of cereal on display. They're tiny with just enough to fill up a bowl, and they're all the brands we never buy because Mama says they're too expensive and too sugary. Feeling a little guilty, I reach for a blue box with a cartoon tiger on it and a carton of milk. The lady at the cash register says, "Honey, you can get more than this here with the meal ticket. Why don't you get you some juice and a nanner, too?"

"Thank you," I say. She says "banana" the same way Nanny does, which makes me feel more comfortable somehow. I sit down at a table by myself, which feels weird, pour my cereal into a Styrofoam bowl, and open my milk carton.

"If I were you, I'd slice the banana and put it on top of my Frosted Flakes," says a foreign-accented voice.

I look up and see Dr. Nasour from the ER. She's holding a paper cup of coffee. I feel shy and my hello comes out as a whisper.

"Mind if I join you?" she asks.

I nod, and she sits down across from me.

"I heard your mom is getting a C-section this morning," she says, sipping her coffee.

"Yes, ma'am," I say. "She's always had her babies at home before. She's scared."

"She'll be fine," Dr. Nasour says. "Could you remind me of your name again?"

"Libby. It's short for Liberty."

"Pretty," Dr. Nasour says, and I notice for the first time

that pretty is a word you could use to describe her, too. Her eyes are big and brown, with the longest, darkest eyelashes, and her black hair is a sleek curtain. "How many brothers and sisters do you have, Liberty?"

"There's six of us. Well, I guess there's about to be seven. Then there were two angel babies, the ones that didn't make it. I'm scared this new one's gonna be an angel baby, too."

"The baby should be okay," Dr. Nasour says. "He or she will just need medical care for a few weeks." She looks down into her coffee cup, then looks up at me. "I don't mean to pry, and you don't have to answer if you don't want to, but your family is very religious, yes?"

"We're Christians."

"Yes. Most people in this area are, but you're a different sort from them, aren't you?" She's looking at me hard, but her eyes are still kind.

"I guess so. I mean, the only Christians I know are the ones that go to my church. Daddy says the so-called Christians that go to the big downtown churches are a bunch of Pharisees."

Dr. Nasour smiles. "And you believe everything your father says?"

"Yes." I say it, but my voice goes up like a question. Do I? "I don't know. I used to. He's supposed to be head of our family like God is the head of the church."

Dr. Nasour nods. "In my home country, the religion gives men all the power, too. Women aren't allowed to show their hair or even their elbows. They can't drive cars, can't go out without a male chaperone, like a father, husband, or older brother. I wanted a different life, so I left. I miss my family, but it was still the best decision I ever made."

I nod, but I'm not sure why she's telling me this.

My confusion must show because she says, "I suppose what I'm saying is . . . Liberty, if you want a different life for your-self—one that lives up to the beauty of your name—you won't have to leave your country like I did. You'll just have to step outside the door of your house and into the world."

"Daddy says we're in this world but not of this world."

Dr. Nasour shakes her head. "Your father says a lot of things, doesn't he? So did the men who made the rules in my country. But you know what? None of those men are God."

I feel a jump in my belly because I've thought the same thing before and can't believe somebody else thinks it, too. I try to speak, but no words will come out.

Dr. Nasour reaches out and puts her hand on my forearm. "Liberty, I left my country and my family, but I did not leave God. I still carry God in my heart, but this God doesn't want to lock me in a cage for my supposed protection. He wants me in the world, spreading light, helping all the people I can. Which is why I am working in a hospital in one of the poorest counties in the state." She gives my arm a pat and then pulls away. "I know you must think it's strange, me talking to you like this, but when I saw you here, I couldn't let the opportunity pass. I can tell you're a smart girl, Libby. You need to know there are better ways to serve God than to live under some man's thumb and have babies until your body wears out. Promise me you'll at least think about what I've said."

It's too much to take in. The past ten hours have all been too much to take in. But I manage to say, "I promise."

ZO

CHAPTER 18

I SLEEP TILL ALMOST NOON. It seems stupid to eat a real breakfast so soon before lunch, so I grab an apple from the fruit bowl and go see Mom in her workshop.

"Hey, you," she says when I come in. "Did you get some rest?"

"Eventually. It took me a while to settle down after all the drama." I always think Mom looks pretty sitting behind her loom. With all those different strands of wool in front of her, she looks like a musician playing a harp.

"I wish I could check and see how Becky's doing," Mom says, not missing a beat in her weaving. "But given our history with that family, I don't guess I can. Your dad says they'll probably have to go ahead and deliver the baby by C-section, which worries me a little. Babies can have all kinds of problems if they're born too early."

"Like Owen?" I take a bite out of my apple.

"Oh, Owen got off pretty easy for being a preemie. Mild ADHD and a little small for his age. Maybe this baby will get lucky like that, too. But between you and me, I wish the doctors would just take out that woman's uterus when they take out the baby and put her out of her misery."

This is harsh for Mom, and I'm a little startled. "I thought you believed women should be able to choose how many children they have, whether it's zero or a dozen."

"I do believe that. But in this case, I think it's the man's choice, not hers, and the man thinks he's speaking for God."

"Like in *The Handmaid's Tale?*"

"Exactly." Mom concentrates on her weaving for a minute, then says, "You realize you've been in those pajamas for quite some time, right?"

I raise my arm and sniff. "I stink, too. Maybe I'll go take a shower."

"Maybe you should, in the interest of health and public safety."

After my shower, I put on shorts and my *Aladdin Sane* T-shirt. Then I figure I might as well put on the album to match. I wonder how Libby and her mom are. I wonder if Libby will bring me my phone in person or if she'll just leave it on the porch without talking to me.

"Zo!" Mom calls from downstairs. "You have a visitor!"

The only person it could be is Libby. I turn off the music and head downstairs to the kitchen.

It's not Libby. Claire is sitting at the kitchen table, wearing a pink Powerpuff Girls T-shirt.

"Hey," I say. I know I should sound more surprised, but the past several hours have been full of surprises.

"Hey," Claire says, getting up for a hug. "I've been calling and texting you like crazy. When you didn't answer, I got worried. Mom let me have the car today. At first I thought I was just going to hit the thrift stores, but I found myself driving here."

"And you told your mom where you are?" Mom says, setting two cups of tea down on the table.

"Spoken like a true mom," Claire says. "Yes, I texted her. Thanks for the tea."

"You're very welcome," Mom says. "I'm going to head out to the shop and try to get some work done. Zo, if you hear anything about Becky, let me know."

"Becky?" Claire asks.

"That's Libby's mom," I say. "She's the reason I've not replied to your texts. I had to loan my phone to Libby."

Claire crinkles her brow like she does when she's confused. "Okay. This is all very mysterious."

"Dad and I had to take her mom to the hospital last night. Complications from pregnancy."

"Hasn't she been pregnant like a million times? Seems like she'd have it down pat by now." She sips her tea. "Sorry, did that sound bitchy?"

I smile. "Kinda, but you have a good point."

"I didn't think your family was on speaking terms with them anyway."

"We're not. But Papa Patriarch wasn't home, and Mrs. Hazlett collapsed. Since Libby does have some sense despite all the brainwashing, she remembered Dad's a nurse and ran over to get him. We ended up driving her to the county hospital."

Claire nods. "So basically your dad saved Fertile Myrtle's life?"

"Well, he helped. He got her to the place where they could save her."

"And you helped, too."

I shrug. "I drove. And I let Libby borrow my phone so she can check in with Patience and try to get ahold of her dad. No big heroics on my part."

Claire grins. "Well, it's a good thing I haven't been sending you any dirty texts."

"You never send me dirty texts."

"Not by your definition, but I bet Libby's definition would be a lot different."

I laugh. "True. One good thing about last night was that I got to talk to Libby. I hadn't spoken to her since Patience caught us together, and that was a bad note to leave things on. Not that her mom almost dying is a good note. I just mean I feel like we're on better terms now, even if we never talk to each other again."

"Well, she does have to give you your phone back. Stealing's a sin, right?"

I laugh.

Claire reaches out and touches my arm. "So are you feeling better now? Less depressed?"

"Things are a little better, I guess. Mom's taking me to look at used cars this week, so that'll help. But I still feel lonely sometimes. I'm over Hadley, but I still miss what we had when it was good."

"Which is when you should remind yourself of how it was when it was bad."

"True. But you never liked Hadley."

"I had my reasons, but as long as she was making you happy, I kept my mouth shut."

Rationally, I know there were many reasons not to like Hadley; I knew that even when I loved her. "I know she had her faults, but sometimes I'm scared that I'll never have that kind of closeness again, that nobody will ever be interested in me that way."

Claire looks me in the eye. "Maybe somebody already is."

"Who? I'm out here in the middle of nowhere. The only people I see are my family."

Claire pulls away her hand. "For a smart person, you can be really dumb sometimes."

"I don't understand."

Claire leans forward, putting her face close to mine. "Zo, what about me?"

"You?" All the confusion of the past twenty-four hours is weighing on me. It's too much.

"Did it ever occur to you that one reason I didn't like Hadley is because I was jealous?"

"But you were crushing on what's his name—that guy with the long hair and gauges."

"Oh, him. That was just physical. He looked like a guy in a band I like. But you and me, we've been best friends so long, and I've watched you grow into this beautiful androgynous creature. Girl and boy and neither and both and points in between. I never said anything because there was Hadley, and then you were hurt so bad I didn't want to risk messing up our friendship." Tears glitter in Claire's eyes. They're beautiful.

"I don't know what to say."

Claire wipes at a tear. "You don't have to say anything. Just think about it. I mean, I wasn't born with the right parts. I don't know if that's too much of an obstacle for you. It's sure one for me."

I hadn't even been thinking about that part. I had been wondering how I could have been so blind to Claire's feelings and maybe blind to my own, too. "You're a girl. It doesn't matter what accessories you come with."

Claire smiles. "So to speak."

I grin back. "A dirty girl."

"That too." She takes my hand and holds it tight this time. "Listen. You're my best friend no matter what, and I love you no matter what. I can keep on being your best friend without doing anything different. But if you want, there could be more. Think about it, okay?"

"I'm already thinking. And I love you no matter what, too." Funny, smart, beautiful Claire, in love with me, of all people. Life is full of surprises, good and bad. This is a good one.

LIBBY

Chapter 19

"How's the baby?" Mama asks as soon as her eyes open.

"She's tiny but okay," the doctor says. "A little jaundiced, and it's hard for her to breathe on her own. She needs to grow bigger and stronger and have some supplemental oxygen for a little while." He takes a deep breath, and his look turns more serious. "Our policy regarding premature babies is to transfer them to the children's hospital in Johnson City. It's a much larger facility, with a NICU."

"I don't know what that is." Mama sounds groggy, like her tongue is thicker than it needs to be.

"Please forgive me," Dr. Kumar says. "In the medical field we spend too much time speaking in acronyms. NICU stands for Neonatal Intensive Care Unit. It's designed for newborns who need special care."

Mama's eyes tear up. "So she's gonna be all the way over there while I'm still here?"

"Mrs. Hazlett, assuming your blood pressure returns to normal, you may go home the day after tomorrow. Then you can go see your baby."

"Hope," Mama says in a near whisper.

"I beg your pardon?" the doctor says.

"I'm naming the baby Hope."

"That's lovely," he says. He gives her a pat on the arm. "I'll be back to check on you in the morning."

After he leaves, Mama looks at me and whispers, "I feel weird. I feel high. Why do I feel high?"

"They gave your morphine for the pain," I say. "That machine next to the bed is a morphine pump. You push the button when you start to hurt."

Mama smiles and shakes her head. "I didn't know they were gonna get me high. I've not been high in a long, long time."

I must have heard her wrong. "Pardon?"

"Oh, I shouldn't have said that, should I?" She gives a strange little smile. "Libby, don't tell your brothers and sisters, okay? But before I met your daddy I was a bad, bad girl."

I can't picture Mama looking or acting different than she does now. Maybe because she never talks about when she was younger. "But how? You're so good."

Mama closes her eyes. "I was bad because I was sad. Hey, that rhymes, doesn't it?" She really must be high. "It was right after I graduated from college."

"Wait—you went to college?" This is too much. Daddy says college is a waste of money and a hotbed of secular humanism and no place for a Christian, especially a Christian young lady.

"East Tennessee State. I've got a bachelor's in business. No wonder I can make our budget stretch so far. Your daddy didn't want me to tell you kids." She winces and then presses the button on the morphine pump. "Oh, that's better." She closes her eyes and smiles. She looks like an angel, which is what I always thought she was.

She's quiet for a few seconds, then she says, "A few months after I graduated from college, my daddy got diagnosed with pancreatic cancer. He was dead four weeks after the diagnosis, and I just couldn't handle it. I loved him so much, and the pain of losing him so fast . . . I started drinking, popping pills, smoking pot—anything to numb the pain, you know?"

It's like a stranger is talking to me. Mama drinking? Taking drugs? I can't even imagine what that would look like. "I thought your parents died when you were little."

"No," Mama says, her voice all calm and floaty from the morphine. "Daddy died when I was twenty-two. And when I think about the risks I took for a whole year after that, it's like I was trying to join him. I was working at a bank in downtown Johnson City—"

"You had a job?" If she wasn't right where I could see her, I wouldn't think it was Mama I was talking to.

"I did. I was a loan officer. I put on high heels and a short skirt and makeup every day. I was good at my job, too, until the booze and pills got to be a problem. Then I was late or absent or present physically but not mentally." She looks at me with heavy-lidded eyes. "My boss basically told me to get help or get fired. And soon after that, your daddy came to the bank. He was good-looking and charming, and he invited me to his church. I thought, why not? I knew I was lost, and I figured maybe church would help me find my way back."

"And that's how you got saved?"

Mama nods. "I was a Methodist growing up, but this church was so different. Not boring and quiet but full of feelings—excitement and love and praise. I stopped drinking and popping pills and prayed instead. I washed off my makeup and let my hair grow. Your daddy sat with me at every service, and then we started going out for coffee or ice cream and having these long talks. Of course, it was him doing most of the talking. We were married three months later, and two months after that, I was pregnant with you."

"Well," I say, "that's a lot to take in."

Mama smiles. "It's hard for kids to think what their parents were like before they were parents. But for you, it must be even harder because I was so different." She hits the morphine pump again. "You know, other than this baby, you were the only one of my children to be born in a hospital."

"I always thought Daddy just caught me at home."

"No," Mama says. "You were born in the hospital in Johnson City. Your daddy and me lived in an apartment then. This was after those animal rights people got the horse farm where he was working shut down, and he got a job at Orkin. And then after about a year there, he had his vision about moving to the country and starting his own business. Your daddy and his visions." She closes her eyes again. "I'm tired, Libby."

"I know. Why don't you get some more sleep?"

I sit in the armchair and have almost dozed off myself when Zo's phone rings. I look at the number on the screen. "Daddy!" I answer.

"Hey, Libby-lou," he says. "Your sister finally got me on the phone. There ain't a signal to be found out in the woods. It's a good thing we had to make a run to Walmart. How's the baby? Have you seen her?"

"No, sir. They took her to the children's hospital in Johnson City. The doctor said they have the equipment to help little babies there."

"So me and Just are on the road, you and your mama are at one hospital, the baby's at another, and Patience and the Littles are at home." He sighs. "That's not the way it ought to be. Family ought to be together."

I can hear how upset he is. "I know, Daddy. But it was an emergency."

"Family ought to be home taking care of each other instead of getting tended to by strangers in an institution."

He can't be right, can he? Didn't we do what we had to do to have the best chance of saving Mama and the baby? "Mama needed medicine."

"Well, that's what they told you. Let me talk to your Mama."

I look over at Mama. "She's asleep."

"She can go back to sleep after she talks to me."

"Yessir."

"And Libby? You pray for your new baby sister, you hear?"

"I will." I shake Mama's shoulder gently. "Daddy's on the phone."

"Oh," she says, her voice heavy with sleep. "Good. Libby, honey, why don't you give us a little privacy for about five minutes? Go out and get some fresh air."

I walk down the long hall, through the lobby, and out the front door. I blink in the bright sunlight. The air's not as fresh as I'd hoped because a woman with heavy makeup and unnatural red hair is standing by the door, smoking. She smiles, but I can't tell if she's being friendly or not.

She looks me up and down. "Church girl, huh?" Her voice is low and raspy.

"I guess so," I say.

"I used to be one, too," she says. I must look at her funny because she says, "Don't be so surprised. A person can live all kinds of lives before they die. You won't be the same person you are now when you're my age."

I don't say anything to her, just go back inside. I want to be with Mama, to feel safe, even though she doesn't feel familiar to me after what she's told me. When I go back to the room, she wipes at her eyes like she doesn't want me to see she's been crying.

"Are you okay?" I ask, putting my hand on her shoulder.

She nods and presses the button on the morphine pump. "Your daddy was really concerned that there might be something wrong with me now so I can't have any more babies. I said let's make sure this baby's okay before we start worrying about making any more."

She doesn't spell it out, but I can tell her feelings are hurt. She almost died having this baby, and Daddy mostly seems more worried about whether she can have more. He never even asked me how she was.

"He and Just are headed to Johnson City to pray over the baby," she says. "He wants to take her home, but I told him the hospital wouldn't let him, that they'd call in the social workers."

"But if he did take Hope home, wouldn't she—"

"Die?" Mama says. "Maybe. I don't know if she's strong enough to breathe on her own, but your daddy says it's all in the Lord's hands. He wants me to check myself out, but I told him I can't even sit up in bed yet, and I've still got a catheter and an IV." She closes her eyes for a minute, then opens them and looks hard at me. "Libby? You know the things I was telling you about back when I was a wild girl?"

I nod. How could I forget?

"I was telling you about it for a reason. For the past few months . . . I don't know, it's like this pregnancy's done something to me . . . I've started to have doubts. Not about God, but about your daddy. Maybe it was because he made us all fast. Or maybe it's because he can't stand to have anybody disagree with him. And it sure didn't help when he whipped you the way he did. But I've found myself wondering—when I gave up booze and drugs for church and your daddy, was I just swapping one addiction for another?"

I can't bring myself to say anything.

"I love your daddy, but he's just a man. Is it right that a man be treated like God?" Mama says. "There's only one God, right?"

I still can't speak.

"Have I shocked you?" she asks.

"Yes, ma'am," I say. "But I understand. I've been feeling some of those doubts, too. I thought it was because I'm a bad, sinful person."

"No, baby, you're a good, good person." Mama breathes out a long sigh. "I knew of all my children, you were the one I could talk to. There's something about you that reminds me of my mom, the way you listen to everything a person has to say without judging."

"I bet you miss her." I can't imagine what my life would've been like if I'd lost Mama when I was little.

"I do," Mama says. "And I've been lying here thinking I know it would be going against your daddy's wishes and against the vows I made to him before God, but I still really feel like we should call your grandmother."

"Nanny? I don't think Daddy would care if you called Nanny."

"No, I mean my mom."

I'm hopelessly confused. Has the morphine scrambled Mama's brain? "Your mom is dead."

Mama shakes her head. "A little bit after you were born," she says, "your daddy decided we shouldn't have anything to do with my mom, that she was a bad influence. He said it wasn't a lie to call her dead because she was spiritually dead. I haven't spoken to her since. But as far as I know, she's still living in the house where I grew up in Johnson City."

Chapter 20

Mama is pumping breast milk when my new grandmother arrives. Mama quickly turns off the machine and pulls up her gown. "Well, this isn't exactly how I dreamed you'd see me after all these years," Mama says, covering herself more with a sheet.

"I'm glad to see you any way I can," my grandmother says, her eyes welling up. "I was afraid I never would." She leans over Mama's bed and hugs her, saying, "Becky, Becky." When she stands up straight, she turns to me. "And you're Libby!"

I nod. She and I look each other over. She's a little woman, shorter than me and small-boned. Her gray hair is cut almost as short as a man's, and she's wearing a pink track suit with tennis shoes. Her eyes are the same blue as Mama's. She steps forward and gives me a big, close hug. It starts out feeling like hugging a stranger and ends up feeling like hugging family.

"I . . . I don't know what to call you," I whisper over her shoulder.

She pulls away, holding my hands in hers and smiling. "I was thinking about that on my way here. How about Grandma Jean?"

"I like it," I say, smiling back at her.

"Well, then, that's who I'll be." She gives my hands a squeeze before she lets go and turns to Mama. "I did stop by the hospital and check on your little one like you asked me to. She's beautiful. Tiny but beautiful."

Mama wipes away a tear. "It's so strange to be separated from my baby like this. That's why I'm pumping. I want to keep my production up so I can feed her when she's ready. I figure that's at least something I can do for her while we're apart. The doctor on the phone told me she's doing okay. Did you talk to anybody while you were there?"

"I talked to a nurse. She said they put the baby on the respirator not because she can't breathe but so she won't have to work so hard to breathe. They'll take her off it in a few days, and then she'll just need to get bigger and fatter until she's strong enough to go home." Grandma Jean takes Mama's hand.

The way Mama and Grandma Jean are looking at each other, it feels like they need a mother-daughter talk, so I say, "Grandma Jean, can I get you a cup of coffee from the cafeteria?"

"Honey, I'd just about sell my soul for a cup of coffee." She digs through her purse and pulls out a ten-dollar bill. "Here, get something for yourself, too."

I'm not used to being responsible for money, so I clutch the bill tight in my fist as I walk down the hall. In the cafeteria, I'm overwhelmed by the choices. It's past lunchtime, and my belly's growling, but how much of Grandma Jean's money is it okay to spend on myself? I finally end up with a grilled cheese sandwich and an apple juice, which comes to less than half of what she gave me. I pay and sit at a table by myself to eat, feeling independent, which is fun but also scary.

"I got you lots of cream and sugar packets because I forgot to ask how you like your coffee," I say to Grandma Jean back in the room.

"One cream is plenty, thanks, honey," she says. "And I think you and me are going for a little ride."

"Really?" I look over at Mama.

"I want you to stop by the house and check on the Littles before your daddy gets there, just to make sure he's not walking into chaos," Mama says. "And I want you to bring me a few things." She holds out a sheet of notepaper.

The list is mostly ordinary stuff: hairbrush, toothbrush, clean underwear. But the last item is confusing: *cardboard box in basement labeled* HOMESCHOOL SUPPLIES.

"I know the last thing seems weird," Mama says, "but there are some things in that box I want you to see."

GRANDMA JEAN'S CAR FEELS TINY COMPARED to the van. I'm pretty sure, too, that this is the first time I've ridden somewhere with just one person.

"I bet you're feeling pretty overwhelmed," Grandma Jean says.

"Yes, ma'am."

"Me too," she says, offering me a stick of gum from a little compartment between the two front seats. "I'm overwhelmed and nervous and worried, but I'm happy, too. Happy to finally know you and to have my daughter back in my life. You know, I lost my husband, then I lost your mama to drugs. I thought I'd get her back when she found Jesus, but that ended up taking her even farther away from me than the drugs did."

"You don't believe in Jesus?" I ask, unwrapping the gum.

She stops at a red light and turns toward me. "Oh, I believe in Jesus. It's your daddy's interpretation of Jesus I have problems with. It seems like there are always men who want to put words in Jesus's mouth to suit their own purposes."

Her words hit me hard. "I've been thinking about that a lot."

"Good," Grandma Jean says. "You need to. That way you won't let some man turn you into a baby-making machine like your daddy did to your mama. You should have an education and a career first and then marriage and babies later if you decide you want them."

It's like she's said my most secret longings—the things I've been afraid to even say to myself—out loud. And she says it like wanting these things isn't sinful, that these are the things that I should want. "You know, with what happened with Mama and her being in the hospital, I keep thinking I might want to be a nurse." I'm surprised to hear these words come out of my mouth, even though they're true.

"Well, Libby, I think you'd be a great nurse. I don't know you well yet, but I can tell already that you're caring and smart. If you want to be a nurse, you should damn well go to a real school and do what it takes to be one."

I don't know what shocks me more—my grandmother cursing or hearing her say I have the right to choose what to do with my life. I can't think of anything to say so I just lean over and kiss her on the cheek.

She laughs. "Well, that was a nice surprise. This day seems to be full of them."

The rest of the way to the house Grandma Jean tells me about herself, about how she grew up in Bristol, a town where you could stand in one part of the street and be in three states at the same time. About how she was on the girls' basketball team in high school and how she went to secretarial school after that and got a job at an insurance company in Johnson City, which is where she met my granddaddy. She tells me about my mama when she was little, and how she and my granddaddy never felt like they needed to have more babies because they got it right the first time.

When she pulls into the driveway of the house she says, "It feels awfully strange to know I've got four other grandkids I've never met in that house. I'm not gonna ask you to lie, but I think it might be better if you don't tell them who I am yet. Maybe a nice lady you met at the hospital offered to give you a ride to get your mother's things."

"Okay." It isn't really a lie. Grandma Jean is a nice lady I met at the hospital.

"I'll wait here. After you've gotten your mother's things, you might want to grab a change of clothes and a toothbrush for yourself, too."

"Yes, ma'am." Until she said it, I hadn't even thought about the fact that I'm wearing the same clothes as yesterday.

Once I hit the door, Faith and Charity and Val run up and hug my legs.

Patience comes in from the kitchen, looking exhausted. "Thank the Lord you're back," she says. "Did Daddy bring you? Is he here, too?"

"No. A lady from the hospital brought me to get some of Mama's things."

Patience knits her brow. "On the phone Daddy said he was going to bring Mama home, so why would she need her things at the hospital?"

"Patience, Mama can't come home yet. She had surgery. She needs to recover. She still has a catheter in."

"I don't even know what that is," Patience says.

I whisper an explanation in her ear so the Littles can't hear me.

Patience gasps, and her face turns red. "But that's not decent!"

"It's not indecent. It's medical," I say. From being with Mama the past several hours, I've learned that when a woman's life is in danger, she has to throw modesty out the window.

I go to Mama's room and find her things. There's no suitcase to put them in because Daddy and Just took it for their trip, so I put her clothes and toiletry items in a paper grocery sack. I go in Patience's and my room and grab a change of clothes and my toothbrush. I look around our room, the pink walls, the white Bibles on the nightstand. It feels strange, like I've been away a lot longer than I have.

There's one more thing I have to get. I come back downstairs, go in the kitchen, and open the basement door.

"Are you sneaking out through the basement again?" Patience asks. She's at the kitchen sink, washing the lunch dishes.

"No, there was something down there Mama wanted."

"What is it? There's nothing down there but Daddy's pest control stuff."

"I don't know." I open the basement door, pull the chain that lights up the bare bulb and go down the steep steps. Just like Patience said, all around me are boxes and boxes of Daddy's pest control stuff, marked "Danger" and "Toxic" and "Keep away from children." And then I see on a shelf on the back wall a lidded cardboard box with HOMESCHOOL SUPPLIES printed on it in Mama's handwriting. I grab it.

I know I need to hurry, but I have to take a quick look. I lift the lid.

There are piles of loose photos: a grinning little girl with brown pigtails on a candy-apple-red tricycle. An older little girl in a green Girl Scout uniform. A teenaged girl with lip gloss and styled short hair wearing a long pink dress that shows her bare shoulders, standing with a boy in a tuxedo who is definitely not Daddy.

Mama, all of them. Mama before she was Mama. There are papers, too—letters she's saved from Grandma Jean, her high school diploma. Another, stored in a cardboard tube, is a diploma showing she earned a Bachelor's of Science degree from East Tennessee State University. I feel like I've been given a gift. Mama wants me to know her as a whole person, not just as my mama.

I carry the box upstairs, away from all of Daddy's poison. "I'd better get on back," I say to Patience and the Littles. "My ride's waiting."

"When will we meet the baby?" Charity asks.

"Soon," I say, making my way to the front door.

"When will Mama be back?" Faith asks.

"Soon, too," I say. "They both just need a little more time to get well."

"What's in the box?" Patience asks.

I'd hoped I'd get out without having to answer this question. I hold the box so she can read the label HOMESCHOOL SUPPLIES.

"Oh," she says, sounding disappointed.

When I walk outside into the light, Grandma Jean is still sitting in the car with the windows rolled down. "I popped the trunk so you can put everything back there," she says. "You found the box, I see."

"Yes, ma'am. There are some cards and letters from you in it."

She smiles, but somehow it's a sad smile. "Good. She saved them. She never wrote me back, but at least she saved them."

I put the bag and box into the trunk. Next door, Zo gives me a shy little wave from her porch. There's another girl standing there with her—a pretty Asian girl. They're holding hands, right there on the front porch where anybody could see. "I'll be right back, Grandma Jean," I say.

I run next door and give Zo a big hug.

"Well, hi," she says, laughing. She nods toward the other girl. "This is my friend Claire, by the way."

"Hi, Claire," I say, and Claire gives me a little wave. I turn back to Zo. "Thanks for the phone," I say, pressing it into her hand. "And for everything else. Thank your dad, too."

"I will," she says. "How—"

Before she can finish, I blurt out, "Mom and the baby are okay, but both of them need more time in the hospital. And in that car over there is my grandma who I didn't even know about until today, but don't tell anybody."

"Okay," Zo says, looking at me like I'm crazy.

"There's too much to explain, and I've got to go." I give her one more quick hug. "I'm glad you're my friend."

"I'm glad you're my friend, too."

"Nice to meet you, Claire," I blurt out as I run down the porch steps.

"You, too," she says.

I run back to Grandma Jean's car. When I slide into the passenger seat, I'm breathing hard. "That was Zo," I say. "Her daddy's the one who saved Mama's life. But my daddy doesn't want me to be friends with her because she's homosexual and he says that's an abomination. Do you think it's an abomination, a girl that likes girls that way?"

"I don't think God put us here to judge each other," Grandma Jean says, starting the car. "I think He put us here to love."

WHEN WE GET BACK TO THE hospital room, Mama is sitting up in bed. The morphine pump is gone, and she looks tired but more alert. "Are Patience and the Littles okay?" she asks.

"Yes, ma'am," I say.

"The doctor was here," Mama says. "He says my blood pressure has improved and my kidneys are functioning. They took me off the morphine, and he said they'd take out the catheter in the morning. If I can go to the bathroom like a normal person, they'll let me go home."

Grandma Jean pats Mama's arm. "You remember what I said, right? That you always have a home with me."

"I remember." Mama has tears in her eyes.

"And that goes for you, too, Miss Libby, and all your brothers and sisters."

"Thank you," I say, meaning it.

Grandma Jean looks back at Mama. "Promise me you'll think about it."

"I am thinking about it," Mama says, wiping under her eyes like she's trying to stop tears at the source. "It's just complicated."

"Life is complicated," Grandma Jean says, "and most of the time when people try to make things simpler, they just end up making them harder." She takes Mama's hand with her right hand and my hand with her left. The Bible says woman is the weaker vessel, but joined with the two of them, three generations of women who share the same blood, I feel like we're strong together.

"Bill's on his way," Mama says. "He'll probably be here in half an hour."

Grandma Jean lets go of our hands. "Well, then I reckon I'd better make myself scarce so he won't see me. I'm going to go nurse a cup of coffee in the cafeteria. Libby, you come and get me if you need me."

Grandma Jean gives me a hug. I guess we have a lot of hugging to catch up on.

"THERE YOU ARE. PRAISE JESUS!" DADDY says. He swoops in like he's about to take over the whole hospital. He's wearing his church suit and tie.

"I thought you'd have Just with you," Mama says.

"I dropped him off at home. I figured there needed to be a man of the house, and he's my second-in-command." Daddy comes to the edge of the bed and takes Mama's hand, which lies limp in his. "I went to see our new little blessing at the hospital up in Johnson City," he says. "She's tiny, but the Lord's watching over her. They wouldn't let me hold her. They said she ain't strong enough yet. But they couldn't stop me from praying! I put my hands on the plastic box she's laying in, and I said, 'Dear Lord, if it's in your will, please let this little girl grow up to be a virtuous woman and a Godly wife. Let her ovaries grow healthy eggs, and let her womb provide a safe place to plant the seed to grow God's mighty warriors! Please—"

"You prayed for her uterus and ovaries?" Mama says.

Daddy looks startled. Mama never stops him in the middle of a big speech. "Of course I did. I've been praying for yours, too, honey."

Mama shakes her head. "And if the baby was a boy, would you pray for his testicles?"

I've never heard such plain language about body parts come out of Mama's mouth.

Daddy looks at Mama like he doesn't even know her. "Well, not in those words, probably. But I would pray for him to grow up to be a strong Christian patriarch, a righteous warrior for the Lord as befitted his role. Why are you asking so many questions? You don't seem like yourself."

"I'm tired." Mama says it softly, looking down at the blanket instead of up at Daddy.

Daddy pats her arm. "Of course you're tired, honey. You just had a beautiful little baby."

Mama looks up at him. "It's more than that, Bill." She wipes away a tear. "It's . . . it's this life. It's wearing me down. I don't think I want to have any more babies. I've had enough."

"God decides when you've had enough!" Daddy's voice is so loud I'm sure people can hear it in the hallway. "You see how it is. You spend less than twenty-four hours in a god-less place like this, and already it starts corrupting you. You need to get back to your Christian life and your Christian home."

"Everybody in this hospital isn't godless," Mama says. "There are lots of different kinds of Christians other than the kind we are."

Daddy's face is red. A vein bulges in his forehead. "There's only one kind of true Christian to be!"

I wonder if that could be right. How many people in the world are Christians like us? I think of the size and number of the downtown churches compared to our little church. If we're the only true Christians, heaven is going to be almost empty, no matter how many babies we have.

Daddy sits down on the edge of the bed next to Mama. He looks over at me like he's just remembered I'm there. "Libby, honey, why don't you run to the cafeteria and get your daddy a cup of coffee?"

I look over at Mama. She says, "I'd like Libby to stay."

Dad takes a deep breath like he's trying to calm himself down. "Becky, do you remember when I first met you? You were lost, chained to drugs and alcohol. It was like you were lost in a big, dark forest and couldn't find your way home. Isn't that right?"

Mama nods. It's hard to tell what mixture of feelings are behind the tears in her eyes. Sadness? Love? Fear?

"Well, the Lord and me led you home. And that's what we're gonna do now, too. The first thing you need to do is get up out of that bed and get your clothes on. Then me and Libby are gonna take you home, and everything's gonna be the way it's supposed to be again." He's smiling, stroking her hair. "After we get you settled, I'm gonna go back to Johnson City and bring home our baby!" He squeezes her hand. "So first thing's first, get on up out of that bed."

My mouth opens before my brain can stop it. "I don't know if she can get up yet, Daddy. She's still got staples in her belly from where they did the surgery, and she has a catheter—"

"The Lord will help her get up." He takes both of Mama's hands and pulls.

She gasps in pain, lets go of his hands, and falls back on the bed with a groan. "I can't, Bill. I can't. Right now I just can't do what you want me to do." She is sobbing.

"It's the dope again, isn't it?" Daddy looks around frantically, then finally looks at me. "What kind of drugs are they giving her in this place?"

"They gave her morphine after the surgery," I say, "but now I don't think she's on anything."

"Well, what's this then?" Daddy jabs a finger at the IV bag hanging over the bed.

"Just fluids," Mama says so softly I can barely hear her.

"I bet there's something that's in these fluids," Daddy says, "something that's making you turn against the Lord's authority." Faster than I can even process what's happening, he grabs Mama's hand that's connected to the IV, tears the tape from her skin, and jerks out the tube and needle. Blood sprays his face and the clean white sheets.

"Bill, no!" Mama yells.

I scream.

The heavy nurse who helped us when Mama was first admitted runs in. "What in the Sam Hill is going on in here?" she says.

"He pulled out her IV," I say. I look over at Mama. Her right hand is covering her left one, blood seeping between her fingers.

"Do you know this man?" the nurse asks.

"I am her husband," Daddy says.

The nurse looks at Mama. "Is this true?"

Mama nods.

The nurse looks Daddy up and down. "Well, sir, even if you are her husband, we can't have you interfering with her medical care and creating a disturbance. I'm gonna have to ask you to leave."

Daddy looks back at the nurse like she's the dirt underneath his feet. "It's not your place to ask me to do anything."

"Daddy, please—" I say.

"Not your place either, little girl." He points his finger at me. "There's only one place I take orders from, and that's from on high."

"Here." The nurse gives Mama a piece of gauze. "Use this to press down on your wound. I'll be right back." She looks at Daddy. "Sir, this is your last chance to leave peacefully. Then I'm calling security," the nurse says.

"The Lord is my security!" Daddy hollers at her as she leaves. "With His protection, I fear no man!"

It seems like the nurse is gone for less than a minute before she's back with two huge guys, one black and one white, wearing blue uniforms with badges. They're mountainous men, so tall and wide they seem to take up most of the space in the room.

"That's him," the nurse says, pointing to Daddy.

The white security guard moves in and takes Daddy by the arm. "Okay, sir," he says, "we've been asked to escort you out of the building."

"I am not leaving without my wife!" Daddy yells.

"Well, sir, I don't know as your wife's ready to leave yet," the security guard says. He looks over at Mama. "Ma'am, do you want to leave with this man?"

"The doctor says I'm not ready," Mama says.

"Well, you heard the lady," the black security guard says, moving in to take Daddy's other arm. "Time to move along."

"That woman is my wife!" Daddy hollers, his face turning purple. "She was created by God to harken to me and obey me!"

"If I talked about my wife like that, she'd be changing the locks on me," the black security guard says. "Come on, let's go."

At our house, Daddy always has so much power, second in command only to God Himself. But out here in the world, he's nobody. The two guards look at him like he's just another crazy person that they run into in their line of work.

"I will not be silenced!" Daddy yells as they drag him out the door. "The judgment of the Lord is sure and swift!"

Daddy is still yelling and raging as they drag him down the hall. The guards are still on either side of him, each holding one of his arms. Each guard is a head taller and a lot wider than Daddy, and something about the way he's dwarfed by them and hanging from their arms makes me think of a puppet. I never noticed it until today, but Daddy is a small man.

I peek in the room where the nurse is working on Mama's hand. The security guards are still dragging Daddy down the hall, and I walk in the opposite direction.

Grandma Jean is sitting in the cafeteria with a cup of coffee just like she said she would be. When she sees me, her forehead crinkles like she's worried. "Is there trouble?" she says.

"Not anymore," I say. "Daddy's gone."

"You look wrung out," she says. "You want to sit down for a minute?"

"Yes, please." I sit across from her. Her track suit is powder blue, my favorite color. "Grandma Jean?"

"Yes, honey?"

"Did you mean it when you said I could have a home with you any time I wanted?"

Grandma Jean smiles. "Yes, honey, I meant it with my whole heart."

I take a deep breath and feel a sudden calm. "I think it's time."

ZO
(Ten months later)

CHAPTER 21

IT DIDN'T TAKE A FULL YEAR for my family to decide that we like rural life more in theory than we do in practice. Groundhogs ate most of the vegetables we planted, and all of Dad's unfinished projects proved that he's much better at fixing up people than places. Owen and I both missed hanging out with people our age. And we all hated that there was no place to order Chinese food.

So once Dad's contract with the health department was up, we moved back to Knoxville, where he got a lower-stress job teaching in the nursing program at the community college. And even though we got a house in town, we still got to keep our rabbits.

The downtown farmer's market in Knoxville has just as many people selling crafts as produce. Mom and I staff a booth selling her handwoven clothing every Saturday in the spring and summer. Today Claire's helping, too. She says she'll cover for me while I entertain my company—that I should have one-on-one time with a friend I haven't seen in so long.

Even though I know they're meeting us here, it still takes me a couple of seconds to recognize them. Libby's mom has ditched her big hoot-owl glasses, has shorn her hair so it's short and stylish, and is wearing jeans and a spring sweater instead of a shapeless jumper. She's carrying Hope, an adorable, chubby-cheeked dumpling, in a baby sling. The Littles are less little than when I last saw them, and they're all wearing shorts, even the girls.

Val and Owen stand and look at each other like they don't know if they should shake hands or hug or what. Finally, Owen says, "Hey, you wanna go play in the fountains?"

Val says, "Can we?"

"Sure," Libby's mom says. "It's a warm day. You'll dry off sooner or later."

And that leaves Libby and me. We've e-mailed back and forth a little, but this is the first time we've met in person since we were neighbors. Looking at her, it's hard to see the same girl who was my unlikely friend. Her hair's been cut to a chin-length bob, and since it's not so weighed down now, the natural waves have turned into soft curls. Tiny silver studs sparkle in her earlobes. She's wearing jeans—not skinny jeans but not Mom jeans either—with a solid pink T-shirt and baby-blue canvas slip-ons. She could step into any high school in the nation without looking like an outsider.

"Hi, Libby," Claire says, probably because I'm just standing there like an idiot.

"Hi, Claire," Libby says. "It's nice to see you."

Claire nudges me. "Now it's your turn to say something to Libby."

"You look so different," I say and immediately feel like even more of an idiot.

"You look the same," she says, smiling.

"Yeah," I say, looking down at my jeans and purple Converses. If she'd seen me a few months ago, I would've been wearing all black out of mourning for David Bowie, a black star pendant Dad bought me hanging from my neck. But then one night, Bowie, in full orange mullet and lightning bolt *Aladdin Sane* drag, came to me in a dream and said, Don't wear all black on my account, love. Be as colorful as you are. The next day, I bought the purple Converses.

There's an awkward pause between Libby and me until Mom says, "You two have time to grab an ice cream before your movie starts" and waves a ten-dollar bill at us.

"Claire, would you like to come, too?" Libby asks before I can. It doesn't seem right to go off for ice cream and not invite her.

"No, I'm good," Claire says. "You two have fun."

WE SIT AT A TABLE OUTSIDE the frozen custard store, licking big chocolate cones.

"Knoxville's nice," Libby says, looking around at the crowded square, where people are walking dogs or pushing babies in strollers. "Do you like being back here?"

"Yeah. I think maybe we all just needed some time away from here to see what's good about it. And it's different than before. Mom's weaving full-time, Dad's new job is way less stressful than hospital work, and Owen's in Montessori now and really likes it."

Libby looks up from her cone. "So that's everybody but you."

I smile. "I guess it is, isn't it? I'm good. I'm back at the same high school, but I hardly ever see Hadley and when I do, it's like, 'what was I thinking?' I'm also taking a film class I really like, and Claire and I are still together."

"That's great." If she's uncomfortable with Claire and me being a couple, she doesn't show it.

"But what about you?" I gesture toward her with my ice cream cone until a stray drip convinces me this is a bad idea. "You're the one whose whole—everything—has changed."

"That's true," she says, sounding happy and a little sad at the same time. "It's been a lot to go through. At first I was the only one who moved in with Grandma Jean, but after about a month and a half, Mama and the Littles showed up, too. Mama said she had to get her strength back and know the baby was going to be okay before she could leave. She said it took me being brave for her to find her courage."

"You were very brave," I say.

"I think I was just desperate." Libby looks down for a moment. "Daddy hasn't made any of this easy, but I wouldn't have expected him to. In his mind, Mama's fallen into sin and is trying to drag us to hell right along with her. He's fought the divorce every step of the way, and he wants full custody of all of us."

"But he doesn't have it, right?" I figure Libby wouldn't be sitting here wearing jeans and talking to me if her daddy had anything to say about it.

"No, he doesn't. That fit he pitched at the hospital when he tore out Mama's IV didn't do him any good. The nurse called social services on him, and since then, Mama's had a social worker and a lawyer helping her. The system is on her side. But Daddy says that's because it's a godless system."

It dawns on me that two of Libby's siblings aren't with her today. "Where are Patience and Just?"

Libby sighs. "They chose to live with Daddy. Just says he wants to grow up to be a strong Christian patriarch and work in the family business. And Patience has promised to live with Daddy and take care of him until the Lord decides it's time for her to marry. She says if Mama won't be Daddy's helpmeet, then she will."

I almost choke on my cone. "That's kind of creepy."

"Yeah, well, that's Patience," Libby says, smiling. "It's been hard, but it's been good, too." She looks around again. "I go places. I talk to people. I read books. I watch TV. And thanks to the social worker, we're all in counseling to help us recover from what our therapist says is called 'spiritual abuse' and adapt to living in the world."

"As opposed to living on another planet?"

"It is like I lived on another planet. I didn't tell you this in our emails because I was kind of embarrassed, but the high school I go to now held me back a year because I'm so behind, especially in math. Knowing that Noah measured how to build the ark in cubits doesn't do me a lick of good in algebra. My regular knowledge needs to catch up with my Bible knowledge."

"I'm sure it will." I dab the ice cream from my face with a napkin. "And if you really catch on to that math stuff, let me know. I can use all the help I can get."

"No promises on that yet. You know what's funny? Daddy thinks we're godless, but we've not missed a Sunday of church since we moved in with Grandma Jean. It's so different from what I'm used to—women with short hair and lipstick who have jobs during the week, a youth group where kids my age go bowling or go out for pizza."

I nudge her arm. "I don't know. That sounds pretty sinful."

She grins. "Yeah, it's pretty wicked. And I don't know . . . I'm starting to think about my future. I can because I have choices now, you know? I really think I'd like to be a nurse. When Mama went into labor early, something inside me just kicked into gear so I knew what to do. I feel like I might be good at taking care of people in an emergency."

"I think so, too."

Libby looks at me intensely. "Zo, can I ask you something?"

"Of course."

"You remember that night in the tent when Patience caught us?"

I wince. "That night's pretty hard to forget."

"Before Patience interrupted us, you were about to tell me something else about yourself. Do you remember what it was?"

I nod. It's time to tell her, even if it feels kind of silly to say something so important while holding an ice cream cone. "Well, I told you that I had dated a girl. What I didn't tell you is that I don't really identify as a girl."

Libby looks confused. Not upset, just confused. "So . . . you're a boy?"

"No, not that either. I'm gender-fluid. I don't feel all the way male or female. I kind of feel like parts of both. Except when I feel like neither. Which is why it's fluid."

Libby nods like it's no big deal. "Okay."

I burst out laughing. "'Okay' is all you say? I've been nervous about telling you this ever since we met!"

Libby reaches over and pats my arm. "You know, from the time I was born until I left Daddy's house, I got told how girls were supposed to be. You shouldn't tell people what you think they're supposed to be. You should accept them as they are."

I breathe a sigh of relief. That's all I needed to hear. I glance down at my phone. "Oh, crap, it's five minutes till movie time. We should probably scoot."

Libby stands up. "You know, this'll just be the third time I've seen a movie in a theater. Mama and Grandma Jean and me have taken the Littles to see a couple of cartoons, but this'll be the first movie I've seen in a theater with real actors on the screen."

The movie Libby wants to see is an adaptation of the final installment of a trilogy of teen dystopian books she got hooked on once she was allowed to really read. She got to see the first two movies on TV, she told me in an e-mail, but she wanted to see the new one in the theater.

By the time we've bought our tickets and popcorn and found our seats in the dark, the previews are over. Libby stares wide-eyed at the big screen, at the characters who are enslaved and oppressed by the very rules that are supposedly designed to protect them. I can't help thinking it's a story she knows well. When the main character, a girl close to our age, appears on screen, Libby gasps in excitement. The girl is wearing a tunic and tights, and her hair is in a long braid down her back.

"Doesn't that look like my hair used to?" Libby whispers.

I nod.

"I wouldn't have been allowed to wear clothes that tight, though." She smiles and turns back to the movie.

Onscreen, the girl, a warrior, raises her bow and pulls an arrow from her quiver. She looks up, aims, and shoots it into the sky.

ACKNOWLEDGMENTS

WRITING THIS BOOK REQUIRED A LOT of research into the Christian Patriarchy movement, both to get the theology right and to capture the details of Libby's family's everyday life. There were more helpful sources than I could possibly list here, but I would especially like to acknowledge Kathryn Joyce's book *Quiverfull: Inside the Christian Patriarchy Movement* and Vyckie Garrison's blog *No Longer Quivering*, an excellent resource for survivors of spiritual abuse. Thanks to my insightful and encouraging agent Janna Bonikowski at the Knight Agency, to my editor Constance Renfrow, and to the brilliant Peter Carlaftes and Kat Georges at Three Rooms Press. And as always, thanks to the family and friends who were kind enough to read drafts of this novel.

About the Author

A native of Southeastern Kentucky, Julia Watts has written thirteen novels for adults and young adults, most of which explore the lives of LGBT people in rural and small-town Appalachia. Her novel *Finding H.F.* won the 2002 Lambda Literary Award in the Children's/Young Adult category. A novel for for adults, *The Kind of Girl I Am*, was a finalist for a Lambda Literary Award in the Women's Fiction category, and her 2013 young adult novel *Secret City* was a finalist for a Lambda Literary Award and a winner of a Golden Crown Literary Award. Julia's other titles include *Gifted and Talented*; *Hypnotizing Chickens*; and most recently, *Rufus + Syd*, co-written with Robin Lippincott. Julia holds an MFA in Writing from Spalding University and has spoken at various national and regional conferences, including the AWP Conference, the NCTE Conference, the Appalachian Studies Association Conference, and the Denham Symposium on Appalachian Literature. She lives in Knoxville and teaches at South College and in Murray State University's low-residency MFA in Writing program. She was recently inducted into the East Tennessee Writers Hall of Fame.

RECENT AND FORTHCOMING BOOKS FROM THREE ROOMS PRESS

FICTION

Meagan Brothers
Weird Girl and What's His Name

Ron Dakron
Hello Devilfish!

Michael T. Fournier
Hidden Wheel
Swing State

William Least Heat-Moon
Celestial Mechanics

Aimee Herman
Everything Grows

Eamon Loingsigh
Light of the Diddicoy
Exile on Bridge Street

John Marshall
The Greenfather

Aram Saroyan
Still Night in L.A.

Richard Vetere
The Writers Afterlife
Champagne and Cocaine

Julia Watts
Quiver

MEMOIR & BIOGRAPHY

Nassrine Azimi and
Michel Wasserman
Last Boat to Yokohama:
The Life and Legacy of
Beate Sirota Gordon

William S. Burroughs & Allen Ginsberg
Don't Hide the Madness:
William S. Burroughs in Conversation
with Allen Ginsberg
edited by Steven Taylor

James Carr
BAD: The Autobiography of
James Carr

Richard Katrovas
Raising Girls in Bohemia:
Meditations of an American Father; A
Memoir in Essays

Judith Malina
Full Moon Stages:
Personal Notes from
50 Years of The Living Theatre

Phil Marcade
Punk Avenue:
Inside the New York City
Underground, 1972-1982

Stephen Spotte
My Watery Self:
Memoirs of a Marine Scientist

PHOTOGRAPHY-MEMOIR

Mike Watt
On & Off Bass

SHORT STORY ANTHOLOGIES

SINGLE AUTHOR

First-Person Singularities: Stories
by Robert Silverberg
with an introduction by John Scalzi

Tales from the Eternal Café: Stories
by Janet Hamill, with an introduction
by Patti Smith

Time and Time Again:
Sixteen Trips in Time
by Robert Silverberg

MULTI-AUTHOR

Crime + Music: Twenty Stories
of Music-Themed Noir
edited by Jim Fusilli

Dark City Lights: New York Stories
edited by Lawrence Block

Florida Happens:
Bouchercon 2018 Anthology
edited by Greg Herren

Have a NYC I, II & III:
New York Short Stories;
edited by Peter Carlaftes
& Kat Georges

Songs of My Selfie:
An Anthology of Millennial Stories
edited by Constance Renfrow

The Obama Inheritance:
15 Stories of Conspiracy Noir
edited by Gary Phillips

This Way to the End Times:
Classic and New Stories of
the Apocalypse
edited by Robert Silverberg

MIXED MEDIA

John S. Paul
Sign Language: A Painter's Notebook
(photography, poetry and prose)

FILM & PLAYS

Israel Horovitz
My Old Lady: Complete Stage Play
and Screenplay with an Essay on
Adaptation

Peter Carlaftes
Triumph For Rent (3 Plays)
Teatrophy (3 More Plays)

Kat Georges
Three Somebodies: Plays about
Notorious Dissidents

DADA

Maintenant: A Journal of
Contemporary Dada Writing & Art
(Annual, since 2008)

HUMOR

Peter Carlaftes
A Year on Facebook

TRANSLATIONS

Thomas Bernhard
On Earth and in Hell
(poems of Thomas Bernhard
with English translations by
Peter Waugh)*

Patrizia Gattaceca
Isula d'Anima / Soul Island
(poems by the author
in Corsican with English
translations)*

César Vallejo | Gerard Malanga
Malanga Chasing Vallejo
(selected poems of César Vallejo
with English translations
and additional notes by
Gerard Malanga)*

George Wallace
EOS: Abductor of Men
(selected poems in Greek & English)

POETRY COLLECTIONS

Hala Alyan
Atrium

Peter Carlaftes
DrunkYard Dog
I Fold with the Hand I Was Dealt

Thomas Fucaloro
It Starts from the Belly and Blooms

Inheriting Craziness is Like
a Soft Halo of Light

Kat Georges
Our Lady of the Hunger

Robert Gibbons
Close to the Tree

Israel Horovitz
Heaven and Other Poems

David Lawton
Sharp Blue Stream

Jane LeCroy
Signature Play

Philip Meersman
This is Belgian Chocolate

Jane Ormerod
Recreational Vehicles on Fire
Welcome to the Museum of Cattle

Lisa Panepinto
On This Borrowed Bike

George Wallace
Poppin' Johnny

Three Rooms Press | New York, NY | Current Catalog: www.threeroomspress.com
Three Rooms Press books are distributed by PGW/Ingram: www.pgw.com